SPLINTER
&ASH

MARIEKE NIJKAMP

SPLINTER & ASH

 GREENWILLOW BOOKS
AN IMPRINT OF HarperCollinsPublishers

Greenwillow Books is an imprint of HarperCollins Publishers.

Splinter & Ash
Copyright © 2024 by Marieke Nijkamp
All rights reserved. No part of this book may be used or reproduced in any manner whatsoever without written permission except in the case of brief quotations embodied in critical articles and reviews. Printed in the United States of America. For information address HarperCollins Children's Books, a division of HarperCollins Publishers, 195 Broadway, New York, NY 10007.
www.harpercollinschildrens.com
The text of this book is set in Berling LT Std.
Book design by Sylvie Le Floc'h

Library of Congress Cataloging-in-Publication Data

Names: Nijkamp, Marieke, author.
Title: Splinter & Ash / Marieke Nijkamp.
Other titles: Splinter and Ash
Description: First edition. | New York : Greenwillow Books, an Imprint of HarperCollins Publishers, 2024. | Audience: Ages 8–12. | Audience: Grades 4–6. | Summary: "A chance encounter throws Ash and Splinter into each other's orbits, and they find friendship in their shared loneliness and their desires to prove themselves"— Provided by publisher.
Identifiers: LCCN 2024010344 (print) | LCCN 2024010345 (ebook) | ISBN 9780063326262 (hardcover) | ISBN 9780063326286 (ebook)
Subjects: CYAC: People with disabilities—Fiction. | Gender—Fiction. | Friendship—Fiction. | Family life—Fiction. | Fantasy. | LCGFT: Fantasy fiction. | Novels.
Classification: LCC PZ7.1.N55 Sp 2024 (print) | LCC PZ7.1.N55 (ebook) | DDC [Fic]—dc23
LC record available at https://lccn.loc.gov/2024010344
LC ebook record available at https://lccn.loc.gov/2024010345

ISBN 978-0-06-332626-2 (hardcover)
24 25 26 27 28 LBC 5 4 3 2 1
First Edition

 Greenwillow Books

To Tonke and Tamora, who taught me how to dream.

And to all the kids who build castles out of stories.
This one's for you.

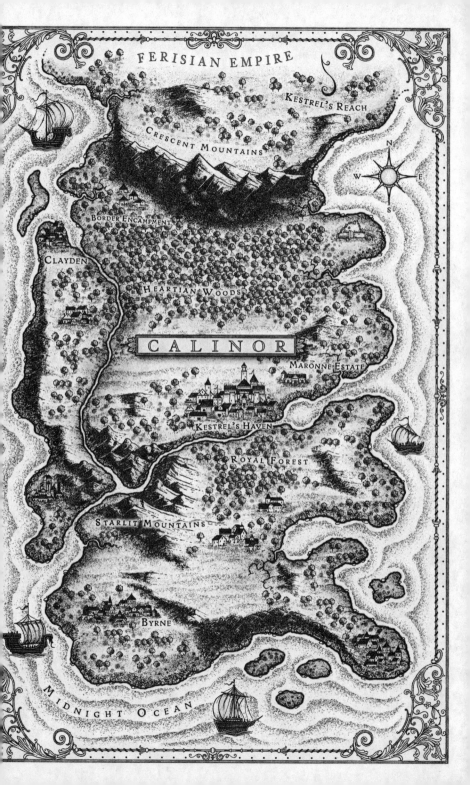

SPLINTER
&ASH

PROLOGUE

The sun set behind the Starlit Mountains, casting the sky in pale purples and blues. The peaks formed jagged shadows. The stars blinked to life. And a carriage driver, who was on her way to deliver her passenger from a small garden estate to the royal city of Kestrel's Haven, decided to take a long-forgotten mountain path instead of the high road.

After all, the driver, a stout woman with a tender heart, had promised her youngest son that she'd be home for the Winter's Heart festival. And the high road was the long way around.

A kingdom's fate is quite often decided by coincidence and happenstance and such small individual decisions.

The girl inside the carriage approved of the change

of route. She didn't mind the cold, even though the superstitious saw it as a warning sign and muttered about unlucky stars shining on the year ahead. Especially with the war at the northern border. The girl had no misgivings about the way the wheels clattered over the uneven stones. She didn't remember the last time she had trekked across icy mountain paths in a carriage, the night of the accident that killed her father. She was bundled up in a thick woolen blanket, and her thoughts were on something quite different than tragedy and war. She was returning to Kestrel's Haven for the first time in nearly six years, and she couldn't wait to be home.

After a long, freezing night amid the cliffs, the carriage wound its way down toward the royal capital, and the girl sat glued to the window. Kestrel's Haven was the type of city that had once centered around a palace and a market square, but over the years it had grown. New districts crawled along the riverbanks. Countless houses and stores pushed past the confines of the city walls and tumbled across the fields. Tall temples provided children a place to learn their letters and numbers, while schools served those who had the coin or the title to demand a finer education. In every district, statues honored the kings and queens of old.

Atop a hill sat the palace, overlooking everything. Like the city, the palace had grown from a handful of buildings to great halls and towers and keeps and pathways that crossed over and under each other. Walls and gates kept strangers out. But the girl's carriage passed through all without delay. It was eagerly awaited at the royal gate. Not by the guard, who kept the palace safe. Not by the knights, who served the crown. Not by the girl's brother, who'd been counting the days until her return and wasn't thrilled at all.

The girl's mother, the queen, stood outside the gates in a simple blue dress with a woolen overgown, fur-lined boots, and leather gloves. She didn't fumble with the hem of her sleeve, because it would not do for the queen to be caught fumbling. She didn't pace, for that would have been improper too. She didn't let her guard come close, though that might have been wise in light of recent threats. Instead she *ran*, out of the cover of the guardhouse and into the falling snow, as soon as the carriage pulled up. She opened the door before the horses came to a complete halt, and when the girl leapt out, the queen gathered her daughter close, held her tightly, and prayed that she would be safe here.

The princess was home at last.

Thanks to the shortcut, she'd arrived two full days earlier than intended.

Now, if that hadn't been the case, perhaps everything would have been different.

If the princess had arrived at the palace on the morning of the masquerade, she'd have been awed by the celebrations, without worrying that she didn't belong. She'd have spent the evening with her brother and her mother, delighted to be reunited, without any concern for the nobles around her, with their cutting glances and snide remarks. She wouldn't have run deep into the snow-covered garden, and she wouldn't have met the squire.

The kingdom would have remained unchanged.

That was not what happened.

Instead the princess discovered that the palace might be awe-inspiring—but it *wasn't* home. She barely had time to talk to her mother, the queen, who kept being shepherded away to more pressing matters. To preside over the royal council, to settle disputes, to talk to merchants and visit Haven's shelters and hospitals, to give the blessings in the royal star temple.

The princess got into the first of many pointless fights with her brother, the crown prince, who wished she'd stayed away.

And the court did not welcome the princess either.

Two days later, instead of enjoying the masked ball, she was plotting her escape back to her aunt's estate, certain that Haven held nothing for her. Until she stumbled into the squire, who longed for a friend and a home, and the trajectory of both their lives—of the royal family and even the kingdom itself—changed forever.

This is how legends start.

Once upon a time, there was a city, a princess, and a squire.

CHAPTER ONE

ASH

Beacons were set up all throughout the royal city of Kestrel's Haven. Along the city walls. In the streets. On the floating docks. In front of the star temples. Around the bell tower that commemorated the citizens who'd fallen defending Calinor. And in the princess's walled garden.

At midnight, every beacon in the city would be lit to celebrate the birth of the new year. And along with the new year, the princess's twelfth birthday.

The masked ball was the social event of the winter, because the princess had only just returned to the palace and the vibrant, chaotic, *wonderful* city. She was new. She was *different*. It was the first time any of the city's nobles would get a chance to talk to her and perhaps influence the girl to sway her mother's opinions in their favor.

Which is why Princess Adelisa—Ash, to her friends, although she had none here—found herself at the center of attention. She wore a midnight-blue velvet dress, sensible boots, and a mask decorated with black feathers and tiny beads to symbolize the stars. Her unruly brown hair had been tied into a braid, but strands kept escaping it. Long gloves obscured the silver bands and rings she wore around her arms and hands, and she leaned ever so slightly on a finely carved cane, which had flowers and woodland animals etched in oak.

Ash felt ill at ease. She didn't know where to go, what to say—or even where she belonged. The night sky was cold, and the questions and comments of her guests were colder.

A knight captain in a long light-brown coat, with deep purple knots embroidered along its sleeves, frowned when she passed him. "Look how fragile she is. The crown needs to be strong, especially in times of war," he said, not softly enough to be subtle.

His dance partner scoffed. "She has no right to call herself princess. And the queen? She spends more time with the common folk than with the knights and nobles who fight for her. Disgraceful."

Lord Lambelin, the commander of the guard, had warned Ash before the celebrations started. "Don't worry about malcontented nobles. The war has made everyone grumpy, and your mother has to make hard choices to take care of her people. The palace is a brighter place for having you back. But try not to lose your guards. It makes it so much harder on them to protect you."

Her mother had straightened her mask and flattened a wayward strand of hair. "It's custom, my love. It was custom to send you to Byrne to be educated, like many princesses before you, to remind ourselves that our responsibility is not only to the city but also to the kingdom. And it's custom to present you at court now that you're home, to remind our nobles that we will always do our duty. Try not to get into any arguments with them."

Back in Byrne, Aunt Jonet had promised Ash that she knew all a princess needed to know. Languages. History. Etiquette. All her tutors praised her work. The problem was, none of that helped her navigate the court.

She didn't laugh at jokes she didn't like. She didn't put on a smile while half of the nobles in the city insulted her, and the others offered sugary words to curry royal favor. She wanted to talk archery or history or the midwinter mystery plays that Haven's theaters put up every year, not gossip.

The queen was charming and graceful. Aunt Jonet was brave and fair. Ash was only some of those things some of the time. She had no idea what kind of princess she wanted to—or could—be.

Lute and zither players in the central square started the next song, the playful winter tune enticing all those present to leave their drinks and sweets behind and join a long circle of dancers. Laughter mingled with the music, and a flutist offered a mocking counterpoint to the main melody.

Ash sidestepped the squires running over to join the dance and withdrew to the wooden tables with spice cakes and sugared winter berries set up along the garden wall, where those nobles who claimed to be too old and too dignified to dance gathered.

An elderly lady in a luxurious fur-lined dress, whose soft brown complexion glowed in the torchlight and whose gray hair was brushed to a shine, tsked at Ash's retreat. "Girl, don't stand around with us old folk. Enjoy the night. Find a dance partner and let yourself be swept away by the music."

Hovering at her elbow, a young gentleman in his early twenties, with a knight's sword at his side, coughed. He tugged at her sleeve and whispered something in her ear, but the lady simply shook him off. "I don't care if she is a princess or our stars-blessed queen herself or even the Ferisian empress, Idian. It's good advice and she would do well to heed it."

She pinned Ash with a stare. "If you don't have a dance partner, my reluctant grandson would be much obliged. He's too old for you, and sadly taken, but he knows how to swing."

"*Grandmother.*"

Ash blushed, both at the suggestion and the young man's discomfort. "Maybe another time, Lord Idian."

She had turned to the table with cakes when another lady spoke up. "You know she's *hardly* a princess. She's been away from Haven half her life. Longer than any royal before her. I've always thought the queen should have gotten rid of her. Having a crippled girl close by is a constant reminder of the accident that killed our beloved prince consort—"

"Wendalyn, *hush*," someone tried to interrupt her.

Wendalyn continued without the slightest hesitation. "She isn't fit for noble society. In the old days, she would never have been brought back."

Ash shrank with every bitter word. Her hands trembled, and her heart hammered. She barely heard the elderly woman's shocked gasp. She hardly registered that Idian strode over to Wendalyn, hooked his arm through hers, and none too gently marched her away.

She retreated. A young guardsman followed her, so she made sure he saw her escape to a garden bench at the farthest edge of a snowy lawn, where it stood hidden in the shadows between two lanterns.

A slender black-and-brown cat lay dozing on the bench. She woke when Ash sat down next to her. She stretched languidly and leapt to the ground, where she butted Ash's legs and walked in circles around her cane.

Ash bent down and let the cat sniff her hand. The cat investigated the girl before flopping onto her back, allowing Ash to pet her.

Ash grimaced. "You're the first palace resident who's happy to see me."

The cat purred contentedly.

"You're the bravest royal mice hunter, aren't you?"

The cat pushed her head into Ash's hands, and Ash relaxed a little.

"Will you be here to watch the new year? Or is it too loud and chaotic for you?" Ash scooted off the bench and crouched next to the cat. "I used to dream about coming home. This feels more like a nightmare."

Back in Byrne, Ash had been expected to rise with the sun, do her chores alongside the household, and start her lessons after breakfast. Everyone knew her, simply, as Ash. The girl who didn't know how to mend her own clothes, until Aunt Jonet's housekeeper taught her to sew and darn. The girl who didn't know how to hunt, but she'd pestered the guard captain to help her craft her own bow and shoot it. The girl who challenged the cook's son to a race to the top of the tower—and won. She'd had friends, back in Byrne. People who saw beyond her cane and her title.

In the royal palace of Kestrel's Haven, people bowed to her and never quite met her eye. When the bells struck dawn, everyone fell into their roles like pieces of a puzzle. The knights fitted tightly into their suits of armor. The queen's council followed her in formation, and the royal guard wore long lines in the stone floors to protect the royal family from danger.

Perhaps there was a place for Princess Adelisa—but she wanted to be Ash.

"How pathetic. Your own party, and you hide like a coward." A clear voice rang through the night.

The cat scurried away.

Ash's nearly-fourteen-year-old brother, Lucen, sauntered over to her, footsteps crunching through the snow.

Underneath a mess of brown hair he had the same bushy eyebrows as her, the same lanky figure, the same snub nose. Like her, he wore an outfit made of midnight blue: dark breeches and a long tunic with silver stars along the edges. On his left shoulder, he wore the royal stars embroidered in gold.

Ash got to her feet and smoothed her dress before she curtsied, mockingly. "*Prince* Lucen."

"Sister *dearest*." Lucen claimed the bench and perched on its backrest, looking down at his sister. He was flush with music and dancing, and snow clung to his boots. "Aren't you impressed by our power and grandeur?"

She shrugged. "The stars aren't impressed, so why should I be?" It was something the star priest at Byrne had said on an almost daily basis, whenever someone tried to find excuses to get out from under his teachings.

Lucen flicked a speck of snow from the cuff of his pants. "Did your peasant friends even know how to celebrate the birth of the year? Did no one teach you how to act like noble people do?"

Ash forced herself to count. First to ten. Then to twenty.

She'd tried—and failed—to figure her brother out. When she came home, she expected him to be happy to see her, like she was happy to see him. They used to play together, before she left to live with her aunt. Unlike Ash, Lucen had never been sent to Byrne, but he'd visited, along with their mother, and he'd made fast friends with Sterne, the cook's son. The three of them had built tree huts together in the apple orchard. Ash had regaled Lucen and Sterne with all the ghost stories of the garden estate and all the myths and legends Master Ebed, her history tutor, had taught her.

Until the Ferisian Empire crossed the northern border, claimed the fiefs that lay beyond the mountains, and her mother and brother stopped visiting. Ash wrote letters, sharing her adventures and misadventures, talking about the progress she had made in her studies and inquiring about the war. She had asked Lucen if he was scared. Last year, with her pocket money, she'd bought him a birthday present from a traveling merchant. A small silver sword pendant, to wear as a necklace and a luck charm. She wanted him to think of her. But replies were few and far between. Her mother was too busy being queen, while Lucen had started his duties as squire and crown prince.

Ash straightened her shoulders. "What do you want, Lucen?"

He glowered. "The squires say Byrne is a backward town. And you haven't answered my question."

The first night after coming home, Ash had sneaked into the palace's throne room, with its dome full of colorful stars. The heart of the crown's power. A symbol of her family's duty to serve Calinor, and a reminder of all the best and worst decisions of those who had come before them. Of war and death. Of peace and prosperity.

"When you're home," Aunt Jonet had told Ash, "remember that your words can make a difference. Use them to make Calinor better."

Ash made her way over to her brother. She pointed the cane at his heart like she was wielding a sword, forcing him to balance precariously on the backrest. "If you care so much about power, you should get to know Calinor instead of insulting it. Winter's Heart in Byrne is far better than in Haven." Ash had always loved Byrne's festivities, because everyone, from stable hand to noble and cook to tutor, danced and laughed together. She doubted Lucen would understand that. She doubted anyone here at court ever let go of their stiff formality.

Lucen pushed the cane away. "*Fine.* It was only a question. You don't have to get all defensive."

He got to his feet and dusted off his tunic. When he glanced up, his eyes held a challenge. "If it's so much better, you should have stayed. Byrne is where damaged princesses like Aunt Jonet and you belong."

Ash forgot her good intentions.

The words cut, and without thinking, she pushed off with her strong right foot and flung herself at her brother. Her fingernails grazed his tunic, but he sidestepped her and tugged her sleeve. Ash lost her balance and went sprawling. Her shoulder slammed into the bench, and her foot twisted underneath her. She bit her tongue to keep from crying out at the pain.

Lucen pulled her up by her arms. His face was close to hers when he snarled, "Mother should have left you there."

Then he turned on his heel and stalked away.

Ash scrambled to her feet, spotted a gate that led away from the main garden—and fled. Away from the music. Away from her brother. She was done.

Ash used her cane to steady herself as she sped deeper into the gardens, disappearing between the trees and the flowers. No beacons. No guests, no guards, no one to stop her from leaving this whole masked mess behind her.

But as the night embraced her, the path sloped steeply downward, and the ground underneath her feet suddenly disappeared. Ash's cane found no purchase, and it slipped from her fingers as she tumbled face-first into the grass.

CHAPTER TWO

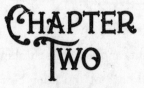

ASH

Ash pushed herself up on her hands and knees. Crushed blades of grass clung to her hair, and she couldn't see her cane anywhere. She patted the ground with no success. She could only imagine what people like Wendalyn would say if they heard about this. Or her brother, for that matter.

Footsteps crunched through the plants. In the low light, Ash could make out the scrawny figure of a squire, dressed in scuffed leathers and wearing a flowery mask. He shouldn't be here, but she might not have another chance to get help until the guests began to miss her. And who knew how long that would take?

She called out, "You, squire!"

The squire startled and steadied himself on a low stone wall. He hadn't seen her. "Yes?"

Ash swallowed. "I need help." She hated to admit it.

The squire spotted her. His eyes widened, and he rushed over. "What happened? Are you hurt?"

"I could use a hand," Ash said.

With a soft groan, she let the squire pull her to her feet. She brushed the grass from her hair and the dirt off her dress. Her heart hammered. "My cane lies here somewhere. Find it for me. Please."

Ash braced herself for the squire to start laughing. She hated how reliant she had to be on him. But he only grumbled while he scoured the grass around her.

Eventually the squire reached for a long dark shape. "Found it!"

Ash sighed with relief. *"Finally."*

Immediately, she realized how rude that sounded, and when the squire came back to her, she grimaced. She'd kept her guard up at the party, but that was no reason to be mean. "I'm sorry. You were kind to me and I'm horrible."

The squire offered the cane to Ash, and she accepted it gratefully. She felt more certain with her cane to lean on, more like she could figure out her next steps. She glanced over her shoulder in the direction of the musicians and pretended to be embarrassed but fine. "It was my own fault too. I shouldn't have wandered off, but I couldn't stand the crowds in the main square."

The squire tilted his head. "You don't like parties either?"

Ash studied him. It was an odd thing to ask, given the circumstance. But that wasn't the only odd thing about him. He looked different from the other squires she'd seen. His mask was made to accompany a dress instead of leathers. His armor was old, and it didn't quite fit, like it was someone else's.

"I don't like crowds," Ash said. Especially not crowds where, if people didn't laugh at her, they *wanted* something from her. An introduction to the queen. A promise to visit someone's estate or store. It made her feel like a means to an end.

"Me neither," the squire admitted. His pale skin turned bright red under his mask, and he pitched his voice softer—and lower.

It only intrigued Ash more. "Then why are you here?"

"Probably for the same reason you are."

"*Court.* All these nobles whose gossip is sharper than their blades, but both are pointless." The words tumbled out of Ash's mouth, unintended but true nonetheless.

The squire didn't scoff at her. Instead her comment

teased a smile from him. Mischief sparked in his eyes. "Parties are a way to show loyalty, my uncle claims. So we're here. But we have the whole evening. We could walk the maze and stay away from the main square."

Ash pushed a lock of her hair behind her ear. She heard the relief in his voice, and she felt certain the squire couldn't be one of the noble sons who lived at court and studied to become knights. They were used to these events. If not one of them, who was he? "What's your name?"

The squire paused before he answered. "Splinter."

Ash frowned. "That can't be a real name."

"Then what's yours?"

The question was so unexpected, Ash nearly laughed. He didn't know her. Giddiness surged through her, because that ignorance felt like freedom on a night like tonight. "My name is Ash."

"Of course *that* is a real name."

"It's the only one you'll get." Ash let her relief shine through. Relief at Splinter's plan. Relief at not having to go back. Relief at finding someone in Haven who didn't care about titles or positions first.

If she could spend the rest of the party with this strange squire, the night looked a whole lot brighter. "Lead the way, Splinter."

◆ ◆ ◆

The flower maze had been Ash's grandfather's favorite place. At least that was what Ash's mother had always told her. Ash understood that well. She loved its winding paths and the winter blossoms. She could *breathe* here. Still, she pretended to let Splinter lead.

He marched across the path and pushed away thorny stems that had crawled over the uneven stones. "None of the secrets of the maze will be safe from us. Anyone who can find their way around Haven can find their way around a simple flower labyrinth too."

Ash raised her eyebrows. Splinter walked with purpose, like he could leave his worries behind if he outpaced them. But at every corner and every crossway, he waited to make sure Ash was close by, and together they picked the most overgrown paths. Occasional snatches of music drifted out from the main square and settled between the flowers.

When Splinter ducked underneath the snow-covered branches of a willow tree, Ash pried. "You know Haven well?" She'd only ever gone into the city surrounded by guards. It was hardly the same as knowing a place.

Splinter spread his arms wide. "I know every street and every secret. I know the best market stalls to buy candied berries. The easiest shortcuts to get from the floating docks to the palace, and the quickest way to get from the palace to the Shallows." He picked another path, surrounded on both sides by holly bushes and wintergreen roses. "Haven is my home."

"I wish I could feel that way," Ash admitted. "I spent a lot of time with my family outside the city." It wasn't exactly a lie. "I'm not sure I could even find my way to the market, let alone find the best stalls."

"I could show you," Splinter offered. "In the market district, everyone has decorated their shops and stalls for the festival. And the docks are lit up at night to celebrate the new year. My brother always used to take me there, to watch the ships and drink spiced lemonade."

"Won't he—" Ash started.

Splinter ducked around a corner. "He left to fight in the mountains. At the border." His enthusiasm made way for worry—or grief. "I miss him. And my uncle doesn't care about the festival. He only cares about power and our family name." Splinter spat out those last words. "Maybe he should try to care more about our *family* instead."

"I'm sorry." Ash reached out a hand to Splinter. "Family is complicated sometimes."

She used her cane to shake some snow from the bushes,

opening up a path before them. "I hope the other squires treat you better?"

A shadow crossed Splinter's face, and he pushed through the gap.

Ash followed, uncertain of what to say, but determined that she didn't want to see him hurt. "When you're a knight . . ."

Splinter raised his chin. "I'm not just going to be a *knight*, I'm going to be a *hero*, like in Calinor's oldest stories." He took his ornamental dagger and spun it around on the tip of his finger, before he offered it to Ash with a flourish. "Like Sir Beril the Valiant, who defeated a dozen assassins with nothing but a piece of rope and a candelabra, saving Queen Eliane's life when she was a little girl. Or Lord Lyon, who crossed the Midnight Ocean twice." He visibly forced himself to grin.

Ash wanted to wrap her arms around him and find a way to make him laugh, both at the same time. She accepted the blade—which was old and blunt but beautifully crafted, with tiny stars etched in the metal—and tried to copy Splinter's move. The weapon spun once before it tumbled to the ground. "What about Sir Riven of the Cats?"

Splinter scooped up the dagger. "Riven of the Cats?"

"Don't tell me you've never heard of him."

Splinter's eyes sparkled. "Tell me, please?"

Ash cleared her throat. "Once upon a time, when the stars-blessed kingdom of Calinor stretched out far beyond the peninsula, and the royal family lived in Kestrel's Reach instead of Kestrel's Haven, Sir Riven of the Cats was the youngest and smallest of the queen's knights. He was barely strong enough to wield a sword, and not very tall. Most people thought he should never have been knighted. When Sir Riven and a handful of other knights were ambushed and captured by Ferisian soldiers, even the Ferisians considered leaving him behind. After all, he was wounded, and no one thought him valuable.

"But Sir Riven knew his captors underestimated him. As the soldiers brought the knights deeper into the empire, Sir Riven used their misjudgment to help his fellow knights escape. One by one. Night after night. Until Sir Riven was the only one left, and under heavy guard. But he managed to slip away too.

"Sir Riven tried to walk back to Kestrel's Reach with the stars for guidance, even though he was injured and the city was far away. He walked until he couldn't walk anymore. Until he saw the shape of buildings, and that is where he fainted.

"When he came to, he found himself not in Kestrel's Reach, but in a misty ruin of an old star temple. His injuries were healed, but no matter where he turned, he saw no exit. What he did see was a cat."

"A cat?" Splinter bit his lip. "Are you making this up?"

Ash laughed and circled around Splinter, spotting the path that led out of the maze.

Splinter ran after her. "Well, what happened next?"

"The cat led him to an altar in the middle of the temple, and on it lay a beautifully made sword. It was graceful and lithe and the blade shone brightly, as if it was forged from starlight. Sir Riven grabbed the hilt, and it fitted his hand perfectly. The sword made him feel stronger. The moment he picked it up from the altar, however, the mists around him solidified and ghosts attacked from all sides.

"Sir Riven fought. The sword struck the ghosts as if they were corporeal. The cat fought alongside him, hissing and clawing.

"The fight lasted for a long time, but neither the knight nor the cat tired. With every specter they vanquished, the mist cleared, and soon only the ruin remained. The ruin, the knight, the cat—and the sword made from starlight.

"Sir Riven simply kept walking home. When the people of Kestrel's Reach saw his sword, legends soon followed.

"He offered the starlight sword to his queen, but she let him keep it, and with it, her gratitude and a trusted place on her council. He was given a hero's welcome and a knight's respect. The cat stayed with him too.

"People forgot that Sir Riven had once been the smallest and unlikeliest of knights. Instead they knew him as brave, fierce, and above all, kind. With his legendary sword, he continued to fight for his queen and for all who needed his aid. And on days when he walked the city with his magical cat by his side, every stray cat followed them, like their own feline honor guard."

Ash's throat was dry and she licked her lips, but she congratulated herself on a plan well executed when she saw how intently Splinter was listening. "The starlight sword is rumored to be in the royal armory still."

Splinter *stared* at her, his expression a mixture of disbelief and longing. "Is *any* of this true?"

Ash glanced at the garden around her, as if to make sure no one else was close, then leaned in. Her heart gave the slightest twinge when she said, "Of course not. My brother and I made it all up."

Splinter blinked. Then he snorted. Finally he laughed, and Ash laughed with him.

CHAPTER THREE

ASH

Midnight crept closer, and with it, the lighting of the beacons. Time had flown by in Splinter's presence. It was so *easy* to talk to him. For the first time since coming home, Ash wasn't lonely. She wanted to take Splinter up on the offer to go to the market together. She wanted to spend more time with him, even if it meant they had to share their true identities.

Splinter hadn't identified anyone in his family, but Ash quietly went through everything her aunt had made her learn about the powerful noble families in Haven. The Labannes, who'd made their fortune investing in merchant ships that sailed from the floating docks. The DuLacs, who could trace their lineage back to the birth of the kingdom, and whose youngest had gotten into a fight with Lucen at the market late last summer and punched him. The lords of Divon, who oversaw the Royal Forest until the war called them north. Too many of them had lost relatives to the war, and countless knights were stationed in the mountains to keep Haven—and all of Calinor—safe.

Her new friend might belong to any of them.

"Splinter?" Ash scratched at the leather bands that held her mask in place. "Who are you squired to? Who are your parents?"

Splinter's hands clenched by his side, and he shook his head like he'd been caught in wrongdoing. A hint of unease tugged at the back of Ash's thoughts. But before she could wonder what secret Splinter could be hiding—

A scream tore through the quiet garden.

A tall guard appeared at the edge of the lawn, his fingers digging into the shoulders of a servant girl.

The girl fought to get away from him. Her face was blotched and tearstained. Her golden brown braid danced angrily as she tried to punch and kick at him. She screamed again. "Help! Let go of me!"

Splinter's eyes widened. He ran. Without hesitation. Without stumbling.

Ash's blood grew cold. She didn't always know how to

stand up for herself, but she would *not* tolerate anyone else being hurt. "Not at *my* party." She ran too, using her cane to propel herself forward.

The girl stamped on the guard's foot just as Splinter dove for the man's arm, trying to give the girl a way out. The guard caught the squire easily and sent him flying across the roses. Splinter landed in an awkward heap but scrambled back to his feet and charged with a shout.

"Stop it!" Ash's voice drowned in the chaos around her. She slammed her cane against the back of the guard's knee. Instead of making him stumble, she lost her own balance. By the time she'd straightened, Splinter had punched the guard *hard* and the girl broke free. Other guards, alerted by the shouts and fighting, came running across the grass.

With a loud roar, the rogue guard, blood streaming from his nose, rushed toward Ash. Splinter jumped in front of her, arms raised to protect her.

The guard swung at him, fury making him reckless.

Splinter blocked the first blow, his arms trembling under the impact, and the guard pulled back to swing again.

Ash seized the opportunity. She tore her mask down. "Don't you *dare*."

Her words echoed across the night and cut through the guard's anger. She peeled off her gloves to show the royal crest on her finger, and he froze.

Two guards descended on him and dragged him to the edge of the lawn. A third guard tried to pull Splinter away from Ash, and when he resisted, the guard roughly pushed the squire's mask aside.

The guard's face tightened. *"You."*

Underneath the mask, Splinter had freckles. A thin scar above the right eyebrow. And *she* scowled at the guard. "I didn't do anything. Let me go."

The guard tightened his grip. "Captain! It's the DuLac girl!"

Splinter flinched, and a broad-shouldered guard with a blue captain's band on his sleeve and a pronounced limp made his way over to the three of them. He'd been unsuccessfully trying to calm the servant girl. She was telling her story with big gestures, trembling hands, and loud determination. The captain handed her over to one of the other guards. He scratched his ear and frowned at Splinter before he turned to Ash.

Time slowed down as he recognized her. He sighed his relief and straightened, and that finally caused Splinter to turn as far as the guard would allow and *really* look at Ash.

The youngest DuLac. Ash shook her head. That was why Splinter's leathers didn't quite fit. They weren't—they couldn't be—hers. Though she had fought as bravely as any knight. "You're the one who punched my brother."

"You're the princess," Splinter said, at the exact same time. She looked confused and sad.

Ash pinned the guard holding Splinter with her gaze. She squared her shoulders. "Your captain heard what happened. Let . . ." Ash hesitated, remembering Splinter's flinch at being identified. Her discomfort with Ash's questions. She didn't even know what Splinter's given name was. "Let *go*."

The guard wavered. "But highness . . ."

"No," Ash said.

The guard captain cleared his throat. "It's good to see you safe, but we should get you back to the party. We have to take statements, my lady. And this girl has a history of violence."

Again Splinter flinched.

Ash narrowed her eyes. Maybe it wasn't just the family name. But that wasn't a conversation to have with guards present. "You should concern yourself with the violence of your guard and leave us."

"Your highness . . ."

"Leave. Now." She spoke the command the way her mother would. Expecting to be obeyed.

To her surprise, the guard captain tilted his head, then bowed. "As long as you stay in the flower maze, we can keep an eye on you." His men withdrew, the guard with the broken nose between them. The captain watched Ash for a moment longer, then returned to the servant girl and gently guided her back to the palace.

Leaving Ash alone with Splinter in the quiet garden.

Splinter shook out her arm and winced. "I wish I could be that strong." Her voice trembled, and she didn't meet Ash's gaze.

"Apparently you looked like a threat to them." Ash kept her voice light.

"They'd get along well with my uncle."

"The crown prince too, probably," Ash said. She pointed back at the flower maze. "Come on."

This time she didn't bother hiding how well she knew her way around. She walked toward the nearest stone wall and sat down to observe her companion. Splinter still seemed shaken, and nervous about what the rest of the night would bring. It was as if she'd shrunk in her leathers.

Ash took a deep breath. "What *is* your name?"

Splinter bit her lip and didn't answer.

Ash tapped her foot against the stone wall, uncertain of Splinter's reaction. "Are you ignoring me?"

Splinter shook her head. "No, my lady."

"Whose armor is this?" Ash asked, trying a different tactic.

"My brother's."

"He's off to the northern front?"

"Yes."

"And you're not a squire."

"No." Splinter's voice grew softer with every answer.

"But you want to be?" She'd heard of tales like that. Of boys who were assumed to be girls and took the long way to their swords. She was certain Splinter hadn't lied about her dream of becoming a knight.

Splinter shrugged. "I'm not a boy."

Ash mulled it over in her mind. Splinter's words. Her name. Her reactions. "But you're not a girl, either." It was part question, part statement. There were stories like that too. The people at her aunt's estate had told of a traveling physician many years ago, whose apprentice had been neither girl nor boy but a great hand with herbs and poultices and that was what mattered.

Splinter's breath caught. She went pale, then bright red. "No one just *says* that."

"I do. I'm not as ignorant as people think," Ash said. The words felt heavy, because she'd *thought* them, but she'd never spoken them before. "They see my cane and believe that's all of me. To them, I'm fragile and unfit." She managed half a smile. "And when I do speak up, they think I'm rude. They're not completely wrong. But I'm more than most people want me to be."

Splinter's hands twitched by her side. "Court is going to hate you," she blurted out.

Ash felt the cold of the night wrap around her like a cloak. "I know."

She wished she could find a way to navigate it. To find her place, and make a difference. To solve it, just like the flower maze.

Splinter plucked at the leather armor. "This was a midwinter night's dream. When word gets out about what happened, my uncle will have me on a cart to the star convent before sundown tomorrow."

"But you won't be happy there."

Ash's words were met with a pained silence. Splinter's heartbreak made Ash want to march to Lord DuLac and give him a piece of her mind. She narrowed her eyes, grasping at the barest threads of an idea. "You didn't answer my question. Do you want to be a squire?"

Splinter rubbed her swollen knuckles. "I want nothing more. I want to be a squire. I want to be a knight someday.

I want to be able to fight for what I believe in."

"What do you believe in?" Ash pressed.

Splinter thought about that. "I believe in my brother. I believe in putting an end to the war. It may not feel that way to you in the palace, but the war . . . it takes so much from so many people." She met Ash's gaze, and fire sparked in her eyes. "And I believe that I should be allowed to be who I want to be—who I *am*."

"Those aren't small dreams."

"Not everything worthwhile is easy."

It wasn't, but perhaps they could make it a little easier together. Splinter wasn't afraid like Ash could be sometimes. She'd jumped in front of Ash to protect her. Splinter was more like the knights in the legends Ash had learned than any of the squires she'd met. All she needed was a chance.

Ash wanted to give Splinter a chance.

This was the kind of princess she wanted to be. "Do you think you could believe in me?"

Splinter didn't hesitate. "Yes."

"Good. You'll be my squire, then. I'll sponsor you." Ash considered the rings on her fingers: two, alongside the royal crest. One had been given to her by her aunt. The other by her mother: a silver-and-gold feather, twisted around a small ruby. She pulled that one off and held it out to Splinter. "It's not just a simple solution because your uncle can't say no to me," she continued. "I *want* you to be my squire." Her voice trembled only slightly.

Splinter opened her mouth and closed it again.

Finally she managed, "Princesses don't *have* squires."

They didn't, but Aunt Jonet had made Ash study the laws of court until she could dream them. Every member of the royal family had a right to companions. Ash felt certain there was no exception for princesses and squires.

And she didn't want to face life in Haven alone. "Princesses don't normally attack guards either."

"You like to make things difficult for yourself," Splinter offered. It made her sound like one of Ash's tutors.

Ash let herself smile. "I like to make things difficult for the people who deserve it." She reached for Splinter's hand and dropped the ring in her palm. "I want to be able to fight for what I believe in too. I don't want to be alone here. Life at court terrifies me. Life in the city terrifies me. And I can't promise you you'll ever be allowed to be a knight, but I promise you'll never have to be anyone you're not."

When Splinter curled her fingers around the ring and comfortably dropped her other hand to her dagger, something settled deep within Ash. Something *right*. It felt new and dangerous and adventurous.

Splinter's eyes sparkled. "I'll be your squire."

"You will?"

Splinter took her hand. "I promise on the broken nose of your guard. I'll be your squire . . . Ash."

"Thank you . . ." Ash realized she didn't need to know her new squire's given name; she knew exactly who she was. "Splinter."

Splinter's joy was as radiant as the stars, and as bright as the beacons that were lit on the battlements of the palace. The music in the main square rose. The beacons in the gardens were set alight too, to be met with cheers and laughter and wishes for the new year. One beacon at a time, an avalanche of lights rolled from Palace Hill all the way down to the Shallows.

Splinter slipped the ring onto her finger. "I can't wait for our brothers to find out."

Ash watched the stars above them dance over the lights below, and smiled. She had a feeling this was the beginning of something legendary. "Splinter, I think we'll make a fearsome team."

CHAPTER FOUR

SPLINTER

Starlight reflected off the blanket of snow that covered the city, and the soft glow filtered in through the dusty windows. The rest of the study was clad in shadows and memories when a twelve-year-old squire-to-be with big dreams slipped through the door and opened her lantern far enough to bathe the room in light.

It didn't look any different from the last time she'd been inside, nearly four years before.

Splinter shivered. The room even *smelled* familiar. Of large maps and ink, and of oil used to polish daggers.

It was almost like nothing had changed.

But *everything* had changed. And had again at the princess's party, five days ago. And tomorrow, it would change once more. She almost couldn't quite believe it, but that was why she'd come here tonight. She had to say goodbye.

"Mama? I know you probably can't hear me," she said. "But do you remember the stories you used to tell me about how you met Dad when he was a squire at the palace? And how proud he was when Anders became a squire? You told me they sat vigil together, even though no one is required to sit vigils anymore. I stayed awake all night after you told me that. I stole one of Anders's practice swords and placed it on a windowsill and pretended it was an altar. I thought if I could sit vigil, I could become a squire too. But the next morning, I had to wear my dress and the weapons master still wouldn't teach me sword fighting."

Splinter's voice echoed in the empty room.

The room didn't reply.

"I never told you about it. I never told you I kept the sword and I started practicing when I could, with forms from Dad's books. With exercises I learned from spying on the guards. I thought I'd try to sit vigil again tonight. Here. Uncle Elias will have a fit if he finds out, but . . ."

Splinter ran a hand over the large desk that covered one side of the room. Her fingers remembered the grain of the wood. And there—a burn mark from a winter's night seven years before, when she had woken up from a nightmare and run here. Lady DuLac, who'd trained with the palace scribes, was focused on her translation work, and Splinter had climbed onto the desk to get to her and accidentally pushed over a candle. Splinter still carried a scar on her wrist from trying to shove the burning candle away.

"I miss you, Mama."

She pulled her mother's chair back from the desk. It scraped across the floor, and Splinter winced. Her uncle *would* have a fit if he found her here, and even though he couldn't do anything about her move to the palace, Splinter didn't want to leave with another fight. They fought about everything. The dresses Splinter refused to wear. Her friendships with the servants. Splinter's less-than-perfect scores in her lessons. She was never proper enough—or good enough.

She climbed into the chair and curled up. The leather was cracked and worn and comfortable. She loosened Ash's ring on her finger and turned it around and around.

"Tomorrow will be different. I'm going to the palace. I'm going to be a squire. Like Dad. Like Anders . . ." Splinter smiled, even though her vision swam. "The *princess's* squire. There's never been such a thing before, but Ash asked me and Lord Lambelin looked into it and said she could. Every member of the royal family has the right to sponsor a squire, and she wanted a companion. Even the queen agreed." As a result, Lambelin had arrived at her uncle's doorstep, with a letter from Ash to Splinter, and orders for her to report to the palace after the next rest day. Her uncle had been furious, but the commander had reminded him that royal orders were royal orders.

Lambelin had placed his hands on Splinter's shoulders. "She will do her duty to Calinor, as will we all. *Do you understand*, Elias?"

Perhaps her uncle didn't. As far as Splinter was aware, the only things that mattered to Lord DuLac were political power and prestige. He'd lamented that their family's manor, their ancestral home, was too far from court to be convenient. That the family's influence at court had dwindled as a result of Splinter's mother's unseemly scribe work. That everything used to be better, that traditions used to be kept. He never talked about duty or honor, but with the commander of the royal guard—and the queen's best friend—towering over him, he'd relented.

Splinter had clung to the commander's words. She'd do her duty. She'd be loyal to Ash and she'd stand by her side and protect her from harm. "And Ash, Mama, she's *magnificent.* Most of the other nobles don't care for her. I saw the way they sneered at her. They think she's weak and quiet and weird. But I think you'd like her. She's kind. She pays attention to the people around her. She knew me for who I was. Immediately."

After her parents died and her brother left, not a lot of people did.

Splinter blinked and rubbed her nose. "It doesn't mean I'm a *boy.* Did you know no law explicitly bans noble girls from becoming squires? It's just *custom,* Ash said. Old stick-in-the-mud lords deciding only their sons could be like them. As long as the master of squires thinks I do my duties well, I can be a squire and no one can stop me."

Outside the study, the floorboards creaked. Splinter fell silent. She dug her fingers into the arms of the chair, and she waited for the stillness of night to settle over the house once more.

"It doesn't mean I'm a girl either. I wore Anders's squire armor for the Winter's Heart festival, and I carried your dagger. I felt like *me* for the first time. I don't know exactly what that means yet, but I want to figure it out. Camille told me, living someone else's truth isn't living. So I hope you don't mind, but I'm leaving my dresses here. And my name too. I'm Splinter now."

The room said nothing. Splinter tilted her head, like if she could focus hard enough, she might hear a reply.

"You always taught Anders and me it's our duty to serve Calinor and the crown in whatever way we can, and I *will*. I'll protect Ash. I'll fight for her, if I have to. I know I can be brave. The weapons teachers at the palace will teach me to fight alongside the other squires, and I'll learn everything I can, until they accept me as a knight one day." Splinter made a warding sign with her hand. Even Ash couldn't promise that. "I hope they will, in any case. Because when I'm strong enough, I want to go to the border. To the Crescent Mountains. I want to see Anders again."

The silence in the room grew deeper, and Splinter frowned.

"I guess no one told you. Anders went to fight in the war. Just like Dad. He wrote us last year to say he plans to stay in the mountains. He keeps being sent behind enemy lines, and he feels more at home there than he ever did in Haven. But I'll find my way back to him, I promise. I know you'd want us to stick together, and we will. I don't want to lose him too."

Splinter swallowed. She bit her lip. Even when talking to a ghost or a memory in the middle of the night, some words felt too big to speak.

She sat back in the chair, until the candle in the lantern burned all the way down to a tiny stump and an even smaller wick. What was left of the flame danced and protested before it extinguished.

Outside, cold starlight made way for the rose gold of the dawning sun. The red glow lit up the ice flowers that had grown on the glass overnight.

When the city of Haven began to yawn and creak and wake, Splinter stretched and rose.

"I'll come back if I can," she whispered. "If Uncle Elias will let me."

She took one last look at the study, at all the familiar nooks and crannies, and all the secrets it still held in its locked cabinets and drawers, and she smiled. "Anders and me both. I'll make you proud. You'll see."

Splinter had closed the door with a soft *snick* and hung the key on a leather band around her neck when behind her, someone cleared his throat. "Leave that here. You'll have no need for it in the palace."

Splinter's hands went cold. She swung around and found Lord Elias DuLac towering over her. Despite the early hour, he was dressed for the day, wearing a caramel-brown tunic with fur lining, breeches, and leather boots that came up to his knees. He had a dagger by his side and dark lines across his forehead. He kept his dull brown hair at chin length, and not a strand of it was out of place.

"Uncle . . ."

Elias's mouth pulled into a thin line, and he held out his hand. "The key, please."

"It's mine," Splinter protested. The key had been a gift from her mother, given to Splinter so she would know she always had a safe place to go if she needed it.

Elias took a step forward. "The key belongs to this manor. And you, if I remember my orders correctly, now belong to the royal princess."

Splinter winced.

When Splinter's mother died, Uncle Elias had been recalled from the mountains to serve as head of the family and guardian to Splinter and Anders until Anders completed his mandatory service to the crown and could inherit. Despite her grief, Splinter had been relieved. She'd met her uncle twice before, and he was young and brave and the spitting image of Lady DuLac, with the same sharp eyes and immovable conviction. Splinter had expected him to be as kind as her mother too.

He wasn't.

After Lord Lambelin's visit, Uncle Elias had sent

Splinter to her room. He hadn't spoken to her for the rest of the day or in the days that followed. And perhaps Splinter should have been grateful—it meant they didn't fight, at least—but it had only made her feel more alone.

She wanted him to be happy for her. She didn't just want to make her parents proud. She didn't just miss her brother. She missed feeling like part of a family.

Elias shook his head. "Perhaps if your brother—by some miracle—manages to survive the war and claim his inheritance, he will tolerate your foolish notions. But I certainly won't. As long as I am head of this family, I will not support your making a mockery of our knighthood. If you leave now, you do not have to return."

A hundred different responses thundered through Splinter's head. A hundred different emotions too. Anger. Determination. Hurt. Heartbreak.

Splinter bit the inside of her cheek. She refused to give Uncle Elias the satisfaction of seeing her cry. She yanked at the necklace. With blazing eyes, she deposited the key in her uncle's hand. "I will go, and you can't stop me."

He pocketed the key with a cold smile. "I'm not unreasonable. You'll come to see sense. Once you do and make amends, you may find your way back here. But not before."

He turned on his heel, leaving Splinter in the hallway, her hands balled into tight fists and resolve straightening her spine. There was only one path forward.

She would not see sense. She would not make amends. She would show him. She would show them all.

By late morning, snow still covered the city of Kestrel's Haven. The youngest children in the neighborhood—nobles and commoners—were playing outside, making snow stars and starting snowball fights.

Under other circumstances, Splinter would have joined them. Snow was rare in Haven, and twelve was never too old for a snowball fight. But not today.

Splinter rolled her shoulders. Her new leather armor smelled of wax and tanning, and while it was made to fit, it did so uncomfortably. According to the armorer, the leather would chafe until it settled.

"You're creaking," Camille whispered with a twinkle in his eyes. As the son of the housekeeper, he had overseen the packing of Splinter's belongings and was now busy double-checking the packs on her piebald mare, Owl.

"Hush." Splinter tried not to move around too much, aware that Camille was right. She pulled a short letter she'd written after her fight with Uncle Elias out of her pocket. "Will you give this to the messenger service? I want to make sure Anders knows where I am."

Camille smiled. "Of course."

She glanced in the direction of the mansion's entrance. When Anders had become a squire eight years before, her parents had joined him on his way to the palace, to officially present him. The whole household—including a curious four-year-old Splinter—had seen him off, and it was a day of excitement and celebration.

Now her uncle's words swirled around Splinter. If she left, she didn't have to come back.

But she couldn't stay.

The door opened, and Splinter's heart skipped a beat.

Camille's mother walked out into the courtyard. Veridia wore her thick black hair tied back in a braid, and the keys on her belt clanked as she moved. She carried a small paper bag with Splinter's favorite snow caramels. She smiled, and it transformed her whole face.

Maybe this—too—was why Splinter no longer felt at home here. Everyone had smiled more often when her parents were still alive.

"Look at you, the very picture of your brother." Veridia held out the sweets to Camille, who hid them away in

Splinter's saddlebags. "He would be so proud if he could see you now. We're all proud."

She pulled Splinter into a tight hug.

Splinter blinked hard. "Thank you."

Veridia pushed a strand of hair out of Splinter's face. "You're a near image of your mother too. But with your father's grit and heart. Our princess is lucky to have crossed paths with you."

A shadow passed over her face, but it was too fleeting for Splinter to identify.

"You need to remember—your determination and your loyalty are your best qualities. It may not always feel like that, but they will serve you well."

Splinter nodded. "I'll remember."

"It's not an easy path you've chosen. You and the princess. Many nobles care deeply about tradition. They prefer power and appearance to truth and loyalty."

"Like my uncle?" Splinter hadn't meant to ask that, but once the words tumbled out, she wanted to know the answer.

Veridia grimaced. "At the palace, you'll have far more powerful enemies than your uncle." She shook her head. "Once you're in the princess's service, you're her first line of defense. You stand between her and danger. Trust your princess. Everyone else has to earn your trust five times over."

Splinter pulled a face. She'd heard stories like that about the palace, often from her mother, and it was the one thing she didn't look forward to. Well, that and seeing the crown prince again after giving him a black eye.

"What about the other squires?"

Veridia placed a calloused hand against Splinter's cheek. "They may see you as a threat, starling. As someone who tricked their way into this position. Perhaps some of your teachers will agree. You're going to have to prove your worth and show that you're willing to work hard."

Splinter nodded slowly. "I'll prove myself to them."

"I know you will." Veridia smiled. "Now, what are you waiting for? The day isn't getting any longer, and you have to report at the palace before the midday bell."

Splinter risked another glance at the door, but then she nodded. "Thanks, Veridia."

She walked toward Owl. The armor creaked and chafed when she mounted up, but once she settled in the saddle and tightened the reins, Splinter felt as knightly as she ever had. Once she passed through the gate, there would be no going back.

Though it ached to leave home like this, she smiled.

And she couldn't stop smiling when she nudged Owl into a slow trot and set out on her way toward Ash. She would work hard to be the best princess's squire the palace had ever seen.

Chapter Five

Splinter

The cobblestone road that wound its way up along Palace Hill, past the curtain walls, and to the royal palace was covered in a thin layer of slush and ice. At the first gate, a raven-haired woman with the shoulders and arms of a blacksmith, carrying a bundle of tools, fought to keep her balance. Two guards who patrolled the road watched her struggle until she threw a sharp look and sharper words at the younger of the two, who laughed and hurried to assist her.

At the second gate, where most travelers left the road for the palace's outer ward and secondary buildings, such as the kitchens and the servants' quarters, an older gentleman with sandy brown skin and a leather carrier full of books slipped a few paces away from Splinter. He managed to shield the books but slammed his left shoulder into the ground. Splinter slid out of the saddle to help.

He took her outstretched hand, and behind a pair of thin glasses, he squinted at her. "Thank you, Squire . . . ?"

Splinter hoisted the carrier with books over Owl's saddle. She bit back a joyful laugh at his question. These steps on an icy road. This was where she left her old self behind.

"Splinter, sir. Squire to the princess."

"Ah. I've heard of you." He didn't elaborate whether that was good or bad or nothing at all. Instead he set the pace toward the palace's main buildings. He kept his eye on the books hanging over the saddle, not on Splinter walking next to her horse.

An awkward silence stretched between them all the way to the third and final gate, where a fortified gatehouse protected the entrance to the royal ward.

The gentleman reclaimed the carrier and draped it over his right arm. He nodded at Splinter. "My name is Master Elnor, tutor to many a wayward squire. I imagine we'll see each other again soon." Without so much as a glance at the guards, who stood aside to let him pass, he disappeared into the palace.

The guards closed ranks again in front of Splinter.

One of them, a young man whose helmet slanted over bright red hair and whose green eyes were attentive and kind, shook his head. "That man is impossible. Trying to make a good impression on your teachers, squire?"

"I didn't know he was a teacher," Splinter said. She'd settle for not making a *bad* impression. Plenty of people inside the palace would have made up their minds about her already. She didn't want to add to that.

"Why are you here?" the guard prompted carefully. His companion snickered, and Splinter felt the blood rush to her cheeks.

She straightened, remembering the words Ash had given her. "My presence is requested by Princess Adelisa. I'm reporting as ordered."

The guard stepped aside. "Carry on to the courtyard, squire. One of the grooms will see to your horse. You are to report to the master of squires, who is an even more intimidating sort than Master Elnor, if you can believe it. Servants will show you the way."

"Thank you," she said. "Guardsman . . . ?"

"Jasse."

"Thank you, Guardsman Jasse."

He winked.

Splinter grabbed Owl's reins and walked to the wide,

open courtyard of the royal palace.

This part of the palace, closed to all except those with permission to pass through its gates, came straight from any legend.

Surrounding the courtyard were structures as tall as any Splinter had ever seen. The palace's central keep, with its majestic stained glass windows and turrets on all five corners, towered over her. Long stone buildings embraced the southern and western sides of the courtyard, and bridges and gateways led to the rest of the ward. Her brother had once described the palace as a city within a city, and he hadn't been wrong.

One of the stable hands, wearing the sensible gray of palace service and hay stalks in his auburn hair, sauntered up to take Owl to the stables. "The royal stables," he said. "On account of you being the princess's squire."

"How many stables are there?" Splinter asked. Her family's manor wasn't small, but this was a whole different world.

"Too many."

"What about my bags?"

The boy barely refrained from rolling his eyes. "I'll make sure your belongings are brought to your rooms."

He took Owl's reins, and she came willingly, leaving Splinter to face the palace on her own. But before the boy and the horse were out of sight, the doors of the keep slammed open, and a familiar figure came running out.

Ash wore a simpler dress than the night Splinter had met her—a russet-brown woolen gown with sleeves tied at the shoulders. Her leather boots were laced up to her knees, and she'd swapped her carved cane for a smooth one. She might have been any noble daughter in the palace, if it weren't for the royal crest on her finger and the determination in her eyes.

Splinter felt a rush of worry. What if Ash had changed her mind? What if she had decided she didn't want a squire at all? What then?

But Ash stopped an arm's length away from Splinter and beamed at her. "I wasn't sure if your uncle would let you come or if I'd have to send a detachment of guards."

"Despite this horrifying break with tradition, Lord DuLac would never disobey a royal order," Splinter said, affecting her uncle's mannerisms. She shoved her nerves aside and bowed. "And neither would I."

Ash nodded regally. "Well then, welcome to the palace, Squire Splinter. I'm glad that you're here."

Squire Splinter. Splinter would not grow tired of those words. "My sword is yours, your highness."

Ash glowered at the honorific, and Splinter smiled at

her, as servants crossed the courtyard around them. Splinter knew from her brother's stories that when Anders had reported for duty, five other boys had been with him, and they'd all been ceremoniously welcomed by the knights who sponsored them as well as the squires they would learn and study alongside for two years, before they left to serve their knights. But with the war calling so many fighters north, that had changed. Even though the empire was far from Haven, the city had lost some of its color. Now squires reported like Splinter did, without fanfare or ceremony.

Well, the two of them didn't need it. Still, "I *am* yours to command, Ash."

Ash shook her head. "I don't need someone to command. I need someone to stand beside me."

Splinter reached for Ash's hand. "I can do that too."

Ash squeezed Splinter's fingers. "Come, I'll show you to your room. It's next to mine. You'll need to present yourself to Lord Brenet, the master of squires. And tonight you'll meet my mother and brother for dinner. Although . . ." A mischievous smile played around Ash's lips. "You've met Lucen already, of course."

"Don't remind me," Splinter muttered. She didn't relish the idea of seeing Lucen again after she'd punched him in the marketplace—even if she still thought she'd been right to stop him from bullying a girl at one of the stalls. She was intimidated by the idea of meeting Queen Aveline too. She didn't want to disappoint the queen after she had allowed Splinter to come to the palace.

She let Ash pull her into the keep, and when she saw the entrance hall open up before her, everything else was forgotten. The winter sun shone through star-shaped windows, casting colorful shadows on the light gray walls. Roughly hewn steps led to the heavy double doors that guarded the throne room.

On either side of the hall, high above doors that led deeper into the keep, were the worn and battered shields of knights whose actions had changed the course of Calinor's history. Knights whose bravery had changed battles, whose loyalty was unmatched. Knights who had kept the royal family safe from danger. Knights whose adventures were studied by squires longing to be heroes.

No DuLac shields were part of this collection, but Splinter only needed to close her eyes to imagine her own shield there one day.

Lord Brenet, master of squires, leaned his elbows on his desk and folded his hands. Tiny scars ran across his face, and his hair was so light it was nearly colorless. His pale blue eyes drilled through Splinter.

She forced herself to stand tall, her hands behind her back.

Once Ash had showed her to a room—a room that was twice the size of her chambers back home—she'd guided Splinter to the office of the master of squires. She could've asked a servant to lead Splinter, but instead she showed her the way through the winding hallways and passages herself, and when Splinter commented on it, she shrugged. "I'm still learning my way too. I like knowing where to go."

"Like the maze?" Splinter offered.

"Like the maze." Ash had grinned.

Lord Brenet pulled Splinter back to the present. "Other squires . . . other nobles . . . may look at your position and imagine it is one of ease and comfort." His voice was deep and measured. "*You* may look at your position and think the same. With the princess as your sponsor instead of a knight, your service may look different. But I will not let you tarnish the reputation of squires in this palace."

Splinter pushed her shoulders back. "I'm willing to work hard, my lord." She wasn't looking for any special treatment.

"I would work you hard even if you weren't willing,

squire," Brenet said. "You have your duties to your princess. You also have your duties to me and to the palace. All junior squires—including you—take lessons from the palace tutors. You will learn to fight. You will learn etiquette and service. You will learn strategy and history. And you will perform admirably, or you'll answer to me."

"Yes, my lord."

Brenet pushed his chair back and wheeled it around the desk. He maneuvered himself closer to Splinter. Ash had told her that Brenet had been one of the queen's fiercest field commanders until his legs had been crushed in an ambush. After his recovery, he had returned to the palace and taken over teaching the squires.

"Have you trained with swords before?" he asked.

Splinter didn't think that following exercises from a book counted to this man. "No, sir."

"Bows, blades?"

Splinter shook her head. "Nothing, sir."

"A squire without experience in times of war and uprising." He sighed. "Let's see if you have an aptitude at all. Follow me."

Splinter knew about the war, and she wanted to ask about the uprising, but Brenet had already left the office. She had to run to keep up with him, as they followed a gently sloping hallway down to a broad corridor and east toward a secondary building.

He kept talking. "You'll be expected to learn your way around. Tardiness because you were lost is not acceptable. You'll be expected to keep your gear clean, your weapons sharp, and your horse well groomed and well fed."

At a tall set of doors, one of which stood slightly ajar, Brenet turned to Splinter. "Every squire who passes through these halls dreams of becoming a knight. That decision is not mine, nor would I want it. It's the queen's, and the queen's alone. But it *is* my responsibility to ensure that every squire knows what it means to *be* a knight. To follow the queen's orders in times of peace, and to fight for her in times of war. If I do not think you have it in you, if I think your presence dishonors or threatens the royal family, I don't care what the princess wants, I'll send you back home before she can muster a protest. Do I make myself clear?"

Splinter swallowed. "Yes, my lord. Perfectly."

"Good."

He pushed open the door, and a wave of sound crashed over Splinter. A shiver of anticipation coursed along her spine. On the indoor practice courts, at least two dozen junior squires were practicing their weapons skills. Some with pole arms and daggers, others at the archery lanes, and the vast majority in circles drawn for sword fighting. In four different circles, all marked with chalk borders, squires holding wooden practice swords were paired off. Some attacked with abandon, while others were more cautiously trying to find the right opening. The squires waiting for their turn shouted tips, cheered for their friends, or heckled their opponents.

In the midst of the group stood a tutor Splinter already knew—Master Elnor, this time without the carrier full of books. He wore a practical tunic and held a slender stick like it was an extension of his arm. He looked dangerous. Far more dangerous than out on the street.

Where the other weapons masters on the practice courts had assistants, Master Elnor focused on all four fights at once, turning from one circle to the other, squinting through his glasses, offering commentary where it was needed. "Keep your guard up, Ilsar!" "Meren, you are too slow!" "It's a deadly weapon, not a breadstick!"

Brenet coughed at those last words, but when Splinter glanced at him, she couldn't make out a smile. He kept his face impassive. He called out, "Master Elnor, I have another student for you."

Immediately, the room quieted as every squire in the practice courts stopped their work to watch. Splinter heard the whispers. "It's the princess's squire!" "She doesn't belong here." "She's only here as a favor to the princess. People like her will *ruin* Calinor."

Splinter tried to pinpoint who had said that, but none of the squires would meet her eye. Nor did she recognize any of them, except for one. At the farthest end of the court stood a squire with a bow several inches taller than he was. Prince Lucen scowled when he caught her staring.

Closer by, two of the older squires, lanky boys with short-cropped sandy hair who appeared to be twins and who were both holding practice swords, laughed at her. "She looks like she's never held a weapon in her life."

Master Elnor slammed his stick to the floor with a resounding crack. "Did your tutors give you leave to stop? Get back to work." His voice echoed through the room. He pointed at the squires with swords around him. "That holds true for you too. Meren, Corwen"—he indicated the twins—"leave your swords and take five laps around the room."

When the two handed in their swords, Elnor turned to Splinter. "Take one of the practice swords, squire, and let's see what you've got."

The air got sucked out of the room, and Splinter swallowed hard. Vaguely she noticed that Elnor stepped into the abandoned circle and every squire who wasn't practicing gravitated toward it, determined to watch. Someone pushed a blade into her hand, and she tested its weight and grip. It was lighter than the wooden swords she'd used at home, and the hilt was still warm.

Splinter's hands were damp and rivulets of sweat ran down her back as she stepped into the circle. She'd only ever tried paper exercises. She had never fought against anyone before. Not with swords.

Elnor's stick shot toward her, faster than she could anticipate, and it cracked across her ribs. "*Breathe*, squire. It won't do anyone any good if you faint here."

Splinter gulped in a breath of air, and her head cleared a little.

Elnor beckoned her forward. "Have you ever sparred before?"

Splinter shook her head. "No, sir. But I've practiced forms."

Her words were met with muffled laughter from the other squires.

Elnor didn't mind them. "Mastering forms is essential to good swordplay. Try to hit me with your sword. Widen your stance. Shoulders back. And fight."

Splinter relaxed her grip on the sword. She observed

Master Elnor. The books she'd found in her father's study had taught her that everyone had a weakness. That there was a strategy for every opponent, no matter how strong.

Maybe the writers hadn't met Master Elnor, because she didn't have a clue what his weakness was. He stood with the comfort of a man who feared no sword.

"*Fight*, squire!"

Splinter leapt. She arced the sword up high and threw her whole body into bringing it down toward her tutor. Elnor parried the sword effortlessly. "Big movements will tell your opponent what you're planning. Keep it small."

Splinter lunged forward. Again Elnor deflected. He slammed the tip of his stick against her shoulder. "Sloppy. Where are those forms, squire?"

The words cut. Splinter rubbed her aching shoulder. She reminded herself that he *wanted* her to show her skills. She needed to keep her wits about her.

She brought her practice sword up to shoulder height and cautiously settled into the stance she always used for practice. The familiarity loosened her muscles and sharpened her awareness.

Elnor dropped the tip of the stick, a fraction, nothing more, but Splinter lunged at the opening. This time when he raised his guard, she didn't let herself be pushed back.

She circled around Elnor and thrust low. When he parried and countered, she sidestepped his attack and slashed at him. They fell into a rhythm, where every one of Splinter's attacks glanced off Elnor's blocks, but each time she spotted a new opening, she reached for it.

The sword grew heavy in Splinter's hands. Her aching shoulder protested, and she collected bruises from Elnor's parries, but it didn't stop her. She *laughed*. This was what she'd dreamed of doing.

Elnor's stick slashed out at her. Low. Too low for her to block properly. The stick swept her feet out from under her, and Splinter slammed down to the floor. She tried to cling to her sword, but the weapon slipped from her hands.

Master Elnor stepped in and pinned down her sword hand with his stick. "*Never* let go of your sword, squire."

Splinter nodded. "Yes, sir."

Elnor regarded her. The stares from the other squires weighed down on her. With a start, she realized that Lord Brenet had remained to watch too, his arms crossed as he considered her.

Did he think she had it in her? Did any of them think she could be a squire? Or was she an interloper to them?

Elnor's hand swam into her vision, and the tutor helped Splinter to her feet. He held her when she stood, and slowly, like it took him a long time to decide, he nodded. "You're not hopeless."

He turned to Brenet. "She'll do."

Splinter's breath caught. As praise, it wasn't much, but she would learn. She would become better. She *would* do.

Around them, some of the squires who'd smirked at Splinter frowned. Others raised their eyebrows, and one or two of them—including a tall squire with pale winter freckles and a shock of red hair—grinned. Prince Lucen was nowhere to be seen.

"Raw talent is only the starting point, squire," Brenet said. Begrudgingly he added, "But it's better than nothing. One of the older squires will guide you to the palace stores for your uniforms. Report to your classes tomorrow. Tonight you are expected to present yourself to the queen. Tidy yourself up, and do *not* disappoint us."

"Yes, my lord," Splinter said.

"Ilsar," Elnor barked. "Return your sword and show the new squire around."

The red-haired squire bowed slightly to his opponent. He took his sword and Splinter's and returned them to a rack on the wall. Lord Brenet left the room, Master Elnor returned to teaching, and Ilsar offered Splinter an arm, then laughed when she scowled at him. "Don't look too disgruntled, squireling. No one can get past Master Elnor's defense, except perhaps Lucen. He must see something special in you, to be so lavish with his praise."

"Lavish?" Splinter had to take two steps for every one of Ilsar's.

He led her to another set of doors, opposite the one she'd entered through. "You must have impressed him. Which means you may actually provide us with some entertainment, before you wash out. A princess's squire. What a joke."

CHAPTER SIX

ASH

Ash arrived to the dining room before anyone else. The table was set. The candles in the chandelier and the lanterns along the windows were lit. Outside, twilight covered the city like a blanket. Inside, the fire in the fireplace crackled, and small sparks danced around the flames.

Ash loosened the leather straps of her arm brace and pushed the wide silver bracelet that wound around her wrist back in place.

"I can't believe you did this," Lucen said, slamming open the door and stomping into the room.

Ash tightened the leather straps again. She'd grown adept at tying them one-handed. "Did *what*, Lucen?"

Her older brother walked over to her spot by the

fireplace. He was resplendent in his royal blue tunic trimmed with silver, but his face was twisted in a grimace. "Made that DuLac your squire."

Ash pulled her sleeve down. "Just because Splinter hurt your feelings doesn't mean I shouldn't ask her to be my companion here at court." She didn't add that she didn't have anyone else to rely on, and that included her brother.

Lucen crowded her. "Companion, attendant, *fine*. Have her be your lady-in-waiting for all I care. But you asked her to be your squire. You're not even a knight! You're never going to *be* a knight!"

"And I suppose you are?" Ash shot back. She leaned a hand against the mantel to give herself space. "You're not behaving very knightly."

"To be a knight of Calinor *matters*," Lucen hissed.

"If being a knight of Calinor matters, maybe you should try acting like one," another voice cut in. Splinter appeared in the door opening, scowling at Lucen. She'd changed to a formal squire's outfit: a silver-gray tunic, a dagger, and a badge on her left shoulder that showed her sponsor's crest— in this case, the royal family's gold stars on a midnight-blue patch, with a red circle denoting a younger princess.

Splinter looked every inch the princess's squire, and Ash couldn't be prouder.

Lucen spun around. "Do *not* forget who you're addressing."

"If being a knight of Calinor matters, maybe you should try acting like one, *your highness*." Splinter walked over to the fireplace and placed herself between Ash and Lucen.

Lucen grabbed Splinter by her tunic, pulling her close. "Only one of us will ever be a knight of Calinor."

Splinter grunted. "My mother and my brother taught me what honor and duty mean. You're a bully who throws tantrums every time he doesn't get his way."

"You have no idea what you're talking about. It's my duty to keep the kingdom strong." Lucen pushed her into the rough wall next to the fireplace. "And a knight's sword is for people who deserve it, who respect the kingdom's history."

Splinter kicked him.

As Ash dashed forward to intervene, she saw movement from the corner of her eye. Queen Aveline and Lord Lambelin entered the room side by side. The queen's dark eyebrows were drawn together in a frown.

Lambelin stalked over to the fighting squires immediately, his face pale with fury. He grabbed Splinter and Lucen by the scruffs of their tunics and tore them apart like they were a pair of angry palace cats. "You both discredit the uniforms you wear."

Splinter stopped struggling at once. Lambelin had to shake Lucen before he dropped his fists. "I was under the impression that squires were taught respect and self-control. Perhaps I was mistaken," Lambelin continued.

Ash opened her mouth to defend Splinter, but the queen placed a hand on her shoulder, gently but insistently. "Stay out of this." So Ash kept her silence, and nervously toyed with the silver bands around her fingers.

Lambelin looked at Splinter coldly. "Is there any reason why the queen should not send you home?"

Splinter bit her lip. "No, my lord."

Lambelin turned to Lucen. "And you, you're supposed to set an example for the other squires. Is there any reason why you keep getting into these fights?"

"She—" Lucen started, but Lambelin shook him again. Ash was impressed by the strength it must take to keep the two of them held up by their scruffs. "No, sir."

"Remember that, the next time you think about brawling in front of the queen." Finally Lambelin let go, and Ash breathed a quiet sigh of relief.

Both Lucen and Splinter bowed to the queen, but no one could deny the look of pure disgust the crown prince gave Splinter, or the silent challenge Splinter offered up in response.

Queen Aveline let go of Ash's arm and swept toward the table, taking her place at the head. "We will sit, have dinner, and that will be the last of it," she said in a tone that brooked no argument.

Everyone fell in line around her: Lucen on her left side, Lambelin on her right, Ash and Splinter next to them and opposite each other.

Ash locked eyes with Splinter. "Are you okay?" she whispered.

Splinter nodded.

Lambelin poured wine for himself and the queen and juice for the others. Queen Aveline turned to Splinter. "My daughter tells me you intend to be a knight one day."

Splinter went bright red, but she didn't flinch. "Yes, your majesty. I hope so."

"It's not been done before."

"That doesn't mean it shouldn't be tried," Splinter said carefully.

Lucen coughed.

The queen took a slow sip from her goblet. "It doesn't mean it should, either."

Ash watched her intently. After a day full of meetings and council sessions, where she negotiated with the nobles of the court to provide for Haven's poor and the merchants of the city to keep their prices low so everyone could afford their wares, the queen appeared tired. She had thin lines around her eyes and mouth, and some of her curly copper hair had escaped the intricate braid laced with gold filigree.

She hadn't been thrilled by Ash's request to let Splinter be her squire. It had taken all of Ash's powers of persuasion, with more than a little unexpected help from Lambelin, to convince her.

"You promised to let Splinter prove herself," Ash reminded her now.

"I intend to keep that promise, my love," Queen Aveline replied. She sighed, like she meant to say more, but right then the doors opened.

Two servants brought in the first course of the meal. A soup tureen shaped like a starflower, with a fragrant leek-and-duck soup. Small freshly baked breads with dried herbs and white cheese. A platter filled with small pastries, ranging from small savory pies with chicken-and-lemon stew, to leaves filled with peppers and cloves, to sweet baskets full of spiced berries. They set out the food for all five of them and swapped out a candle in one of the lanterns. Everyone sat in silence until they had closed the door behind them.

Lambelin placed a hand on the queen's arm. "Perhaps

you should tell Adelisa and Splinter why you're concerned, majesty."

Ash had picked up her spoon but put it down again. She frowned. "Mother?"

Queen Aveline shot Lambelin a look of annoyance, and it occurred to Ash that she didn't just look tired—she looked *old*.

Lucen sat up. "Is something wrong?"

Queen Aveline sighed. "I thought we might have a meal first. I've fought hard to keep the war away from you."

Opposite Ash, Splinter clenched her fingers tightly around her spoon, and Ash winced. "No one else can escape the war," Ash said softly. "I don't think we should either."

"I will fight if you want me to, you know I will," Lucen put in.

The queen closed her eyes briefly. "It's not about fighting, my love. At least, not in the way you mean."

She ran a finger along the edge of her plate. "As you know, the Ferisian Empire has tried for years to cross our northern border and take our land. But they do not only fight there, and not merely with swords and arrows. Twice in the past year, Lambelin's guards have managed to foil an attempt on my life. From our own people, turned against us by Ferisian coin and false promises. Lately we've found reason to believe that even one of Calinor's oldest noble families, the Maronnes, has turned spy for the Ferisian empress."

Ash's hands grew cold and her appetite fled. "They tried to *kill* you? Our own people? Are you safe here? Can the guard protect you?" Her words—and thoughts—tumbled all over each other.

"*Adelisa.*" Queen Aveline grabbed her daughter's hand. "I am well protected."

"The royal guard knows its duty, here and at the border: to keep our queen and our kingdom safe," Lambelin said quietly.

"And if, stars forbid, something does happen, my life is less important than the kingdom. Your brother will ascend to the throne, and you will have to stand by his side." Next to Ash, Lucen turned green at the thought. "But hopefully that will be a long way off still."

"The Maronnes were at the royal star temple days ago. Why didn't you arrest them?" Lucen wanted to know. His voice cracked.

The queen shook her head. "To accuse a member of the court of treason is not something we can lightly do."

"But Uncle Lam said—"

"Our suspicions are well founded, but we have no

proof. I cannot and will not act without it," Queen Aveline continued. She squeezed Ash's hand. "That, my love, is where you come in. I hope you'll forgive me when I tell you that I didn't bring you home just because I missed you—though I did miss you. I need you to do your duty and help us unravel what kind of information the Maronnes are gathering for the enemy."

Ash's mind was in an uproar. First at the revelation of threats against her mother. Then at the revelation that she'd been brought home to *help*. Not Lucen. Not the guard or the knights. *Ash*. "What can I do?"

Lambelin explained, "The guard is investigating the family, but we can't get close without attracting attention. The Maronnes have daughters at court. Two girls, of your age. We want you to make friends with them, to listen and learn. I have no reason to believe the girls are part of their parents' schemes, but through them, we may be able to discover what their parents are planning and act against it."

"I'm not good at making friends," Ash protested. "I—"

"What if the Maronnes realize what she's doing?" Lucen interrupted. "She'll be in danger constantly. She has no way to defend herself. Let *me* do it. I will find out what they're planning and stop it. I will—"

"*You* will follow my orders," Queen Aveline said. "There

is no reason for you to seek out the girls. Adelisa is new at court, and she's expected to look for new companions. They will likely see this as an opportunity to get close to the throne as well, which should make it easier."

"Besides, she has me. I will be by her side," Splinter said. She ducked her head when the queen frowned at her and Lucen scowled.

"It's not only that it makes more sense, my boy. You're the heir to the throne, which makes you too valuable a target. Adelisa . . ." Lambelin hesitated.

"I'm expendable," Ash said.

The queen gasped. "You're my daughter, and you're *not* expendable. You are both equally valuable to me. But I cannot trust *anyone* outside this room."

"I understand," Ash said slowly, and she did. She didn't like it. She didn't have any idea how to go about making friends with the daughters of traitors. But she understood why it was necessary to get the information. And why it was necessary that the queen obey the law before she made any accusations. The kingdom would have a revolution on its hands if she didn't.

"I never wanted to get my daughter involved in this. I didn't want you to get involved either," Queen Aveline told Splinter. She picked up a butter knife and squeezed it hard enough that all the thin fencing scars on her hands shone white. "But since Lambelin convinced me your presence could be a boon, Adelisa's safety is your responsibility too."

Splinter nodded. "I'll protect her, your majesty."

The queen smiled at Splinter's fervor, and it softened the lines of her face. "Stay by her side. Keep your eyes and ears open. And serve loyally, as I would expect from one of Evana's children."

Ash glanced curiously at Splinter, but her squire stared at the queen in awe.

Queen Aveline buttered a piece of bread. "Now, to more important things. Despite what the empire may want, we can and will have a family meal without worrying about treason or assassination. You're home again with us, Adelisa. I'm certain you have many more stories to tell us about Byrne, and I want to hear the latest from Lucen's lessons. The cooks have outdone themselves on this meal. Let us eat and enjoy each other's company."

Queen Aveline tasted her soup as if the conversation had simply been the first course of the meal and she was ready to move on to the next.

But when Ash observed her mother at the head of the table, she knew better than to believe her nonchalance. She could see the shadows in her eyes. She brought her hands up to her head and massaged her temples. Lord Lambelin hid his concern better, but Ash recognized the many lines on his face and the tension in his bearing. He'd always been part of the family. He'd been the queen's best friend growing up, and he was still her closest confidant. He was worried. And next to Ash, Lucen was simply angry. Or hurt. Or perhaps he felt overlooked. Or maybe it was all of the above.

Ash pushed her food around on her plate.

On the other side of the table, Splinter locked eyes with her, and she silently brought her hand up to the crest on her tunic.

A small bubble of fear inside Ash's chest popped and dissipated. At least, whatever happened next, Splinter would be by her side. She'd promised.

CHAPTER SEVEN

SPLINTER

For squires in the palace, the day started before dawn. Splinter rubbed her hands to warm them. She'd studied her schedule and the palace map together with Ash, and she thought she knew where to go, but the buildings sprawled across Palace Hill and she was starting to wonder if she'd made a wrong turn somewhere when she heard voices ahead of her.

She straightened her tunic and rounded the corner to find the other squires gathered at the gate to the outdoor practice courts. They were huddled together, chatting and laughing and clinging to their coats, because outside the sky had turned a pale purple and icy mists rose up from the ground.

Like the day before, the squires quieted when they saw Splinter. The sandy-haired twins, Meren and Corwen, smirked, and Splinter's former guide, Ilsar, raised his eyebrows. Lucen pushed a few of them aside so he could better glare at her.

Splinter plastered on a smile like none of their actions bothered her. "Good morning."

Her friendly greeting was echoed by a few of the squires, while others hushed them. "She doesn't belong here."

"Impostor."

"Freak."

"My brother says being a squire used to mean something, but her presence is destroying it all, for all of us. And the broken princess too."

Lucen swirled around to face the speaker. "Shut your *mouth*, Tobias," he snarled.

The other boy flinched. "Yes, highness."

"And you . . ." Lucen turned back to Splinter. He pulled himself up. He had dark circles under his eyes. Splinter couldn't help but feel bad for him and how worried he must be for his mother and for his sister. She wondered if any of the other squires knew to look out for him. Perhaps now that they both knew about the dangers in the palace, things would be—

"Don't expect us to accept you," he said, loud enough for all to hear. "You're only here because people can't say no to my sister."

"And you only have friends because people see your crown and not your character," Splinter immediately shot back, against her better judgment. It had been this way last night and in the marketplace too. Lucen brought out the worst in her.

Her words were met with murmurs. Some of the squires instinctively took a step back. "She *didn't*."

"He's going to murder her."

Lucen dashed forward, his fists balled, but Ilsar grabbed him by the shoulders and held him back.

"Not here. She's not worth it," he hissed.

Lucen snarled, and Ilsar tightened his grip. "Come on. Lord Brenet would be furious."

Splinter winced at the reminder that hadn't been meant for her. If Lord Brenet thought Splinter's presence dishonored or threatened the royal family, he'd send her away. She didn't know if getting into a fight with the crown prince to defend Ash's good name counted as dishonoring anyone, but she couldn't risk it.

The squires waited to see who would make the next move.

Splinter tugged at the collar of her tunic and forced herself to play nice. "I apologize, your highness. That was inconsiderate of me."

Lucen shook out of Ilsar's grip. "It's a disgrace to pretend that you're one of us. You'll never earn your place here."

Splinter bit her tongue. The only skill the other squires needed was to be a boy in a noble family. *That* was the disgrace.

The silence stretched out between them, until the gates swung open and Lord Brenet entered the hallway. He didn't look like the cold bothered him, though the ice that outlined his tunic indicated he'd been outside for the better part of an hour at least.

The squires stilled at his approach, and turned to face him. Splinter and Lucen kept their focus on each other.

Lord Brenet took the situation in, and his face clouded over. "I see how it is. Some time outside will cool you all down. File out. We are going to do two rounds of the practice courts, and I want no complaints whatsoever."

One of the squires closest to Splinter groaned quietly, and she soon realized why. The outdoor practice courts covered a large expanse of the palace's outer ward, with snow-covered fields and sandy circles, and pens and lists for horse training. A single round of the hilly grounds was easily a mile or more.

"If I catch anyone dawdling, we'll go for three," Brenet snapped.

The squires started running, with Lucen taking the lead. He glanced over his shoulder once to see how Splinter was doing and picked up the pace, the other squires following suit.

By the time she passed the archery lanes, Splinter's heart hammered in her chest and she was lagging. She'd loved running with Camille, but they usually just chased each other around the abandoned orchard until they were laughing so hard they couldn't run anymore.

By the time the squires circled around the jousting lists, Splinter's legs and lungs were burning. She'd bound her hair back to keep it out of her face, but errant strands were matted to her temples.

Ilsar fell back to keep pace with her, laughing at her struggles. "If it makes you feel any better, none of us could do this run the first time around."

He paused, then added, "Except maybe Meren. We're fairly sure he's part bird."

"Why do you care what I can and can't do?" Splinter gasped. "You don't want me here."

"I don't want you to get Lucen into trouble. He's my friend."

He started it. Splinter didn't say that out loud.

"But I do want you here," Ilsar said. "Court is boring with all the knights off to the war. For as long as it lasts, your presence is going to liven up these dusty old halls, and I intend to have a front-row seat." He smirked and comfortably rejoined the front of the line.

After the run and two rounds of early morning weapons practice, the squires reported to the mess hall for breakfast. Servants had set out food for them on a single long table, and one by one, the squires found their seats. Splinter's stomach roared. But no matter where she turned, there was no place for her. Every empty chair got snatched out in front of her. All the plates and sets of cutlery were claimed.

As soon as she walked away, the boys moved seats back in place and shook knives from their sleeves, laughing uproariously.

At the head of the table, Lucen filled his cup with fruit juice and watched Splinter's wild dash for a place to eat with a satisfied grin. He lifted his cup in a mocking salute.

Eventually Splinter gave up trying. She snatched a plate from one of the squires, a raven-haired boy with a tawny brown complexion and a slight look of discomfort on his face, then filled it up with food and sat down at one of the unused tables, far away from the others. She twisted Ash's ring around her finger.

She'd barely finished half of her breakfast when the bell rang for their lessons. She downed her juice, stuffed a bread roll in her tunic, and started thinking of a better strategy for lunch.

The tricks and teasing persisted. In the classrooms, none of the squires wanted to share a desk with her unless told to by their tutors. During etiquette practice, they had to be ordered to pair up with her.

The classes weren't great for Splinter. She'd never been good with numbers, and she hadn't read any of the strategy reports the other squires had studied. Lord Adelard, her politics and diplomacy tutor, made it a point to comment that only noble sons had the courage and fortitude to become knights. His words were met with cheers and hoots.

In her history class—the one subject she usually loved and excelled at—her teacher had a low, monotone voice, and he droned on about the kings and queens of old without pause. The squires passed notes and shared jokes, while Splinter squinted and tried to listen so hard she gave herself a headache. She wasn't used to so much noise and other students around her. She couldn't even make out Master Ness's homework assignments. When she asked him to repeat them, he told her she should've paid attention.

At least by the time lunch came around, she knew better than to wait to claim a spot. She dove into the room first, stole another plate, filled it up, and found a quiet corner. She kept her head down and focused on what she'd promised Veridia.

She would prove herself to them all. Even if it would take a long time to get through those thick skulls of theirs.

After lunch, the squires returned to the practice courts for sword practice with Master Elnor, to be followed by blacksmithing and blade theory in the royal smithy. Then they'd have riding lessons and work in the royal stables. And at the end of the afternoon, they had one final hour of classes in the star chapel, after which the squires had the evening off to spend time with their families or sponsors. In Splinter's case, Ash. They planned to read up on the Maronnes together.

On the court, Master Elnor set the boys to doing pattern drills with their blades and brought in guardsmen to keep an eye on their work. He paired off with Splinter himself.

"You show talent," he said. He shut down the whispering around them with a dark look. "But you lack technique."

"My family's weapons teacher refused to teach me," Splinter protested.

"Excuses do not matter in battle," Master Elnor snapped. "And your weapons master was a fool."

Splinter felt a glimmer of hope. "Sir?"

"Talent untaught is talent wasted." He motioned to Splinter to assume the guard position, and when she did, he corrected her grip and her footing. He brought her elbows up higher and pushed her shoulders lower. "You taught yourself from a book?"

"Yes, sir. I know it's not perfect, but—" Splinter stopped herself. He'd just told her excuses did not matter in battle.

"It's far from perfect," Elnor agreed. He considered her thoughtfully, and gestured at her to follow the same patterns as the other squires. She'd memorized the stances from the books she read. The blocks and the attacks. The lunges and the feints. She'd never known for sure if she was doing it right, if she held her blade properly, or if it was a pale imitation of what she was supposed to do.

Master Elnor made her repeat the moves. He met every attack with the right block, every step forward with the right step back. He suggested small improvements. He tapped her fingers with his sword when she gripped the hilt too tightly. He kicked her stance wider.

He picked up the pace, and Splinter met it, and for a few blissful moments nothing existed but the gentle *clack, clack, clack* of the wooden practice swords. The *clack, clack, clack* as they moved quicker and quicker.

If Splinter closed her eyes, she could imagine the sword was made from steel and she was wearing armor, the DuLac flower emblazoned on her chest.

The *clack, clack, clack* of adventure and heroics.

Clack, clack, snap. Elnor's sword cut across Splinter's knuckles, and she hissed at the sudden pain.

She clung to her blade to avoid dropping it. The sword master raised his eyebrows, but although her hand throbbed, Splinter kept silent and pulled back to guard position.

"No daydreaming, squire," Elnor chided.

Splinter's cheeks heated. "No, sir."

She saluted him with the sword and hoped he would continue. Instead he put his own practice blade away and ordered the guard to end the exercises.

He barely looked at Splinter when he repeated his earlier judgment. "It's far from perfect." Then he grinned, and Splinter understood why the guards at the gate had called him intimidating. Master Elnor's grin was feral and dangerous. "But the potential is there."

Splinter glowed. "I want to learn," she blurted out.

"Then I will teach you, squire," he promised, and with a glimmer in his eyes, he raised his voice loud enough that she knew the other squires would hear. "You will curse my name before we're through, but you will learn swordplay like a knight."

CHAPTER EIGHT

ASH

Ash straightened her dress and used her mirror to peek into the adjacent room. Although today was a rest day, Splinter had her practice sword out, and she was going through the motions. Like she was dancing.

After a few seconds, Splinter spotted Ash looking at her, and she grinned self-consciously. She wiped the sweat from her eyes. "Master Elnor says I should practice every day."

Ash smiled. "If he ever worries that you don't practice enough, I can vouch for you."

Over the past week, Splinter had gone through the sword patterns constantly. As soon as she woke up and before they both went to bed, and whenever else she could fit it in.

Every time Splinter picked up the sword, Ash found an excuse to watch. It made Splinter look like a knight.

If Splinter could be a knight, maybe Ash could be a princess.

She had to be. Ash plucked at the hem of her sleeve, and she sighed. Today she would officially join the social circuit of the city's nobility. She would meet her targets—and based on how disastrous the masked ball had been, she did not feel ready at all. "The Maronnes will definitely see through what I'm doing."

Splinter tossed her sword on her bedside table, and she walked through to Ash's room. The royal suites all had rooms for companions or squires built adjacent to them, and ever since Splinter had moved in, they'd kept the connecting door open. Splinter laughed at how messy Ash's rooms were, with clothes and books everywhere. Ash marveled at how clean and empty Splinter's room was, with her bed neatly made and her scant belongings stored in a big wooden chest, so she could swing her sword around to her heart's content.

At night, after they'd both gone to bed, they talked about Splinter's squire lessons, and Ash's morning study with Lord Lambelin, where he'd taught her everything they knew about the Maronnes. They talked about the scornful comments the courtiers made when they saw Ash with her cane and her braces. They talked about their favorite legends and their shared love of history.

The more they talked, the more Ash was grateful for Splinter's companionship.

Splinter flopped down on Ash's bed and patted the spread. "Sit, I'll braid your hair."

Ash grabbed her braces and sat down in front of Splinter. "What if I say the wrong thing? What if I let slip that my mother thinks they're traitors?"

"You won't." Splinter ran her fingers through Ash's hair. She was far better at braiding than Ash—wayward strands always got stuck between Ash's bands and rings. "You pay attention to people. And you're brave."

"Me?" Ash whirled around, pulling her hair from Splinter's hands.

"You and my brother are the bravest people I know," Splinter said seriously. "You stood up to court for me. You're going to spy for the crown and unravel a conspiracy."

Ash felt color rise to her cheeks. "The queen doesn't want to call it spying." Queen Aveline had showed up to her meetings with Lord Lambelin twice, but both times she'd worn her crown and she'd been there as *queen*, not as Ash's mother. And both times, she'd been shepherded away to other meetings before Ash could ask if they could have breakfast together—or go for a walk across the palace grounds. She wanted to spend time with her mother like she'd spent time with Aunt Jonet. She wanted to find a way to tell her that she was afraid, but she'd do her duty anyway.

The bed bounced when Splinter shrugged. "It's still spying even if you don't call it that."

"That's what Uncle Lam said too," Ash admitted. At least Lord Lambelin had listened to her. He'd told her about Lord Maronne's correspondence with Ferisian nobles, which had first raised his suspicions, and how Lady Maronne had bribed her way into the royal archives, though the scribes hadn't been able to uncover what she'd searched for. He'd reminded Ash that all she needed to do was to get the girls to trust her, and to pick up every bit of information she could, no matter how useless. He'd also quietly confirmed that Splinter's uncle wouldn't be part of today's event, as he'd left the city to go on a hunting trip. "Uncle Lam promised he'd keep an eye on me."

"And so will I," Splinter said.

She'd taken her duty to Ash to heart.

"I know." Ash let Splinter pick up her hair again. She began to fasten her braces around her arms. Her fingers ached. "It may be very boring. If it's anything like the masked ball, it's a lot of people complaining about everything they don't like about themselves and everything they don't like about each other."

"You don't have to pay attention to *everyone*," Splinter reminded her. "Just those girls."

"Hazel and Melisande." Melisande was nearly twelve. Her sister Hazel was ten. Their parents were frequent visitors to the theater, where the afternoon would take place, and the girls loved its acrobatics shows. They were both ardent archers, with Melisande outshooting most of the squires. "Did you ever meet them?"

Ash felt Splinter shake her head. "Mama only brought me to court a few times. She preferred to visit the palace scribes. I met the Labannes' son, because he was Anders's best friend growing up, and Briar of Divon, because Mama loved to visit their forest estate and we were forced to play together. But never the Maronnes."

Ash hesitated. "At dinner, Mother said she knew you'd serve me loyally. That she expected no different from Evana's children. What did she mean?"

Splinter's hands stilled. "Mama translated texts for the palace scribes. She studied with them when she was younger."

"*Ferisian* texts? Was she a spy too?"

"Old texts, she said. Stories and documents from centuries past. She showed me once. The words and the letters were jumbled, like a puzzle. . . ." Splinter's voice drifted off.

"But why . . ." Ash stopped herself when Splinter quietly sniffed. Why would the queen have anything to do with translators? Why did she remember Evana as loyal? It was a mystery she intended to solve.

For now, she changed tactics. "What about your uncle? Did he take you to court?"

"Uncle Elias preferred to keep me home." Splinter sniffed again and laughed. "He probably thought I would embarrass him."

Ash's heart clenched. "I'm sorry—"

"I'm not," Splinter said immediately. "I don't know how to mingle. I wouldn't want to be in your shoes. My suggestion is to challenge both of them to a shooting match, and if you win, they have to be your friends."

Ash elbowed her. "That's not how that works."

"Isn't it?" Splinter giggled. "And I was going to try to make friends with all of the squires."

"*All* of the squires?"

"Maybe not Lucen." Splinter tied a leather band around

the braid and tugged it in place. "There, now you look like a princess from any of the old stories. And everyone wants to be friends with a princess, right?"

Ash got up to admire herself in the mirror. She tried to look serious. "Is that why you're here with me?"

"Of course." The corner of Splinter's mouth pulled up into a smirk. "Bragging rights. It's the only reason, your highness."

Ash laughed, and the rest of the day didn't seem so intimidating.

The royal carriage pulled up outside the theater. Ash toyed with the silver rings around her fingers.

On the cushioned bench opposite her, Queen Aveline had pushed the curtains of the carriage open far enough that a sliver of light reached through, and she'd spent the whole journey staring out at the city, lost in thought.

When the horses came to a halt, she patted Ash's knee. "I know you are worried, my love. But you're doing the crown a service."

Ash grimaced. "But what if I can't protect you? What if I fail you?"

The queen blanched. She leaned in close and for a moment focused all of her attention on Ash. "Adelisa, you're my daughter." She tugged at Ash's moss-green skirt. "Our crown comes with the responsibility to keep Calinor safe. From intruders and traitors, from outside and within. It's why we fight, not just at the northern border, but at court, to keep whispered lies and venomous words out of people's hearts and minds, and in Haven, where hunger and poverty are as deadly as any war. This is the duty given to us, and as long as you try your hardest to fulfill it, you could *never* fail me."

Before Ash could say or do anything more than nod, the doors of the carriage opened and the driver bowed to the two of them. "Your majesty, your highness, we've arrived."

Queen Aveline's fingers brushed Ash's cheek as she rose and made her way out. "Thank you, Lilyn."

She straightened the long coat she wore over her dress, and Lambelin—who'd stood on the footboard outside of the carriage—offered her an arm. Ash heard the whispers and gasps from the crowd that had gathered to watch the parade of nobles enter the theater for the afternoon of entertainment.

Splinter appeared in the doorway in her formal wear. She'd ridden along on the footboard too, and despite having her hair in a tight bun, several locks had sprung loose and framed her face wildly. "Are you ready?" she asked.

"Remember, everyone wants to be friends with a princess."

Using her cane to stabilize herself, Ash stepped out and blinked against the bright winter sun. People were gathered around the theater—a cylindrical stone building with tall stained glass windows and a thatched roof—and they all stared at her. Merchants in woolen coats. Guild apprentices in long aprons. A handful of girls in patched dresses, kicking up the snow around them and giggling. A teenage boy Lucen's age, who kept his hand on a dog's rope collar. The spotted mutt was skin and bones, and the boy did not look much better. His hand sneaked into the pocket of one of the merchants, and he pulled out a shiny silver coin.

A girl with long curly hair and piercing slate-gray eyes, roughly Ash's age, grinned at Ash and disappeared into the crowds.

And then Ash was ushered in by the guards. Once she crossed the threshold, she traded in the bright and loud outside for a shadowed and louder inside. From the reception area, where servants in the colors of the Labanne family took their coats, she could see the grand salon where the nobility gathered. A wooden stage graced the north end of the room, and high tables brimming with teas and cakes and biscuits were scattered throughout.

Lambelin took the queen's coat and handed it to a

young man in a light brown tunic with purple trim, while Splinter took Ash's coat and gave it to a slender woman wearing pants and a lilac shirt with a light brown baldric across her chest.

A herald cleared his throat and announced, "Her Majesty Queen Aveline and Her Highness Princess Adelisa."

The salon fell silent. Everyone present bowed low.

The queen clapped her hands and laughed lightly. "Please, continue!" And sound once more swelled around them. The queen swooped down toward Lady Labanne, who stood in the center of the room, talking to the theater troupe she patronized, while Lord Labanne chatted with the knight captain who'd called Ash fragile on the night of her party. He looked as sour and unpleasant as he had then. Lord Labanne clapped his shoulder and laughed.

Ash hung back, as she had been ordered to. Lord Lambelin had reminded her several times that it would look suspicious if she immediately singled out the girls.

Splinter took up position near the wall, where long velvet drapes covered the rough stone. Whispers followed them both.

"Our sons are dying at the border, and the queen doesn't care. All she does is spend money on shelters, mingle with commoners, and scorn our traditions for freaks like *her*."

"Back in the old days, the crown was powerful and trustworthy. Now look at it."

"The queen needs to be reminded where the real power lies."

"*I* think it's quite innovative."

"*You* would. And look at her, she is so fragile."

Ash spotted the elderly lady and her grandson who'd been kind to her at the masked ball, and veered away from them. She paused near one of the tables filled with treats and tried to look lost while she scouted out the position of the girls. It didn't involve much acting, and soon enough other nobles were drawn to her like ants to honey.

"Poor thing, this is too much for you," a middle-aged lady with flowers in her hair and shimmery paint on her eyes told her. "Can I pour you some tea? Fetch you a chair?"

Ash declined both offers, but the woman insisted she wanted to do something for "an unlucky child such as yourself," so Ash asked her for some biscuits. As soon as the woman's back was turned, she slid them—plate and all—into a big potted plant.

A gray-haired gentleman, his skin so white it was nearly translucent, walked by. He regarded her over thin gold-rimmed glasses and scolded her for entertaining such folly as a girl as squire and bringing shame to the crown.

Ash bit her tongue to keep from snapping back at him and telling him Splinter wasn't a girl at all, and she would entertain any squire if she so pleased. In her peripheral vision, Splinter mimed gagging.

The first visitors were followed by a lord and lady whose names Ash didn't catch, who spoke at length about investments in trade and the future of seafaring and whether she would mention them to the queen. And then, by Lord Idian, who simply took up position next to her and munched a slice of cake.

"My grandmother mentioned you might need rescuing, your highness," he said, by way of explanation. "It would hardly be honorable of me to refuse."

She smiled at him. "I'm okay, I'm just . . ."

"Getting used to the beehive?" He nodded his understanding. "I wouldn't be here if not for the old lady, but it's not as intimidating as it seems. Amid all the bluster, many *do* support the queen. You need to find the right people. And perhaps a few companions your own age."

He held out his hand. She hesitated only briefly.

"Have you met Hazel and Mist Maronne?" Idian gently pulled her along. "Let me channel some of my grandmother's busybody instincts and introduce you."

"I don't believe I have." Ash's heart skipped a beat.

This introduction was the point of the entire afternoon, but she'd expected it to be more complicated. Besides, if Lord Idian knew the Maronnes well, was he part of their conspiracy? Was that why he was kind to her? What if the girls had come here with the same goal she had, and Lord Idian was helping them?

She rubbed her nose. This was what her mother had meant when she'd told Ash and Splinter she couldn't trust anyone outside of the family. It made Ash's head and her heart hurt.

The Maronne girls stood in front of the stage, where two acrobats were setting up supplies for a performance. Both sisters wore similar bronze dresses with sensible sandals, though Hazel wore her thick black hair in a long braid, while Melisande had her hair cut short.

"Hazel! Mist!" Idian called out.

Melisande—Mist—spun around. "Lord Idian! I didn't know you'd be here."

"The grand matriarch decided for me." He smiled and indicated Ash. "May I present to you both . . . Her Highness Princess Adelisa? She's new to the city."

The girls curtsied, and Ash tried to remember everything Lambelin had taught her. To remain calm and focused. To make them trust her. "It's a pleasure."

"Hazel and Melisande Maronne are two of my archery students," Lord Idian explained. "And talented ones too."

Unwittingly, he'd given Ash the perfect opening. "I love archery! I practiced with my aunt's weapons master when I lived at her estate. He helped me carve my own bow."

Idian bowed to the three of them. "Clearly you'll have much to discuss. Girls, keep the princess away from all the sweet-talking nobles, please. Let's give her time to adjust to the city before we all make a terrible impression."

"It may be a little late for that," Ash murmured.

Hazel, the younger of the two, giggled. "Mother makes us go to these events, but we'd much rather be on the archery courts," she confided while Idian took his leave. "Especially Mist. She *hates* this."

"I don't *hate* it," her older sister argued. "It just seems pointless to me. I don't get why grown-ups think talking to each other for hours is fun. Especially not when they end up spinning tales to one person and then they have to lie to another and then a third person comes in with *another* lie. I'd rather settle everything with bows."

Against the wall, Splinter gave Ash a subtle thumbs-up.

"I wouldn't mind that," Ash said.

Hazel frowned. "Don't your braces get in the way of shooting?"

Mist jabbed her sister in the ribs. "You can't *say* that," she hissed. She ran her hand through her stubbly hair. "I'm sorry, highness. My sister doesn't have a filter."

"Please, call me Ash," Ash said. "And I don't mind. I'd rather people ask than that they assume." They'd done that all her life, or at least as long as she could remember. The carriage accident that had killed Ash's father had also killed the driver and the queen's companion. Both the queen and Ash had faced many months of recovery.

Brother Nivanil, master of the royal physicians, had given Ash star amulets to ease the pain. But her body had never fully healed. Or at least, that was how Nivanil explained why the princess's joints kept snapping apart. The physician's assistant had once offered the opinion that Ash's illness was inherited, but since no one else in the royal family dealt with these afflictions, that theory was soon dismissed.

It was a star blessing, people said, when they thought she couldn't hear—or if they didn't care—that the kingdom still had a whole and healthy prince.

"I didn't want to make you uncomfortable," Hazel said softly.

Ash wiggled her fingers. "The braces help me. I can't shoot a bow for hours at a time, but I can manage a few rounds."

Mist touched the silver bands that Aunt Jonet's blacksmith had designed for her. "They're beautiful."

"I wouldn't know what to do without them," Ash admitted. But as soon as the words left her lips, she felt the weight of them.

Lord Lambelin had told her, "Keep your conversation casual. Don't give away anything that you wouldn't want an enemy to know."

And she'd done just that.

She breathed in hard. "Anyway . . . will the acrobats start their performance soon?" The young men had hung a hoop from the rafters of the theater, and they'd set up a long beam raised by two standards. They were unpacking a case full of balls and batons.

"It's the same performance every few months," Mist said dismissively. "You should come visit us sometime. We could shoot together."

Ash's mouth was dry. "I'd like that," she said. She hoped her voice didn't sound as hollow as she felt. "Perhaps you could come to the royal practice courts too."

Hazel clapped her hands in delight, and Mist grinned. "We'd *love* that." Mischief glinted in Mist's eyes. "Your squire could join in too. I know most people here are old-fashioned and don't approve, but I think it's beautiful.

About time those grumpy old knights realized far more of us want to join their ranks."

The fierce words made Ash smile despite herself. "Perhaps she will."

"Good," Mist said. Next to her, Hazel mouthed along when she said, "I love outshooting everyone."

By the time Ash and Splinter got back to their rooms, Ash's head was spinning. She'd spent the rest of the afternoon with Mist and Hazel. The two girls had folded her into their conversations and their observations. They joked about the other nobles, they'd made her laugh, they watched the acrobats' tricks together, oohing and aahing, and they dashed through the backstage area of the theater, where none of them were allowed to be. Ash had loved it.

"Come with me?" she asked quietly when Splinter had changed into her nightclothes.

Splinter yawned. "Sure."

Ash grabbed the lantern that stood on the small side table by the door and led the way.

One of the things she loved most about the palace was that it had been rebuilt so often that entire hallways had disappeared or been restructured. Rooms had been torn down and redesigned, leaving hidden nooks and crannies everywhere. When she was still tiny, Uncle Lam had taught Lucen and Ash to play hide-and-seek in the palace's dustiest secret passages. One day, while scouring the royal wing, she'd found a forgotten staircase leading from her father's office.

Now Ash entered the room and made straight for a windowsill decorated with stone leaves. The office itself had long since been stripped of the prince consort's personal effects, but it was brimming with gifts that Queen Aveline had received from state visitors. Glass baubles. Beautiful paintings. Silver candelabras. Gold cups. Even a small doll carved out of gemstones that were held together with fine silver chains.

She located the lever to open the passage, and when one of the bookcases swung open, Splinter gasped. "Amazing."

"I used to hide in here when I didn't want to go to my lessons."

Splinter raised her eyebrows. "Good to know."

"Don't you dare." Ash nudged her. "You're going to be a knight and a hero one day." She slipped into the passage. The air was freezing cold around her. The stone floor was smooth and slippery. It was exactly as she remembered.

She raised the lantern high. "Isn't it beautiful? There are so many passages throughout the palace, but this one is my favorite."

"It's dark." Splinter squinted. "Are the passages protected?"

"The tunnels connecting to the outside are all barred and gated," Ash reassured her. "And Uncle Lam told me the guard patrols the others."

Splinter nodded solemnly. "Good."

"This one doesn't go anywhere, though. It's caved in. This is all that's left." Ash sat on one of the worn-down steps. It was quiet and protected, and she could leave the world and the war outside. "I wanted you to see it because it's safe. From bullying squires and from conspiracies. It's ours."

To Ash's horror, her breath hitched and her eyes welled up.

Splinter sank down next to her. "Ash? Did something happen at the theater?"

The whole afternoon flooded back to her. Every comment. Every detail. The sugary smell of the cakes. The scornful words of the grumpy old man. Mist's laughter. The acrobats' pirouettes. "I like them. And I'm so scared."

"What are you afraid of?" Splinter asked gently.

Ash searched for the words.

"Not of . . . I'm afraid *for* my family. Mother wants me home because she trusts me, but I don't know how to help if I can't tell the difference between nice and dangerous. I don't want anything bad to happen to her. Or to anyone."

Splinter clasped her hand. "The guard will protect your mother, Ash. They'll protect your brother too. And I'll protect you."

Ash shuffled over so that she could lean against Splinter. "What if someone gets past the guard?"

"Lord Lambelin wouldn't let that happen," Splinter said at first. Then her voice grew softer. It barely echoed in the passage around them. "If someone does slip through, your mother is never alone. All the knights in the kingdom are sworn to protect her. They would fight for her, and they would die for her if they had to. For Lucen and you too." Splinter tilted her head. "And for all that he is impossible, Lucen is the best fighter of all the squires. He can hold his own."

She bit her lip and visibly mulled over the next words. "And if that isn't enough, if the stars are unlucky and something goes wrong . . . I will stay by your side, whether you're angry or sad or hurting or scared."

"I'm not sure that helps," Ash admitted, and she felt terrible for it.

Splinter put an arm around her shoulder. "I know."

She did, at that. Ash knew the war hadn't been kind to Splinter. It had been a nightmare for so many, but in Byrne, with Aunt Jonet, the war had felt distant. Any threat to her loved ones was only theoretical. Now the threat came with faces she knew, people she talked to. In Haven, the war was real.

Ash leaned in closer. "Just to be clear, I forbid you from letting anything happen to *you*."

"Yes, your highness."

"Stop making fun of me."

"I would never, O noble princess."

"Splinter."

They sat together, huddled around the lantern, in their own small bubble of light in the darkened passage.

CHAPTER NINE

ASH

"Come on, Ash! Let's see if you can do better than me!"

Ash ran her fingers across the limbs of the bow and found herself smiling. Mist's suggestion to shoot together had turned into an official invite for tea and games in the city, which had led to Ash's first—entirely nerve-racking—visit to the Maronne country estate just outside of Haven, and that was quickly followed by another invite for another visit the following rest day. Today.

Spending time with Mist and Hazel was *fun*. More than that, it was *easy*.

During Ash's first visit to the estate, they'd shared a wintry picnic in the conservatory. Splinter hadn't been allowed to join them inside, because Lady Maronne thought it wouldn't be politic, so today all four of them were spending long hours at the archery lanes behind the sprawling mansion. And the girls had promised Ash to take her riding through the city and the hills around Kestrel's Haven.

They'd said nothing that made them sound disloyal to the crown. They went out of their way to make Ash feel welcome *and* to include Splinter.

They felt like friends, and it worried Ash.

"One more round before tea!"

Splinter stood to the side of the archery lane and yelled, "Show them what you've got, Ash!"

"No one is better than Mist!" Hazel shot back.

Mist hushed them both, laughing.

Ash fixed her eyes on the target and brought the bow up to shoulder height. Her arms and shoulders protested sharply, but as soon as she found her anchor point, everything disappeared. All that was left was the arrow, the bow, and the small blue circle in the center of the straw target.

She squinted, breathed out, and let fly.

The arrow hit the center with a satisfying *thud*, and to the side, Splinter cheered, her arms raised high. Ash had matched Mist's accomplishment of hitting the blue circle on all five targets without misses or retries.

"A tie?" She flexed against the pain that had settled inside her wrists and elbows.

"*Absolutely* not. We'll do this again next time until one of us wins. Who knows? Maybe with enough time, Hazel and Splinter will catch up to us." Mist grinned.

"Lord Idian says I'm talented enough." Hazel scowled at her sister.

"He also says you lack patience," Mist said.

"Well . . ." Hazel's voice trailed off, as she was clearly trying to think of a counterargument and coming up empty. She shrugged.

Splinter shook her head. "It'll be awhile before I'm as good as *any* of you. I'll take a sword over a bow any day."

Mist considered her shrewdly. "I guess you need to excel at sword fighting if you want to be a knight."

"Exactly." Splinter smiled, but it was the careful smile she wore when she and Ash crossed paths with any of the other squires at the palace. The type of smile she wore as armor.

Mist faced Ash. "Maybe Lord Idian could take you on as a student too. At least until he returns north."

"Back to the mountains?" Ash frowned. "I didn't realize he was only here on leave."

"He was wounded at the border, and he was sent back

home to recover. The old lady, as he calls her, brought in as many physicians and star priests as it took to heal him."

"I didn't know," Ash admitted.

Mist lowered her voice. "I overheard Papa talking to him."

"What she means is, she was eavesdropping," Hazel teased.

A shadow flitted across Mist's face, and she growled. "It's the only way I can figure out what's going on. No one ever talks to us. They think we're too young and the war shouldn't concern us. Do they think we live with our eyes and ears closed? There are stories about the war on every street corner in Haven, there are rumors at every social gathering. I want to *know*, otherwise I'm just going to worry." She scooped up her bow and stalked toward the targets to retrieve the arrows.

Ash stared after her.

"Don't worry," Hazel said when Mist was out of earshot. "She just needs a moment to calm down. She has bad dreams a lot."

"Oh." Ash rubbed her arms, and she felt Splinter's attention on her. "That must be really difficult."

"It was worse when Papa was fighting. No one would tell us what was happening or if he'd come home at all. That's when Mist's dreams started." Hazel tugged at her tunic. "And now Papa has nightmares too. He never really laughs, and he doesn't want to come shooting with us. He just stays in the library." Her fingers were curled into tight fists. She looked as though she wanted to say something else, but she settled for, "Anyway, I'm glad you're here. Mist likes having a challenge. And it's nice not to come in last all the time."

Hazel directed those last words at Splinter, who tipped an imaginary hat. "You're welcome."

"I'm sorry." Ash tried to gather her scattered thoughts. Mist's eavesdropping meant she might have overheard just the sort of information Ash had been asked to uncover. This was why she was *here*. But both girls were hurting. She didn't know how to navigate that. "I wish the war wasn't happening."

Hazel leaned in. "I wish we could *end* it."

"We can't," Mist said as she returned with her arms full of arrows. She placed them back in their quivers, and she dusted off her hands. Her eyes were suspiciously red.

"Are you okay?" Ash asked.

Hazel silently handed a handkerchief to her sister, who wiped her eyes and face with it. "I'm thirsty. Let's go inside." Mist grimaced at Splinter. "I'm sorry. I've been trying to convince Mama to let you join us, but she doesn't think it's *proper*."

"It's fine—" Splinter started.

"It's *not*," Mist interrupted fiercely. "But I have an idea." She stood on tiptoe to look out over the courtyard. "Fenna!"

She waved over a broad mountain of a man, carrying a bundle of spears over one shoulder. "Fenna used to be a guard at the floating docks," she told Splinter, while Fenna handed the bundle over to a younger guard before ambling in their direction. "He could show you sword tricks. Can't you, Fenna? You can show Splinter tricks they don't teach her at the palace. Please?"

Fenna folded his arms. He had kind eyes under bushy eyebrows, and a thick, braided scar ran from the corner of his jaw, across his throat, and down to his shirt. Under his gaze, Splinter blushed furiously, and she fumbled for a sword she didn't carry.

"Splinter is going to be a knight someday," Mist declared. "And I think it's wonderful." She nudged Splinter with her elbow.

Splinter straightened. "Please. I'll listen well to everything you can teach me."

"Please," Hazel added her voice to the chorus.

"No squire works harder than Splinter," Ash insisted.

Splinter blushed deeper, and Fenna lifted her chin as if he was looking for something. After a moment, he nodded.

He locked eyes with Mist and gestured at her, twisting his fingers into intricate patterns.

Mist laughed delightedly, some of the tension melting from her stance. "You're the best." She interpreted for Splinter. "He says the guard has a different approach to sword fighting. He'll teach you tricks that you can practice on your own."

"Thank you," Splinter said. This time, her smile was unguarded and full of wonder.

"I could stay and translate . . . ," Mist suggested.

Fenna signed something at her, and Mist rolled her eyes.

"*Fine.* I could stay and translate, but Papa doesn't want us to spend too much time around weapons, and Fenna says swords are all the language you'll need."

"Thank you," Splinter said again.

Ash squeezed her arm.

"Tell me everything afterward," Mist told Splinter. "And show the other squires that it isn't just noble *sons* who can make a difference."

Fenna guided Splinter away, while Mist hooked her arms through Ash's and her sister's. "*Now* we can have tea," she declared, like she couldn't fix the world, but she could make small bits of it better.

As far as Ash was concerned, she had. Her heart swelled

as Splinter and Fenna crossed the courtyard. Her mother's assignment pressed on her shoulders like the guard's bundle of spears. The Maronnes were traitors. Maybe. They were unquestionably kind. She smiled despite the uproar in her mind, and she hoped she didn't look as conflicted as she felt. "Let's go inside."

CHAPTER TEN

ASH

Inside the Maronne estate, the hours passed by with tea and cake and the crackling of the fireplace. Mist and Hazel kept Ash entertained with stories of their favorite midwinter mystery plays at a small theater near the floating docks. When Ash mentioned that she loved the plays but they weren't a tradition in Byrne, they insisted on bringing Ash along.

"You'll love it," Mist said. "You win a silver feather brooch if you're the first to solve the mystery. We've been trying to win one for*ever*."

"And no offense," Hazel said, "but Mama will be thrilled to show you off."

Mist groaned. "She is certain that your companionship

is a sign of royal favor. Which is *not* why we want to spend time with you," she added.

"Mama thinks it's an opportunity to move up."

"Oh." Ash nibbled at her lip. "She may be disappointed. I don't think court much likes me." She hadn't gone back to any of the social events, telling her mother that she wanted to focus on Hazel and Mist instead. It was a flimsy excuse, but the queen let her get away with it.

"Well, we don't care about court, and we do like you," Hazel said. "Please say you'll come? Between the three of us, we could solve any mystery, I'm sure!"

"I'd have to ask my mother." Ash hid behind a teacup and glanced through the window to watch Splinter spar with Fenna in the courtyard. As if she could feel her gaze, Splinter waved at the mansion. Ash pulled the corner of her mouth up into a half smile. "But I'd love it. We should practice. Do you have any plays in your library?"

It was a risk, but one she knew she needed to take.

Mist and Hazel shared a look before Mist nodded at her sister. "I don't think Papa will mind. Can you run ahead and ask him? I'll show Ash the way."

Hazel placed her teacup back on the tray and dashed off. Ash took a last sip to calm her nerves. "What she said earlier, about the war . . ."

Mist got to her feet too. "When Papa left to fight, Hazel cried herself to sleep every night. And now she misses him, even though he's here." She scowled. "Mama told me not to say anything *untoward* to you, and I don't mean any disrespect to the queen, but I hope she finds a way to end the war."

"I'm not sure that she can," Ash admitted. "Not without losing half the kingdom to the Ferisian Empire."

"All the people fighting in the mountains? They're the kingdom too." Mist's face darkened, and Ash realized that Mist's worries and helplessness were like a bruise that couldn't heal. Instead, it just hurt.

She placed a hand on Mist's. "I know."

Mist held the door open for her. "Maybe you should learn to eavesdrop too. Papa only talks to us about ancient history and old treaties. You could learn what's *actually* going on. Aren't there secret passages in the palace? It'd be an adventure!"

The words settled like ice in Ash's stomach. "I . . . I think they're all heavily guarded."

"I would go exploring *all* the time. Find every single way in or out. Perhaps the guards have missed passages. Can you imagine?"

Ash leaned on her cane with force. Mist's excitement

sent her head spinning. She *could* imagine that. She only needed to close her eyes to imagine assassins in the passages, with cruel eyes and crueler blades. "No," she snapped. "I don't want that."

Mist paled. "I'm sorry, your highness, I didn't mean—"

"It's *fine*," Ash managed, through gritted teeth. She rolled her shoulders. "Let's just go to the library, please."

In silence, Mist led her up a flight of stairs and toward a pair of intricately carved doors. She picked at her dress, and she cast furtive looks in Ash's direction, but she didn't say anything.

Ash, meanwhile, felt every step up the stairs echo in her ankles and knees.

In front of the library, Hazel was talking animatedly to an older man. Lord Maronne had the same thick black hair as his daughters, though his was sticking out in all directions. He was paler than the girls, and he had dark circles under his eyes. He held a notebook clutched under his arm, and absently fiddled with a pen. When Ash approached, he bowed deeply. "Princess Adelisa. You do us great honor spending time with our girls."

"Lord Maronne." Ash considered him. He didn't seem to despise or hate her. If anything, he was sad. She glanced over at Hazel, whose face had fallen, and Mist, who grimaced.

"I understand you want to see my library?"

"If it's not too much of an imposition." Aunt Jonet had given her all the phrases of polite society to practice over and over again.

Lord Maronne tousled Hazel's hair. "You'd be most welcome. These two can show you around."

Hazel stared up at her father with hope in her eyes, but instead of turning back to his daughter, he bowed again and wandered away. In that moment before she ran inside, Hazel looked like she'd shatter.

Ash's heart went out to her and Mist both. She disliked lying to them. She hated having to doubt them. That wasn't the type of princess she wanted to be.

She held out her hand to Mist. "I'm sorry I snapped at you. I didn't mean it. I'm just afraid for my family too."

"We'll both do what we can to protect them," Mist whispered. She clutched Ash's hand and gave her an awkward hug before pulling her into the library and leaving their harsh words outside.

"Hazy, have you found the plays yet?"

"Stop calling me that!"

Ash gasped when the library opened up to her. Aunt Jonet had a room full of disorganized books in Byrne. The royal archives were filled with scrolls and contracts and charters. But this was a work of love. A rival to the palace library. Endless rows of tall wooden shelves. Countless leather-bound books in all colors, shapes, and sizes.

"Stars," she whispered. She couldn't imagine why Lady Maronne had had to bribe her way into the archives, if this is what she had at home.

Hazel called out something from between the bookshelves, but the words didn't register.

The library was divided into three different sections, separated by shelves. Comfortable chairs were set out in the first section. In the center space, a huge table was covered with maps. Hazel stood on a spindly ladder that led all the way up to the ceiling, and she was pulling out booklets and putting them back with alarming speed. "I'm trying to find *The Seventh Star*," she told Mist. "I think it has the *best* mystery."

"Only because you guessed it before I did."

"Can I wander?" Ash asked reverently.

Mist climbed the shelves without the aid of a ladder. "Feel free."

"Papa doesn't like us to touch his desk, though," Hazel added. She overbalanced and the ladder tilted precariously.

"I'll be careful," Ash promised. She tiptoed past the table with maps, toward the third section of the library, where a large oak desk took up most of the space. Every available surface drowned under the weight of books, papers, and writing equipment. A blemished and scarred dagger functioned as a paperweight to hold down a stack of notes, and a large mug that had maybe once held cider now held pens, the ink mingling with the remains of the drink.

Ash made note of where Mist and Hazel were clambering on the shelves.

Then she took a deep breath and riffled through the stack of notes. The topmost was a lifelike ink sketch of Mist and Hazel on horseback. The next was a half-finished drawing of Lady Maronne.

"I've got it! I think!" Hazel called out.

Something slammed against the floor, and Hazel's "Oops, never mind!" was followed by Mist's weary sigh.

"You'll get yourself killed."

Ash's heart hammered. She quickly circled the desk.

She ran her fingers across the spines of books, uncertain what she was looking for, when a stack of three volumes caught her eye. A book on the history of Kestrel's Reach—the long-lost twin city of Kestrel's Haven on the Ferisian continent. A Ferisian dictionary. A book titled *The Song of the Lark*, about one of her ancestors.

Letters peeked out of the dictionary.

Hazel and Mist were hidden from view by the endless shelves, so Ash teased out one of the pages. The paper was crumpled, the writing marred by water stains.

But she recognized the language.

Her stomach dropped.

It had been Lord Maronne's correspondence with Ferisian nobles that had first alerted the queen that something was amiss. Lord Lambelin had told Ash it'd been near impossible to intercept any letters, because the messengers carried star amulets for protection. A handful of short coded messages carried by pigeons had been stolen from the sky by the royal hawks, but the scribes hadn't been able to decipher them yet.

Perhaps one of these pages, written in a fine Ferisian hand, could help them crack the code. Because several of the words were scrambled and the order of the words didn't make sense. There had to be some kind of secret design to it.

"Found it!"

Ash's heart skipped a beat at Hazel's jubilant shout. Her hand jolted, and she nearly sent the stack of books toppling over.

She stepped back from the desk. With trembling hands, she shoved the page into her shirt, the paper crackling against the fabric.

Mist peeked around the corner. She held out a booklet, then frowned at Ash, standing awkwardly in the center of the room. "Are you okay? You look like you got lost between all the books."

Ash plastered on a grin. "I could spend whole days here, reading."

"Papa always tells us that books are the most powerful weapons in the world." Mist rolled her eyes. "I'd rather spend my days on the archery lanes, if it's all the same."

Ash straightened her shirt and smoothed out the page underneath. "I think words can cut too," she said.

"But arrows are a lot more dangerous, don't you think?" Mist demanded.

"A lot," Ash lied.

CHAPTER ELEVEN

SPLINTER

"With the kingdom changing around her, she clung to the star-given right of queens. Some historians argue that she forgot about her responsibilities. That she chose power over the welfare of her people. To many, she wasn't queen of Calinor, but merely queen of the noble houses." For the past hour, Master Ness had been droning on about Queen Eliane, nicknamed the Lark for her delicate singing voice. He spoke with dry disdain of the queen who enshrined the nobility's traditions in law, and his words were met with discontented mutters from Ilsar and two others, who came from families who valued tradition over progress.

Splinter sat on her own in the back of the classroom. Over the past six and a half weeks, she'd grown accustomed to her history teacher's manner of speaking. Now that she could decipher his words, she could fulfill her homework duties. She read the books he assigned, and she passed the written tests. She never spoke up in class. Master Ness wasn't the sort who gave squires the opportunity to ask questions or argue points.

She did well with sword practice too. Twice, Master Elnor had told her she wasn't a complete disaster, which she'd taken as high praise. She practiced every spare moment and worked on Fenna's tricks whenever she had the chance.

When it came to her etiquette lessons, she'd been forced to pair up with Tym, one of the boys who'd accidentally greeted her on her first morning. While uncomfortable with her presence, he never sabotaged their exercises. "I don't care about tradition," he'd explained. "I just don't want to disappoint the masters."

Between his careful notes and Ash's help deciphering the different bows, forms of address, and rules for meals and get-togethers, Splinter was certain she would pass that class too. Uncle Elias would be shocked if he heard.

With everything else, Splinter lagged behind. The other squires made no effort to help her or to keep a seat available for her. More than once, Lucen had "accidentally" tripped her during her runs.

Yesterday at lunch, Ilsar had casually confided in her that she'd already lasted longer than any of them had expected. "If the teachers can't get rid of you, we may have to try other methods."

"Go away, Ilsar." She didn't want to rise to his bait.

"Aren't you the least bit intimidated? Or worried?"

"Unless you're here to tell me something useful, leave me to my lunch. I'm hungry." When he left, she clung to her bread roll to hide the shaking of her hands because, despite her bravado, she *was* worried.

But she had other things on her mind too.

The last time she'd accompanied Ash back to the palace from the Maronne estate, Ash had been edgy and upset. As soon as they'd passed the palace gates, she'd pulled a crumpled letter from her tunic. A message written in Ferisian. She'd held it like the paper was burning her fingers, and despite the fact that they'd both been taught basic Ferisian, neither of them could read what it said.

Lord Lambelin had been thrilled. Ash had skipped dinner because she felt ill. Splinter had gone to the kitchens to get fruit juice and dry biscuits for the both of them, and they'd eaten in silence on the hidden staircase.

That had been a week ago. Splinter knew from her mother's work that translations took time. But no one knew what the letter said yet, and Ash had been invited to join the Maronnes for a long ride tomorrow, while Mist and Hazel were supposed to visit the palace the day after.

After her lessons, Splinter would help Ash prepare for the ride. She'd promised to stay close to her. Splinter reminded herself of Veridia's warning every night before bed. A knight-to-be protected her princess. Everyone else had to earn her trust several times over.

She scribbled down her homework assignments, scarcely paying attention to them. She scarfed down her food at lunch. When Lord Brenet set the squires to another run around the practice courts at the start of their weapons drills, Splinter barely noticed that she had an easier time keeping up with the others. She still came in last, but it was a near thing.

She ignored the other squires' whispers and focused on Master Elnor's arrival, and the wooden swords that he carried. They were longer and heavier than the ones she'd used so far. The blade he held out to her showed the wear and tear of use. It reminded her of Anders's blade.

"If you want to succeed, you'll have to build up strength," Master Elnor said. "This will help."

Like most practice sessions over the past weeks, he set the other squires to work and squared off against Splinter, aiding her through the forms and dances. He didn't hold back. He drew her away from her worries.

For the duration of the lesson, there was only the patterns of the blade, Splinter's steps to keep her footing, and the slow-building ache in her arm muscles. Her brother had once told her that this was a good ache. The type of pain that told you that you were growing and learning.

Splinter knew what he meant. All too soon, Master Elnor stepped back, a frown on his face. He surveyed the practice yard and called out, "Ilsar. A moment?"

Ilsar broke away from a mock fight to walk over.

"Master Elnor?" he asked politely.

The sword master indicated that Ilsar should take his position opposite Splinter. "Humor me. I need another perspective."

Splinter's vision narrowed. She heard the faint echoes of whispers around her as the other squires all stopped their practice to watch.

Nerves ran down Splinter's spine like ants. She hadn't sparred with any of the other squires yet. And while Ilsar wasn't as strong a fighter as Lucen, he was the best of the rest. He was twice, maybe three times, the sword fighter she was.

Ilsar stepped into the circle and smirked. "My pleasure, my lord."

"We go until one of you disarms the other," Master Elnor said. "I want a fair fight. No foul play, no dangerous charges. Respect your blades and each other, do you hear me?"

They both nodded.

Splinter's hands felt clammy.

"As for the rest of you—" Master Elnor raised his voice. "If you have time to dawdle, you're not working hard enough."

None of the squires moved.

Splinter stepped into guard position. Master Elnor wouldn't ask her to fight if he didn't think she was ready—right?

They raised their blades, and the moment Master Elnor brought his arm down to signal the start of the match, Ilsar attacked.

Unlike Master Elnor, he didn't trade Splinter blow for blow and form for form. He fought with the intent to beat her. His moves were met with cheers from the squires, Lucen's whoops loudest of all.

Ilsar's blade snaked past Splinter's defense to whack her on the shoulder. He ducked under one of her attacks, and the next thing she knew, his sword slammed into her ribs with bruising speed.

"Focus," Master Elnor called. "Don't be cowed by stronger opponents."

Splinter dodged Ilsar's next attack. Before she could press her advantage, he circled around her and jabbed the back of her knee. She struggled to keep her balance, bringing up her sword at the last moment to block his lunge.

"You are better than this, Squire Splinter," Master Elnor snapped.

Ilsar hooked his blade around hers and pulled her close. He grinned at her, but his eyes were cold. "Are you better than this, squireling? Or is it time to show the teachers you're nothing but a sham?" He kept his voice low so Master Elnor wouldn't hear, but the words burrowed deep under her skin.

Splinter slammed her heel onto the instep of his foot, forcing him to release her.

She adjusted her grip like Master Elnor had taught her. She widened her stance in the way Fenna had shown her, to block more comfortably.

When Ilsar's next attack arced toward her, she parried. The voices of the squires around them dimmed. She followed a low thrust with a sideward slash. Ilsar might be more experienced, but Splinter was quicker, and she had nothing to lose.

Her body remembered the forms she'd practiced endlessly. She dashed in and out of range. She felt, rather than saw, Ilsar's surprise. She pushed when he wavered.

She didn't hear the squires around her anymore, or Master Elnor. She lost herself in the fight. Perhaps it was luck when Ilsar overreached and lost his balance, but she was there to take advantage of it. She feinted to the right and stepped into the left, and her blade hooked around his.

She twisted.

Ilsar lost his grip. The wooden practice blade slipped from his fingers. The blade tumbled to the ground—and the rest of the world roared back to Splinter.

The sword clattered softly before it came to rest outside the practice circle. Then deadly silence.

Master Elnor clapped his hands, the sound echoing across the courts. "Adequately done. Squire Ilsar, thank you for your assistance. Squire Splinter, you are progressing admirably."

Splinter grew hot and cold all over.

Ilsar stared at her, pale and furious.

Lucen picked up the fallen blade. Ignoring Splinter completely, he handed the sword to Ilsar. "Come on," he said. "Let's get back to work. Don't think this means anything."

Splinter knew the words were meant for her. But she also knew Lucen was wrong. She had bested one of the most talented squires in the group. It meant everything.

She raised her head and smiled.

"Look at her. She thinks she deserves to be here now."

"She just got lucky."

"Father says the palace squires are the laughingstock of court now. Wait until he hears—"

Splinter stopped listening. She turned to Master Elnor and raised her sword. "Do we keep going, sir?"

The sword master looked at her curiously before he shook his head. "No, squire, I think I know all I need to know."

He pitched his voice to reach the very corners of the practice courts. "Squires, put down your weapons. Since you all have so much time on your hands, instead of playing around we'll make use of it."

Master Elnor gestured. "Taking care of your equipment extends to these courts. Our master smith has business at the docks today, which leaves me to decide what to do with your afternoon. The dummies need cleaning and the targets need to be refilled with straw from the stables, and let's try to spruce up the fields and lists."

Some squires groaned. The practice courts had gone muddy and disgusting from the melting snow. Corwen sighed loudly, and Meren elbowed him, but that didn't stop his twin from speaking up. "This is servants' work, sir."

Master Elnor walked over to him, staring him down. "Any worthy knight knows how to take care of their equipment. But if you're not willing to put in the work, I'm sure Lord Brenet will be happy to explain that to you."

Corwen blanched. "No, sir. I'll work."

Master Elnor nodded at a handful of stable boys, who brought in rakes and shovels and buckets. The sword master gathered up the practice weapons. When he approached Lucen, he considered the crown prince. "Perhaps some good honest work will give you time to consider the meaning of courteous behavior, your highness." He raised his voice. "Have fun, my doves."

Then he wandered off, deep in thought.

CHAPTER TWELVE

SPLINTER

At first the squires on the practice courts worked in harmony, in case their teachers were watching. Lucen and the oldest squires divided up the tasks, and no one complained—not even Splinter, who was given a shovel and a bucket and told to scoop up the mud from the practice field. She felt her ears burning, and she thought it better not to draw too much attention to herself.

When no one showed up to check on them, the squires slacked. Corwen took his dummy and danced a waltz with it. Two boys took their rakes and pretend to joust. Lucen swung an arm around Ilsar's shoulders and talked to him for a few minutes. Ilsar's sullen pout tightened into a smirk, and he punched Lucen's arm, laughing. They nudged

Corwen, who sauntered over to Tobias, who, in turn, made his way to Meren.

Two guards crossed the courtyard and the squires snapped back to work, but as soon as the guards disappeared, they stilled.

Meren stopped filling up the archery targets and nudged his brother. Together they crossed the courts, stopping by the other squires, exchanging a few words. Some laughed. Others nodded.

Splinter noticed, but she kept her head down. She didn't like this assignment any more than they did, and the mud kept sliding off her shovel, but she wasn't going to get in trouble over it.

Until Lucen walked up to her, hands at his side. The twins flanked him. "You know, if we're to make these practice courts look appropriate for a royal palace, we should do something about all the muck gathered here."

"What—" Splinter started.

Meren and Corwen grabbed her by her arms and hoisted her to her feet. Lucen leaned in close. "You do not belong here. You leach away the masters' time and attention. You'll never be strong enough to protect my family." He picked up her bucket, half full with mud, and tipped it out over her head. "And we'll get rid of you, like the stain that you are."

Splinter spluttered to keep the mud from seeping into her mouth. "Let me go!"

She tried to pull out of the twins' grasp, but they carried her over to the archery lists, out of sight from the gate. With little regard for her struggles, they held her over a muddy puddle at the edge of the lane, where grass met greenery, and let her fall.

Ilsar advanced on her with a sloshing bucket full of dirty water. With a smirk, he threw it at her. The other squires gathered, carrying shovels and rakes, and they began to cover Splinter with filth.

Mud slammed against her head and tangled into her hair. Her tunic was soaked through and freezing. And the chant was like a drumbeat around her. "Stain!" "Stain!" "Stain!"

Splinter curled to protect her head and her face. She squeezed her eyes shut to keep from crying.

Fendar—one of the youngest squires, who apparently acted as lookout—hissed. "Quiet! Someone's at the gate."

Immediately the chant ceased. The shovels and rakes dropped to the ground, and all the squires ran away from Splinter. All but Lucen and the twins.

With her bullies' attention elsewhere, Splinter slowly pushed herself up from the muddy puddle, to see who the visitor was.

A page in palace livery held a note in his hands and scanned the practice courts. "Squire Splinter? I have a note from Princess Adelisa."

Meren stepped in front of her to block the page's line of sight.

Corwen held Splinter down with his shovel. Mud dripped in her eyes and mouth, and she spat. "Let me pass," she croaked.

Corwen pushed until she was facedown on the ground. He tsked. *"Stain."*

Splinter drew breath to shout, only to inhale a mouthful of mud.

Lucen walked up to the page. "A message from my sister?"

The page stammered. "Prince Lucen, it's addressed to Squire Splinter."

Splinter struggled to get out from under the shovel. She needed air. She needed that note.

"I will make sure it gets where it needs to go. Trust me," Lucen promised.

The page hesitated, then he held out the folded piece of paper. "Thank you, highness. Please make sure it gets to her as soon as possible."

Splinter snarled. Mud crept up her nose too.

Lucen saluted the boy and spun the letter around. With a single glance in Splinter's direction, he broke the seal and read it. Then he tore it to shreds.

With a strength born from fury and desperation, Splinter grasped for the shovel again, and this time she found purchase. Her fingers curled around the tool, and instead of pushing it back at Corwen, she yanked hard and rolled away, pulling him off-balance.

She scrambled to her feet. She rubbed the mud from her eyes and nose, spat on the ground, and locked eyes with Lucen. She put her head down and rushed him.

The other squires jumped to Lucen's aid. It was a mess of fists and knees and elbows. One of the squires hissed when an elbow clipped his eye. Another coughed when a foot connected with his stomach.

A fist struck out and caught Splinter on the chin. Her head snapped back, and stars danced across her vision. A knee slammed into her side, leaving her breathless. Fingernails dug deep into the soft tissue of her wrist.

She tried to give as much as she got. She pulled at hair. She punched wildly. She didn't even—really—care about who was on the other side anymore. Not a single squire had helped her. No one had stood up for her.

She was trying to lash out again when strong fingers

clamped around her arm.

She struggled, but the fray around her was letting up. Burly guards in leather armor waded in, professionally avoiding the wild kicks and punches, and pulled one squire after another from the tangle.

"You will cease this disgraceful behavior, or the guards have my permission to throw you in the horses' troughs to cool you down," Lord Brenet said, regarding the chaos. He didn't raise his voice. He didn't have to. He was quietly furious, and the courtyard was eerily quiet.

"This is the most shameful display I have seen in all my years here," the master of squires continued.

Some of the squires tried to straighten. Others scuffed their feet. Two had bloody noses. Tym, Splinter saw to her horror, held his obviously broken arm cradled to his chest, and he had tears in his eyes.

Only Lucen was remarkably unscathed, and that made Splinter feel worse. He'd *deserved* her anger.

"I will have to think about how to respond to this flagrant disregard for your position, for your duty, and for yourselves. I expect I will have a long conversation with each of you. The squires responsible *will* be punished." Lord Brenet stared at the squires in turn.

Splinter couldn't meet his eye.

"For now I simply want to know who threw the first punch." Lord Brenet kept his voice light, like it was a reasonable request. Deep in her heart, Splinter knew that it had been any of the boys, none of them would have tattled.

Those rules didn't apply to her.

She glanced up through her lashes, and found every single squire staring at her.

Lucen schooled his expression to one of regret. "Splinter, my lord. It was Splinter who attacked me. The others came to my aid."

The two guards who'd flanked Lord Brenet stood watch outside his office door, and Splinter had never before felt so much like a prisoner. She'd waited in Lord Brenet's office while the master of squires ensured that the squires who needed aid were seen by the physicians. The others were told to gather on the indoor practice courts. All but Splinter.

She hadn't dared to move. She was all too aware of the mud dripping onto the rug beneath her feet.

When Lord Brenet returned to his office, Splinter folded her hands behind her back and forced herself to meet his gaze.

"Squire Splinter." Lord Brenet's voice was frosty and

his expression thunderous. "When you reported to me, I told you that I would not let you tarnish the reputation of the squires in this palace or dishonor the royal family. Do you have anything to say for yourself?"

Splinter did. That it wasn't fair. If she was a blemish on the good name of the palace squires, then so was the crown prince. So were all the squires who'd fought her, bullied her, stood back and done nothing.

She could still hear their voices in the back of her head. *Stain. Stain. Stain.*

She didn't even know what was in the message from Ash. Splinter needed to get to her.

"Nothing, my lord," she managed.

Lord Brenet frowned. "Was there a reason why you initiated the fight? I heard there were inappropriate comments during practice. If any of the squires acted dishonorably, I will hear of it."

He offered her an opening. It would be so easy to take it.

She wouldn't be the one to snitch.

They outnumbered her. It didn't matter what she wanted, or what Ash wanted. With Lucen leading the other squires, she didn't stand a chance. But she wouldn't become someone she wasn't. Splinter fought her own battles. She didn't tell on people. Not even on Lucen.

"I'm sorry, my lord," she said. "I made a mistake. I got angry. I . . ." She swallowed. "I'm trying to be a good squire."

Lord Brenet ran a hand through his hair. "I appreciate that Princess Adelisa needs a friend at court, but this is not the way. I will speak to the queen about your future here. We will find another means of companionship, but I cannot in good conscience let you keep your position as a squire if this is how you abuse it. Until we decide what to do with you, you shall confine yourself to your quarters. You're dismissed."

Splinter fought hard to keep her shoulders straight and her head held high, when all she wanted to do was curl up and cry.

As she closed the door behind her, she could just make out Lord Brenet's soft voice. "It's a shame. Elnor believed you had the makings of a fine and uniquely talented squire."

Splinter ran.

CHAPTER THIRTEEN

ASH

Ash waited. Her note should have gotten Splinter out of her lessons. But her squire hadn't shown up yet.

Restless, Ash slipped out of her comfortable dress and changed into a wide, flowing tunic and a long woolen skirt. She picked a long leather belt that circled around her hips twice, and she tightened the straps of her braces. Tension made her hands ache. After some hesitation, she clasped a small purse with some coins and a spare star amulet onto her belt, and she pulled her hair back in a ponytail.

She reread the letter from Mist that lay on her desk.

Change of plans. We have to postpone tomorrow's ride because Mama is being called away for business. Please join us for dinner tonight instead? A carriage will be sent to pick you up.

Ash tapped out an anxious rhythm against the desk. Queen Aveline and Lord Lambelin had given Ash their blessing to go. Uncle Lam had assured Ash that no one would blame a princess for a missing letter. Besides, so far, the letter appeared to be relatively innocent correspondence between scholars discussing history.

Worry still churned her stomach.

Lord Maronne had looked scattered and harmless. She had a hard time imagining he was the type of person who'd betray the queen, but that didn't mean he wasn't.

Ash wanted Splinter by her side at dinner tonight, and she didn't have a clue why it was taking the squire so long. The teachers had to obey a royal command too. Even from her.

Ash grabbed her cane and left her room.

The royal wing was empty at this time of day. The queen held court, and Lucen was busy with his studies. Two guards who stood watch at the entrance to the royal apartments saluted when Ash passed.

She never knew whether to acknowledge them. That hadn't been part of Aunt Jonet's lessons. So far, she had erred on the side of politeness. "I'm going to find Splinter," she said. "I'll be back before the carriage driver sends for me."

The guard on the left didn't move a muscle. He was a young man with short cropped hair and pimples on his nose, who seemed permanently on the edge of nervousness. He always blushed fiery red when a member of the royal family was near. The guard on the right—a middle-aged man with long black hair, dark brown skin, and scars along his chin—suppressed a smile. "Of course, your highness."

The royal wing was situated on the fourth floor of the palace, high above other rooms and residential areas. When a younger Ash had complained about the many staircases, Queen Aveline had explained that their rooms were the highest because that made them easily defensible. And, the queen reminded her daughter, they provided the royal family with a good view of the city and the lands around it, and of all the people they served. "All we need to do is look out the windows to be reminded."

Ash held on to that thought. She was doing her duty. She still hated the stairs.

She climbed down to the third floor, where several of the palace nobles—including Lord Lambelin—had their rooms, and then to the second, where the scribes and the royal physicians worked.

She paused. She didn't like the physicians' wing. When

she was still small and the physicians were learning how to care for a princess whose joints easily snapped apart and then grew back crooked, she'd come to associate this place with pain, and with being the royal physicians' object of study and curiosity. When she'd returned from Aunt Jonet's estate, Brother Nivanil had spent a full afternoon prodding and testing every bone, as if she was a warhorse being measured for armor, before pronouncing the silver braces she wore "sufficient."

But the physicians' wing was the quickest route to the squires' practice courts. And there was no sign of Splinter— or of the page she'd sent to deliver her message. If for some strange reason he couldn't locate Splinter, he was supposed to report back to her.

She gathered herself and walked into the winding hallway with its many offices, sticking to the shadows of the statues that stood on either side. Perhaps if she could keep her head down—

"Princess Adelisa?" A slender woman in physician's garb appeared at her elbow. She carried a leather satchel with fresh herbs from the royal star temple's gardens, and mud clung to the hem of her dress. "Do you need assistance? Should I find Brother Nivanil?"

Ash startled. "No, thank you." She lifted her chin and

channeled every bit of *princess* despite the erratic pounding of her heart as she met the woman's curious brown eyes. "I'm on my way to the practice courts."

"Oh." The woman seemed almost disappointed at the lack of an emergency, but then she brightened. "*Oh.* For the squires?"

Ash nodded. "I'm looking for Splinter."

"Of course, your new friend. *Marvelous.*" The woman patted Ash's arm. She began to set out glass jars with pastes and dried herbs, and Ash took the opportunity and dashed.

She passed a secretary desk filled with colorful bottles and jars with animal skeletons in greenish liquid. The desk concealed a passage that wound down to the first floor and provided easy access to the physicians in times of need. A guard lingered nearby, whispering to an apprentice girl. He kept his helmet on despite being inside. Dark brown curls escaped around his ears. He saluted Ash smartly. "Princess."

The apprentice, with a wimple over her hair, dipped into a curtsy.

Ash nodded a greeting and continued on down the hallway toward an impossibly narrow door, which opened up to a dark corridor that led to the battlements overlooking the practice courts. It was one of the few passages that, instead of being swallowed by redesigns, had appeared as a result of them, at a point where old and new buildings intersected.

Ash looked back toward the main staircase to make sure Splinter wasn't on her way up before she ducked into the passage. She used her cane as support, and to make sure she didn't bump into anything. She knew from experience that the stone walls were sharp and they cut.

Something creaked or squeaked behind her, and she picked up the pace.

Quickly, through the darkness. Carefully, across the uneven stones.

She pushed the outer door open, crisp winter air streaming in and sunlight momentarily blinding her. Ash stepped out onto the battlements that ran along the whole perimeter of the castle.

Guards patrolled these battlements, but it was an endless expanse of walkways. No guards were within sight at the moment. Ash was alone.

And the practice courts below were empty.

Ash grimaced. She followed the wall walk to get a better look, but Splinter and the other squires were nowhere to be seen. Only two stable hands, who were repairing a practice dummy.

Then Brother Nivanil walked out onto the courts, supporting a squire with a broken arm, and Ash hissed.

Training accidents happened. Lucen had broken his wrist once, falling off his horse. What if something had happened to Splinter?

The door behind her opened, and the curly-haired guard came out, hand in hand with the apprentice. They were whispering and laughing, and stopped abruptly when they saw her.

The guard straightened. "Princess."

This time the girl didn't curtsy. She stared intently at Ash, with slate-gray eyes that were uncomfortably familiar.

Ash blushed and tried to push around them. "Carry on. I was just on my way again." She needed to get down to the squires' practice courts.

But the girl grabbed her arm. "It's dangerous to be out here alone."

Ash froze. "What are you doing? Let me go!"

Curls had escaped from the girl's wimple, and Ash startled in recognition. This was the girl who'd watched Ash outside the theater. Who had no reason to be here, in the palace. The girl shook her head. "I thought this was impossible."

"Hush, Merewen." The guard's voice came from right next to Ash's ear.

Ash drew breath to scream, but before she could, a

rough hand wrapped around her mouth. "Quiet now, your highness. We don't want to draw attention to ourselves."

Ash struggled. She slammed her cane back, as hard as she could. The guard grunted, but instead of letting go, he pulled her arm to the side of her body, immobilizing Ash. His fingers dug painfully deep.

She kicked out. She wrestled. She screamed again, to no avail.

"So fierce. Nanna would love it." The girl sounded *happy*.

Ash frantically tried to see if any real guards were near, but the girl pulled Ash's arms back and bound them firmly together. She used a piece of cloth and fashioned a gag, weaving it beneath the strong hands of the guard, who kept a tight grip on Ash.

"Don't worry, princess," he whispered gently when the girl stepped back. "We'll take good care of you."

The guard let her go, and for a moment—a heartbeat—Ash thought someone might have spotted them. The guards. Perhaps one of the physicians had smelled trouble.

But then a heavy blunt object slammed against the back of her head.

And darkness took over.

CHAPTER FOURTEEN

SPLINTER

The connecting door between their rooms was closed. Splinter raised her hand to knock—and paused.

Her hands shook. She still had mud stains all over her arms, though she'd toweled most of the dirt off. Her knuckles were starting to bruise from the punches—the other squires' and her own.

Splinter looked like a mess, and she felt worse. Nothing she did lessened the lump in her throat or the ache in her chest.

Ash's words to Hazel, Mist, and Fenna echoed inside Splinter's head. Painful and sharp, like a headache. *No squire works harder than Splinter.*

Ash had stared down court for Splinter. She'd fought

for Splinter's dreams as fiercely as her own.

And Splinter had failed her.

She'd let her anger get the better of her. She'd proven to everyone that she wasn't worthy of being a squire.

Her uncle's words came back to her with a vengeance too. "You'll come to see sense."

Uncle Elias used to tell Splinter it was unseemly to cry. Once she discovered she would get in trouble for it, she learned to cry quietly. And then not at all.

But Splinter wished she could, because maybe it would relieve the pain.

She rested her head against the door.

She could explain herself. Maybe Ash would understand. She disliked bullies too. Besides, Lord Brenet had suggested they would find another place for Splinter by Ash's side, and maybe that would be enough.

She pushed the door. "Ash?"

Silence.

"Ash? Something happened . . ." Splinter's voice trembled as she pushed the door open wider. "I didn't get your message. . . . Lucen . . ."

She stuck her head in. The room was empty. Dresses were strewn across the bed and the floor. A pale blue gown lay propped up against one of the bedposts, while a daffodil-yellow skirt hung over Ash's desk chair. A silver jewelry box, the lid open, balanced precariously on a small stack of books, and one of Ash's braces rested against a set of drawers.

Ash was nowhere to be seen.

Splinter slipped into the room. "Ash?" She peeked around the dressing screen and knocked on the door to the washing room. Splinter didn't want to face Ash and desperately wanted to see her, both at the same time.

An open note on the desk caught her eye. Picking it up, Splinter recognized Mist's scrawly handwriting, and her heart sank.

Please join us for dinner tonight?

This was why Ash had sent her a message. And instead of being by her side, Splinter had left her to face the Maronnes on her own, and who knew how dangerous that could be?

Splinter sank down on Ash's bed and hid her face in her hands. Stars, she was an utter disappointment.

But a small voice in the back of her mind, one that sounded remarkably like Anders, told her she'd only be a disappointment if she gave up now. Although it was late afternoon, perhaps the carriage hadn't left yet. And even if it had, perhaps she could follow it and keep an eye on Ash from a distance. Or perhaps she could go through all the information Lord Lambelin had gathered and find clues that everyone else had missed. Splinter's mother had once told her that when she worked on translating documents for the palace, she always searched for the patterns between the lines. Perhaps Splinter could do the same. Perhaps she could still make herself useful—

A soft scratching sound came from near Ash's door, and Splinter raised her head from her hands. "Ash?" Please, she wanted to add. Please still be here.

A piece of paper had been pushed under the door. Folded in two, the corners crumpled, and spidery ink stained the page. Splinter crouched down to collect it.

With some hesitation, she opened it, and a lock of brown hair fell out. Splinter snatched it up, recognizing the color. The world began to twist and spin around her as she read.

Her heart hammered. Her hands grew cold. She dropped the note and yanked open the door. The wide hallway outside the princess's room was deserted. The doors that gave access to the royal wing were well guarded.

She called out to the two guards. "Did you see anyone enter or leave the wing?"

The older of the two guards—Splinter was quite certain

he was called Ridir—turned to her and frowned. "No one, squire. But Princess Ash was looking for you. You probably just missed each other."

In any other situation, that would've been good news. Right now, Splinter wasn't sure. "She didn't leave by carriage yet?"

Ridir shook his head. "No, squire. She meant to come back here first."

Panic fluttered inside Splinter's chest. She dashed back to Ash's room, grabbed the note, and flew past the astonished guards.

"Alert the other guards!" she shouted at them. "I think Ash has been kidnapped!"

She ran toward the staircase, and the mysterious note with the threatening message burned a hole in her hand.

We have your princess. She is safe and unharmed. If you wish to see her again, our demands must be met. Extinguish the lights at the royal star temple to signal your understanding.

We will be in touch.

Without care for propriety, Splinter had burst into Lord Lambelin's office. His flash of anger had made way for shock and action as soon as she handed him the note. He'd immediately ordered a full lockdown of the palace. No one could leave the grounds without the guards knowing and checking every cart and carriage. He sent for those who'd seen Ash that afternoon. He recalled the crown prince from his private weapons practice, and then Lambelin stalked toward the throne room, where the queen was with the captains of the floating docks, negotiating trade agreements and taxes and job opportunities for apprentices.

Splinter followed awkwardly, half running to keep up with the guard commander. He'd glanced back at her once and nodded, which she took as permission.

But when Lord Lambelin entered the majestic throne room, she had hesitated. The fiery late-afternoon sun poured through the windows like liquid copper, the beams of light reflecting off the star-covered domed ceiling. The din of voices hushed.

Lambelin dismissed the captains, who observed him curiously—and calculatingly. Once they realized how serious he was, they filed out without protest. Guards fell into step with every single one of them, to escort them out.

At the head of an oval table covered in scrolls and cups, Queen Aveline crossed her arms. Her eyes briefly rested on Splinter as thin lines appeared across her forehead. They were the only outward sign of her worry. "Lam? What's going on?"

Lambelin gestured at Splinter. "Close the doors."

She did as ordered and lingered.

"Your majesty, Ava . . . it's Adelisa. Someone took her." Lambelin knelt down in front of the queen and held out the crumpled note.

Reading it, the queen turned a ghostly shade of pale. Her expression twisted in pain—and fear. "No. *No.*"

Splinter swallowed. This was what Ash had feared, that night in the hidden passages.

"Once you're in the princess's service, you're her first line of defense," Veridia had told her.

"I will protect her," Splinter had told the queen.

"I'll protect you," she'd promised Ash.

Splinter slunk into the shadows of the doorway, but Queen Aveline got to her feet and slammed the note down onto the table. "Tell me, one of you, how could this happen? Why weren't you by my daughter's side, squire?" When Lambelin rose, the queen grabbed the front of his tunic. "Why didn't the guard stop anyone from getting close to her? My *daughter*, Lambelin! I demand to know *how*!" Her voice broke on the last word, and her knees gave way underneath her.

Lambelin caught her in his arms, and held her close, until the shaking of her shoulders subsided and the muffled sobs grew quieter. Splinter blinked hard and turned away from the queen's raw pain. She wanted to help. She wanted to run through the palace and *find Ash*.

The queen shook out of Lambelin's grasp. She dusted off her dress. "I want to know everything." Her eyes were red and puffy, but her voice was measured. "Are the Maronnes involved in this? Did we send her into danger ourselves?"

Lambelin guided the queen back to her seat while he remained standing. He beckoned Splinter closer. "My guards have apprehended the carriage driver who came to take Ash to the Maronnes. He only arrived at the gates *after* Splinter found this disgraceful note, so it's unlikely he was involved. But for the Maronnes, I . . . do not know. The letter Ash found in their library appears harmless, though the palace scribes still miss Evana's eye for codes."

Splinter startled at that. Ever since Ash had asked her about her mother, in those quiet moments before sleep, Splinter had wondered about Evana's work. The long texts on her desk. The stacks of notes. Her mother, a code breaker? Ash would want to hear that. She should tell—

She swallowed hard.

"Regardless, these thieves needed help to get into the palace," Lambelin said. "Lord Maronne remains our best lead. With your permission, I want to bring him and Lady

Maronne in for questioning. With luck, we can shield our investigation and Ash's role in it."

"Do whatever needs to be done," Queen Aveline snapped. She rubbed her eyes and focused on Splinter, who wanted to shrink back under her fierce glare. "You found this note?"

Splinter folded her hands behind her back to keep them from trembling. "Yes, your majesty. It was pushed under Ash's door."

"Did you see who delivered it?"

"No, your majesty."

"Did you ask the guards for information? Had they seen anyone?"

"No, your majesty," Splinter said. Heat rose to her cheeks. "I mean, I did ask, but they hadn't seen anyone."

Queen Aveline tapped the note on the table. "Do you know where Ash was when she was taken?"

Splinter shook her head. She couldn't force herself to meet the queen's gaze anymore, so she stared at her boots. "No, your majesty."

"From what we've puzzled together so far," Lambelin interrupted, before Queen Aveline could say any more, "Ash was on her way to Squire Splinter. She was seen on the second floor, in the physicians' wing. She spoke briefly with Sister Beatrice, who believed Ash was on her way to the battlements. But the guards outside never saw her. The guard who stood watch inside is nowhere to be found." His voice darkened at those words.

"You think the guard might have been infiltrated?"

"It's one of many possibilities that we need to investigate, your highness," he said. "If they have been, the traitors will be found and dealt with harshly. I will not fail you again."

Splinter knew how Lord Lambelin felt. He was the queen's best friend. And he didn't want to disappoint her any more than she wanted to disappoint Ash.

"I don't care about failure, Lam, I care about my daughter." Queen Aveline breathed out hard. "And to demand we extinguish the lights of the royal star temple . . . that temple has weathered storms and wars and it's never been brought down. It's a beacon of *hope*. If we give in to these demands, it'll be a clear message to our enemies that we're vulnerable."

"I believe that's their intent. It must be a Ferisian ploy to weaken us. Cruelty upon cruelty."

The queen closed her eyes. "Order it to be done."

"Your highness . . ."

"Lam. Do it."

Splinter had to force herself to not fidget as she felt the weight of the queen's decision. For as long as she could remember, the royal star temple—a building older even than the palace, or the city—had been a bright light against the darkness. In winter, it offered warmth and shelter for all who needed it. In times of famine and fear, it offered food and hope. It towered high enough over the rest of the city that all could see it, and all could use its lights to find their way.

But Ash needed to find her way home too.

"*Squire* Splinter." The slight inflection when the queen called Splinter "squire" was enough to indicate that she was fast reconsidering her promise to Ash. "Why weren't you *with* my daughter? You promised to keep her safe."

The letter. The fight. The crown prince.

It wasn't *fair*. It wasn't her fault.

Splinter opened her mouth and closed it again. Anything she could say would sound like an excuse. It would only make matters worse. "I—"

The door slammed open, and Lucen, dressed in his practice gear, barged in. His pale face was blotched with red. He ran to his mother, discarding his leather braces and dropping them on the floor. "Is it true? They say Ash is gone. Everybody's talking about it. *Is it true?*"

His voice cracked, like Splinter had never heard it crack before. Not even when they fought. He was pleading. He bit his lip.

Queen Aveline took one of his hands in hers and gently pried open his fingers, rubbing circles over them with her thumb. She nodded at Lambelin. "The palace remains locked down. I want the royal council assembled within the hour. I need a moment alone with my son." She regarded Splinter. "We'll talk later." It sounded less like a promise, and more like a threat.

Both Lambelin and Splinter bowed. When Splinter straightened, she found herself staring right into the tearstained eyes of Lucen. He snarled, like he wanted to start their fight all over again. "You should have been there for her."

"I would have been—" Splinter bit her tongue. Her head pounded. She would have been, if it hadn't been for *him*.

Lucen flinched and looked away.

Lambelin grasped her shoulder. "Come. It's best if you return to your room now."

After weeks of squire training and tutors who expected all squires to jump at their commands, Splinter could only mutter, "Yes, my lord."

But she kept her eyes on Lucen—who didn't meet her

gaze—while Lord Lambelin guided her out of the throne room, where the shadows obfuscated the stars above.

Splinter couldn't sit by and wait. She had promised to protect Ash.

Once she had returned to the royal wing, she walked past her own room and toward the prince consort's old office, where she traced the windowsill until she found the lever that Ash had used. She let the bookcases swing open and checked the passage for any sign of Ash.

Nothing. Nothing but darkness and silence.

Splinter hated silence. It was far too easy to fill it with worry.

Everyone assumed it had been the Ferisian Empire that stole Ash. What would they do to her? Would they ransom her? Would they hurt her?

Someone had to go after her. Someone had to find her.

She went to Ash's room to collect the map Ash had used to teach Splinter her way around the buildings. Ash had marked down every passage in case Splinter ever needed a shortcut to her classes.

Splinter planned to make her way through every single one, just in case the guard had missed anything.

But on the third floor, guards were swarming the

hallways, methodically scouring rooms and passages. When Splinter tried to get closer, her practice sword at her side, she was pushed back, like the other nobles who gathered to watch and whisper.

"I'm Ash's squire!" Splinter called. "I want to help."

"You can help by staying out of our way," a blond guard with a gruff voice replied. "We'll do what we can to find her."

Splinter tried another wing, where she was met with similar chaos. Two courtiers, tall young women in flowery dresses, observed the search from a distance, gossiping behind their fans.

"When I was her age, I wanted to run away from home all the time. Perhaps she chose to go back to Byrne. It's a simpler, quieter place for her."

"They say the poor girl was kidnapped. *Kidnapped*. If the palace guards cannot even protect a princess, how can we feel safe here?"

"Don't worry, I don't think the Ferisian Empire is coming for your fake diamond earrings quite yet, Dinah."

Splinter pushed past the squabbling women and approached the nearest guard, who stopped her. "No. We don't need help. We don't need good advice. We don't need rumors from your friend's cousin's neighbor who saw the princess being carried away. We are doing what we can."

"But I . . . ," Splinter started, but the guard had already turned away.

With every passing hour, the gossip grew more outrageous. On every floor, the guard tried to disperse the gathered nobles, but they simply flocked to another part of the investigation.

Everywhere Splinter tried, the response was the same. The guards didn't need help. They wouldn't let her pass.

And Ash was nowhere to be found.

Splinter grew desperate. Once, she saw Lambelin walk past from a distance, but by the time she'd elbowed her way through, he was gone.

She wasn't Ash's squire anymore in the eyes of the palace.

But she *was* her friend.

Splinter knew what she had to do. She returned to her room and dressed in her most comfortable leather armor and a midnight-blue cloak. She grabbed the stash of candies and dried fruits that Ash had stored away for emergencies, munching on a few of them to silence the pangs of missed dinner. And she waited for darkness to blanket the city.

Before she left, she placed her mother's ornamental dagger in the rack above her desk, as a silent promise that she would return—with Ash.

♦ ♦ ♦

Inside the palace, Splinter zigzagged around the gossip and around the worries that the guard had no clues or witnesses. Outside, she cast a longing gaze in the direction of the royal stables, where Owl was housed, but she didn't want to draw attention to herself.

Instead she held her head high when she approached the first gate out. The lanterns were lit, and the soft orange glow formed a barrier against the deep emptiness of the night. "I'm running errands for Lord Lambelin," she lied. "I have to go to the lower wards."

The guard at the gate, the copper band around his sleeve indicating he was a sergeant-at-arms, squinted at her. "Aren't you the princess's squire? Are you the one who let her get stolen?"

Splinter gritted her teeth. "The lord commander won't like to be kept waiting. Let me pass."

The sergeant grunted and stepped aside. "Far be it from me to make sense of who the commander trusts."

At the next gate, Splinter told a similar story. "Lord Lambelin wants the latest information from the curtain walls. Please let me through."

At the third and final gate, Splinter noticed the guard on duty was the same one who'd given her entrance to the palace on her first day. Guardsman Jasse. She picked up her pace and waved at him. "Running errands for Lord Lambelin, I'll be back soon!"

The second guard at the gate stepped forward to stop her, but Jasse shook his head. He furrowed his brow. Some part of Splinter wanted him to demand an explanation. Leaving the palace felt far too easy after she had fought so hard to be allowed in. But she couldn't stay. She had to figure out who had taken Ash, how they had gotten to her, and where she was now.

The guard would search every corner of the palace grounds. Lord Lambelin would interrogate Lord Maronne, who was the crown's best lead. So Splinter would talk to the two girls who—with a bit of luck and eavesdropping—knew everything their parents knew. Hazel and Mist.

Splinter cracked her knuckles.

She *would* bring Ash home.

As soon as she stepped through the last gate onto the meandering road down the hill, a blade flashed in the starlight, a hand pulled her into the shadows, and the tip of a dagger pointed at her throat.

CHAPTER FIFTEEN

SPLINTER

Splinter searched the shadows for the person on the other side of the weapon. A figure in a supple dark cloak stared back at her, a heavy bag slung over his shoulders. Despite the large hood he used to hide his face, she'd recognize that scowl anywhere.

"What are you doing here?" Splinter and Lucen hissed at the same time.

Splinter narrowed her eyes. "I'm going to look for Ash," she said. It should be obvious.

"You're going to run around Haven and hope that someone has seen something?" Lucen's words were sharp, but his voice sounded hesitant. The hand with the dagger dropped.

"It's better than doing nothing!"

As soon as Lucen had lowered the dagger completely, Splinter charged at him. She vaguely registered the sound of the dagger tumbling to the cobblestone road as her fist collided with his arm. "If it hadn't been for you, I would have been with her! *None* of this would have happened."

She shoved him against the outer wall of the palace grounds, and punched.

She expected Lucen to fight back, like he had in the squires' courtyard. Instead he raised his arms to protect his head. He didn't flinch away. He didn't reach for his weapon or block Splinter's blows. "I know."

She barely heard him at first. She only stopped because she refused to fight an opponent who didn't fight back, even one two years older than she was. "What did you say?"

"I said I know." Lucen was still scowling. He lowered his hands. His knuckles were bruised from the fight that afternoon, and red spots and scrapes showed where Splinter's punches had landed. "You're right."

Splinter took a step back, uncertain. She was so angry at Lucen her fingers tingled and the back of her neck itched. This was the last thing she'd expected. "Good. So you know. That's . . . good. . . ."

One of the guards at the gate took a lantern from its

hook and began to walk down the road. Lucen hid deeper in his hood, until his face was obscured by darkness.

Splinter pushed herself closer to the wall too, but the guard noticed the movement, swinging the lantern in their direction.

"No loitering, no lingering! Keep walking!"

This late at night, only a handful of people made the trek from the palace to the city. Servants, mostly, who lived somewhere in Haven. On normal days, it'd be guards too, but Splinter assumed they were all needed in the palace.

Lucen grabbed Splinter's hand, snatched the dagger from the cobblestones, and drew her toward the city. Flabbergasted, she let him, at least until they were well outside the glow of the guard's lantern.

Halfway down Palace Hill, Splinter jerked her hand out of Lucen's grasp. "What do you want, *your highness?*" She spat out those last two words.

Lucen made sure none of the guards had seen them and no one had followed. "I want to find my sister. But I don't know where to start looking. Even though we're not exactly friends, maybe we can help each other. We can help *her.*"

Splinter folded her arms. She didn't want him to be a part of any of this. "I suppose if I say no, you'll call the guard on me?"

The corner of Lucen's mouth quirked up in a wry, humorless smile. "If I call the guard on you, I might as well call them on myself too. They want me locked safe in my rooms."

"So why *aren't* you?" Splinter asked. "Do you feel guilty? Do you want to be a hero? Do you even care about Ash at all?"

Lucen's face twisted in anger. "She's my sister! Of course I do!"

"Really? You told her she's too weak to be a princess. You don't have faith in her and you don't want her in the palace. Don't you think she knows that?" Ash had never explicitly said so, but Splinter had noticed that she flinched every time Lucen scorned her.

Lucen fidgeted. His expression was haunted. "If you say no, I'll find my own way. I'll do what I can to track her down and bring her home safe, I promise."

Splinter didn't believe him. If he cared, he would have been kind to Ash, not belittled her.

The night around them grew darker and colder. Splinter walked past Lucen. In the middle of the night, the trek to the Maronne estate was going to be long and tiresome.

Lucen stood where she'd left him. He fiddled with his tunic, and he stared down at the vast city sprawled below them.

She didn't understand him. He was a bully. He was a sorry excuse for a brother. But he *was* Ash's brother. And the crown prince and the kingdom's future king, stars help them all. Could she leave him out here alone, when the Ferisian Empire may have already kidnapped one of the royal children? She sighed. "We're *not* friends. I don't like you. I think you're cowardly and cruel. But Ash would want you to be protected."

He looked at her. "You'll let me come along?"

"You'll only get in trouble if I let you go by yourself. One of us should know what they're doing."

"I suppose that's you?"

Splinter very nearly reconsidered. She was better off without him.

She started walking. "Come along, highness. We're going to visit the Maronnes."

They followed the road down to the foot of the hill in silence. Twice, groups of guards charged past on horseback, doubtless sent by the crown to search for the lost princess. Guards would also have been sent to the Maronnes to escort the lord and lady to the palace, and Splinter didn't think Hazel and Mist would welcome them kindly.

Splinter's plan was built on ifs and wishes. *If* the Ferisians had taken Ash. *If* Lord Maronne had Ferisian contacts. *If* anyone knew anything. Splinter hoped she could count on Mist's eavesdropping—and the girls' friendship with Ash. She didn't know where else to start.

She kicked a pebble down the road, right as Lucen cleared his throat. "I do care, you know."

Splinter kept walking. "I don't know, and I don't think Ash does either, or she wouldn't have seemed so lonely when I met her."

"Mother *should* have left her in Byrne," Lucen shot back. "None of this would have happened."

"She should have left *you* at a star temple," Splinter suggested. "We would all have been a lot happier."

He was quiet after that.

Splinter kept her eyes on the cobblestones in front of her. The Maronne estate was on the far side of Haven. It would take them an hour or more to cross the city, and another hour to get to the estate itself. By the time they arrived, Ash would have been gone for nearly half a day. She could be anywhere. Splinter pulled her cloak tighter.

When they reached the point where the road that wound down Palace Hill flowed into the streets and bustle of the city, Lucen threw one last glance up at his home.

"You can go back," Splinter muttered uncharitably. She

didn't want him to travel with her. At least that way, she wouldn't have to look out for him.

"I left a note for Mother and Uncle Lam, so they won't worry."

"They will."

"Yeah. I'll deal with that when we're all safely home." He focused on the city ahead.

The roads were lit by lanterns on either side, but Lucen stuck to the shadows in between. Despite herself, Splinter acknowledged that was smart. At this time of night, the city was quiet, and her mother had always reminded her that the people who traveled the streets and roofs by starlight were best avoided.

Besides, once the queen or Lord Lambelin discovered Lucen was gone too, the streets would flood with guards, and Splinter didn't want to be caught. It was far better to not draw attention.

She hurried to catch up with Lucen, and he paused to fall into step with her. He didn't try to talk to her again. In the palace, Lucen had always been loud and present, and silence didn't suit him. But Splinter was sure that any attempt at conversation would only result in harsh words and balled fists.

They passed storefronts that were all shuttered and

closed for the night. Small flowers were painted near some of the doors. A cart with boxes that, come morning, would hold breads and cakes for the market, stood empty in front of a bakery. The smell of sweet and spicy dough clung to it, and a handful of rats scurried around. Overhead, a hungry owl hooted.

Splinter's stomach, empty but for a few sweets, growled. She should've brought more food for the road. She should have gone past the kitchens to beg for bread rolls and turnovers.

Lucen nudged her with an elbow and, without looking at her, held out a cold meat pie wrapped in paper. It was similar to the ones she'd had at dinner with the royal family, and it smelled delicious. Fowl with peppers and spices, in a beet-red dough.

Splinter hesitated.

"Don't worry," Lucen said. "It's not a peace offering."

"Good."

She snatched the pastry and bit into it, the sudden burst of flavors so overwhelming her stomach cramped. She devoured the pie in three bites.

She braced herself for a snarky comment from the crown prince, something about her lack of preparation, but it didn't come. He pushed his hands into the pockets of his cloak and kept walking.

They passed down a long street with shops on one side and a large walled garden on the other. The wrought iron gate was decorated with a thin row of copper and gold stars, and with a start, Splinter recognized it as the royal star temple garden, where physicians grew medicinal herbs and roots and flowers.

On normal nights, the lights of the temple were a beacon to all in the city. Large lanterns outside and candelabras inside illuminated the open square in front of the temple, as well as the trees and the temple garden. When Splinter was younger and her mother had brought her along for the blessings of the year, she'd loved running around the square to try to find star-shaped reflections of the lights.

The royal star temple *was* a symbol of hope.

The lights had been extinguished like the note ordered.

It was darker than the night itself, a void where the stars should be, and it scared Splinter.

Splinter and Lucen turned the corner to the temple square, and a rush of whispered voices crashed over them. Despite the late hour, people were gathering, and they were worried. Guards tried to hurry them along, but in a strange way, the lack of a guiding light still drew people in.

"Did something happen?"

"I heard someone say the queen died!"

"Did we lose the war? What will happen to us?"

Lucen froze. Every inch of him radiated tension. Splinter was certain he would turn and run, and she almost, *almost*, felt sorry for him. Then he took a step forward. And then another. With his arms tightly at his sides, he stalked across the square. He had his hood pulled over his face, but he kept his head high, as if daring anyone to come closer.

No one did. No one paid attention to the two of them. They all stared at the darkened building.

Splinter knew she would've stopped too, if it hadn't been for Lucen. She followed him through the streets, until the whispers and worries were far behind them. Until the night overwhelmed them again.

This time the silence grew so heavy that Splinter was almost relieved when Lucen spoke up again. "Why do you want to do this?"

She frowned. "Highness?"

"Be a knight." He didn't break pace. He didn't look at her. He waved his hand in her direction, at the squire armor she was still wearing. The leathers she technically wasn't allowed to wear anymore after their fight.

She threw the question back at him. "Why do you?"

To Splinter's surprise, Lucen considered it. He tugged at his collar—or at least she thought he did. Then the light from the lanterns glinted off a necklace. A small silver sword. She had never noticed it before.

"I know it's expected of you," she added, "but you said being a knight of Calinor *matters*."

"One day I'm going to be responsible for everyone in this kingdom. Everyone. I need to be strong for them. I want to be able to protect them." More softly Lucen added, "I want to keep them safe."

He turned to her, his expression fierce and defensive. "Now why do you?"

Because, less than a year after their mother died, Anders had looked like a hero when the queen knighted him. He'd smiled at Splinter, and despite the lump in her throat, for the first time in months, she'd smiled too. Mama would've been proud, Splinter was proud, and the light that reflected off Anders's sword and shield was like the first ray of sunlight after a devastating storm.

Because Mama had taught her that Calinor wasn't just a name and a place on a map, it was an idea. A home to all who fought for it.

Because that day when she had punched Lucen in the

marketplace, the girl he'd tripped and laughed at while the other squires stood by and egged him on *smiled* at her.

Because of Ash.

"Because I want to do the same."

CHAPTER SIXTEEN

SPLINTER

The deep inky black of midnight made way for a softer blue. Bright enough that Splinter could see the shape of buildings ahead, dark enough that the edges of the buildings blurred. Predawn fog rolled into the valley past the northern walls of Haven like a ghost army marching silently forward.

Glowing fields stretched out in all directions. The large mansion where the Maronne family lived stood tall and proud on the hillside. Guards with torches stood at the entrance gate, and others patrolled the walls. It wasn't as well guarded as the palace, and the walls weren't as tall, but it was clear people were on high alert.

"Wait." Lucen paused. "If the royal guard is there, they'll send me back home immediately."

"So?" Splinter grumbled.

He breathed out hard. "Can you think of another way in?"

Splinter imagined the layout of the mansion, the courtyard, and the buildings around it. "If we circle around, we can find a place to climb over the walls. We can hide in the stables and sneak into the mansion. I don't know exactly where Hazel's and Mist's rooms are, but we can figure it out."

Lucen looked at her oddly. "Haven't you been inside with Ash?"

"Lady Maronne thought it improper."

When the guard at the gate spun around to pace in the opposite direction, Splinter broke from the shelter of two evergreen bramble bushes and dashed across the field to the walls. She expected someone to call out to her, or for the guards to sound the alarm. But the only sound she heard was the soft crunch of leather boots on frozen grass.

She ducked down near the wall behind the stables, and Lucen skidded to a halt next to her. He dumped his bag on the grass, put his back against the finely hewn white stone, and held out his arms, fingers entwined. "Climb onto my hands. I'll boost you up and over the wall."

She frowned. He pulled a face. "I'm taller than you are, and stronger. Once you make it to the other side, I'll toss you a rope so I can climb up too."

"Yes, your highness."

When she put her left foot in his hands, he sighed. "You can just call me Lucen. All the squires do."

Splinter ran her fingers over the stone wall until she found a hold. "In case you've forgotten, *highness*, I'm not a squire anymore." She wasn't really sure who she was.

"I didn't mean for that—" Lucen started.

Splinter put her right foot on his shoulder. "Yes, you did."

She pulled herself up. She wasn't afraid of heights. She'd loved climbing trees with Camille. She stuck close to the wall and took advantage of every uneven outcropping, every broken stone.

When she reached the top, she made sure none of the guards were coming their way before she slipped over the wall and onto the thatched roof of the stables. The straw itched beneath her palms, and she leaned down precariously.

Lucen pulled a slender rope out of his bag and tossed one end up to Splinter, so she could tie it to one of the protruding beams of the hayloft. She clung to the rope on the other side to anchor it. "Hurry up, highness," she hissed.

The rope pulled taut, and the beam creaked and

groaned, and by the time the prince's head appeared over the edge of the roof, Splinter was as tense as the rope itself. "Come on. We have to get away from here in case the guards heard us."

She scurried along the edge of the roof until she spotted a large cart full of hay leaning against one of the walls.

Lucen crouched down next to her, his eyes bulging. "Are you trying to kill me?"

Splinter's hands itched, the temptation to push him overwhelming. Instead she rose and balanced on the edge of the roof. "Coward."

She jumped.

A hurried heartbeat later, she hit the pile of hay hard. The cart rocked under the impact, and she scampered aside to make room for Lucen. Sharp hay stalks clung to her clothes, her hair, her cloak. They scratched like cat's claws.

Splinter climbed out of the cart right as Lucen jumped—

The moment her feet hit the ground and his body hit the hay, a firm hand clamped around Splinter's arm. "You are, without a doubt, the worst thieves I've seen in twenty years of serving the lord and lady."

Splinter's stomach dropped. She was hauled into one of the empty stalls of the stable, where an abandoned card game had been left scattered across the straw. Two empty cups smelled of spiced grape juice.

A hooded lantern opened, and warm light flooded the area. Splinter struggled against the ironlike grip, but weeks of training meant nothing against the strength of the guard. "We're not thieves," she protested. "Let us go!"

The guard who held her—a broad-shouldered woman with short-cropped hair—laughed humorlessly. "Now *that* I believe." Her expression grew deadly. "So tell me, what are you doing here? It's a strange night, and I have little patience."

Through the stall window, Splinter could make out a second guard, who reached into the hay cart and hauled Lucen out by his arms.

Lucen tried his best to pull his hood over his head, but he was too late. The guard gasped and dragged him into the light.

The woman turned to them, and Splinter recognized Fenna, a sword slung over his back and a heavy war hammer hooked on his belt. He held Lucen like he was holding a snake, torn between doing his job and putting the crown prince down and backing away.

"Stars, what is *happening*?" the other guard muttered. "Your highness?"

"Fenna, it's me! It's Splinter!" Splinter kept trying to pull herself loose. "We're looking for Ash. We need to speak with Hazel and Mist. *Please.*"

"You're trespassing!" her captor bristled. "You put yourself in harm's way, sneaking in. We could have killed you both. Do you know what that would have done to the family?"

Fenna let Lucen go, inclining his head at him. He strode to Splinter and the other guard, signing urgently. Outside the stables, a handful of guards patrolled the courtyard, their presence marked by torches and lanterns.

The guard growled. "The girls are under our protection with the lord and lady taken, and they don't need to deal with an adventure-happy prince with no regard for consequences."

Lucen flushed, picking stalks of hay off his tunic.

"Please," Splinter said desperately. "We just want to talk to Mist and Hazel."

Fenna added his signs to her pleas. He placed his hands on the guard's arms and gently pried open her viselike grip. As quickly as the female guard's temper had flared, it disappeared. Her shoulders dropped, and she rubbed her hands over her face. "Take them. Let her decide what to do. But be smart about it. Hoods up. Voices down. And keep them in your sight at all times, do you understand, guardsman?"

Fenna saluted, fist over heart.

He took a lantern off the hook and held it up in front of him, locking eyes with Splinter.

"Thank you," she whispered.

Fenna led them into the mansion. Inside, the atmosphere was as tense as it had been outside, and Splinter wondered what it had been like when Lord Lambelin summoned the Maronnes to the palace. "Taken," the guard had said. By force?

For the first time, she wondered if they should've come here at all. Theirs was not the only home that had been upended. This was what the queen had meant, all those weeks ago, when she told Lucen that to accuse a member of the court of treason is not something she could lightly do. This was the other side of it. Hurt and mistrust. Anger. And Splinter couldn't make the pain go away.

Fenna guided them up a flight of stairs to a large sitting room, where logs in the fireplace were crackling and popping. Hazel was curled up on a long couch, clinging to a book without turning the pages, and Mist paced past the tall curtained windows.

Fenna cleared his throat, and Mist whirled around. Hazel sat up. She rubbed her eyes. "Fenna! Any news from our par—oh."

Her eyes drilled into Splinter, who pushed back her hood. Fenna retreated to the door, and Lucen stayed close to him, his face cloaked in shadows. He folded his hands behind his back.

Hazel scrambled to her feet. *"Splinter?"*

Mist furrowed her brow. She tried to stare through Lucen's cloak. "Why are you . . . what are you doing here?"

Splinter walked to Mist, her feet squishing the soft carpet. "We need help."

Mist took a step back when Splinter approached. Her face twisted.

"We're looking for Ash. She . . ." Splinter's voice trailed off. She felt like an unwanted guest. She twisted the ring around her finger.

"She got kidnapped. We heard," Hazel piped up behind her.

"She got kidnapped, and within hours, the royal guard burst into our estate suggesting our parents have something to do with it," Mist said, her voice a challenge. "Why is that?"

"I'm sorry about your parents." Splinter couldn't meet her gaze. "Ash was supposed to visit you today. I hoped you might have heard . . . something."

Hazel laughed humorlessly. "I can't believe that was supposed to be today."

"She never made it here. Why would we know anything?" Mist demanded. When she'd argued that Splinter should be allowed to come inside, when she'd convinced Fenna to teach Splinter more swordcraft, Mist had been brave and immovable. Scared, she was even more intimidating. "Tell me!"

Splinter didn't have an answer. From the corner of her eye, she could see Hazel and Fenna arguing silently.

Lucen stepped forward. He found a spot near the fireplace, and all eyes were drawn to him. He folded his hood back. His face was expressionless.

"My mother thinks your parents know more because your father has been corresponding with Ferisian nobles," he said coldly. "No loyal Calinoran noble would. And *someone* had to help the Ferisians into the palace."

Hazel gasped.

The words hung like swords above them all, ready to drop down and draw blood.

Mist's eyes flashed like embers as she spun and stalked to Lucen. "Your royal highness." She made the title sound more biting than Splinter ever had. "My father fought in the mountains to defend Calinor. He survived horrors that we could never imagine. And tonight he and Mama were arrested like *traitors*, for the crime of writing letters? Do you even know what's in them?"

Splinter opened her mouth to speak, but Lucen stepped closer to Mist, who stared up at him with her hands planted at her sides. "Do you?"

Mist didn't flinch. "Papa is trying to *end* the war. He's finding like-minded Ferisian nobles and scholars. He's gathering information about traitors at court. He's trying to *save* Calinor."

Splinter frowned. Could that be true? Could Lord Lambelin's spies have misjudged Lord Maronne so completely? Could they have confused the Maronnes with another noble family? The idea left a pit in Splinter's stomach.

Lucen frowned too. "If that's the case, your family has nothing to fear from the crown's investigation. But if your father has Ferisian contacts, the best thing you could do is share them. Because even if I don't know the horrors of war, I do know what will happen if my sister is brought to the empire. The war will escalate, and far more people will get killed, and you'll be just as responsible."

Mist clenched her jaw. Her fingers twisted the edge of

her woolen gown. "Ash is our *friend*. If you believe she's here, you're welcome to search the mansion. The royal guard didn't find anything, but who knows, maybe you will. You can comb through the rest of the estate. Every grain silo and every hayloft. You can go through my father's office, or what's left of it. The royal guard ransacked it and took all his correspondence."

"I don't believe she's here," Splinter said. Her head spun. She wanted to get closer, but Hazel positioned herself between Splinter and her sister, and Splinter knew they'd broken something by coming here. "I'm sorry. I just . . . hoped you could help us find her."

"Our father would do anything for Calinor," Hazel said. "We are loyal to the crown. And it doesn't matter because you don't trust us."

Mist turned her back to Lucen and rounded on Splinter. "Tell me one thing. Was Ash ever our friend? Or was she just here to spy on us?"

Splinter flushed under the girl's scrutiny. "She was also your friend."

Mist scrunched her face in disgust.

Fenna was signing again. "Fenna says that you were trespassing and that it's up to me to decide what to do with you." She drew herself up to the full height of her nearly twelve years. "If we send you back to the palace, we might gain some favor with the queen for keeping you safe. But unlike some people, *we* don't betray our friends."

"Thank you," Splinter whispered.

"If you need a place to start, find Lord Idian. He knows what Papa was researching, and he is fond of Ash. Ask him about the Larks."

"We appreciate that, more than you can—"

"It's best if you leave now."

"Mist . . ."

"Leave." Mist walked over to Hazel and pulled her close. "And don't ever come back."

CHAPTER SEVENTEEN

ASH

The wagon rumbled. Ash lay on a threadbare blanket, with a burlap sack filled with straw as a makeshift pillow. Her hands were tied behind her back, and her head ached. She blinked against the light filtering in through the gaps between the wooden panels on the sides of the wagon and overhead. She tried to sit up and get her bearings, but the constant rocking motion made it hard to stay balanced. She rolled to her side. Her shoulders protested, and she could feel the rope around her wrists slip past the braces she wore. One of her binds cut deep into her forearm.

She rolled until she hit the side of the wagon. Rough wood scraped against her legs and arms, and the shift of her dress knotted around her knees. Ash used her legs to steady herself, until she was half sitting, half leaning in the corner.

Flashes of memory came back to her. The attack on the battlements. One of the palace guards smirking at her. Being carried down a flight of stairs, with musty fabric covering her face and head. Emptiness.

She tried to breathe through the pain that cascaded through her bound arms and pounded in her head. She wasn't in the palace, that much was sure. She probably wasn't anywhere *near* the palace. She didn't know how much time had passed, exactly.

She was alone.

And she had to figure out what to do.

She tried to remember if she carried anything of aid. Her purse with coins and her star amulet had been taken away from her. Splinter had told her on more than one occasion that she should carry a dagger in a boot, just so she would have means to protect herself. Or get a cane with a sword hidden inside, like in the stories.

Her cane—

Ash sighed with relief when she spotted it on the far side of the wagon. Having her cane would make it easier to escape, and she had to escape.

The wagon didn't offer anything else that she might consider useful. The rope that hung from one of the hooks was so frayed, Ash expected it would crumble if she could find a way to untie it. The pillow wasn't comfortable and too small to do anything much. The blanket had potential, if she could get her hands free and sneak close enough to one of her captors to toss it over them.

Voices from outside the wagon drifted in. Muffled, like Ash was eavesdropping from behind a thick door.

". . . get there on time . . . stuck with *her*."

". . . worth a lot of gold . . . not going anywhere."

The first voice belonged to the guard in the palace. The one who was responsible for taking her. The second voice sounded gruffer. Older. *Odd*.

It took Ash a moment to pinpoint why the voice sounded strange. She'd expected lilting Ferisian accents. But the man sounded Calinoran, guttural and dry. They had to be traitors, criminals working for the Ferisian Empire.

The girl who'd been on the battlements spoke up, her voice ringing loudly. "It's not about gold, it's about family!"

"*Merewen.*" The older man's voice snapped like a whip. "Make yourself useful instead of arguing."

"Uncle . . . ," Merewen protested.

"*Now.* We'll make camp here for breakfast. Check on the girl. See if she's awake yet."

At those words, Ash pushed herself deeper into the

corner, and wished desperately for a weapon. The wagon groaned as it slowed down, the wheels rocking back and forth, and finally it stopped.

Ash pulled at her bonds. She tried to get to her feet. But instead she toppled forward, landing hard on her shoulder. Her arm slipped from its socket, and Ash cried out as tendrils of pain crawled down her arm and back. She rolled onto her side and hoped the pressure would keep her shoulder in place.

The door to the wagon burst open. Merewen rushed toward Ash, her hair bouncing around her head. "What happened? Are you hurt?"

Ash flinched. "Don't touch me! What do you want from me?"

She angled herself away from the girl, to keep her hurt side protected.

"Careful." Merewen propped her up against the side of the wagon. "I'm sorry this is a rough journey, but you must understand it's the only way to get you out of the city," she said, like it was the most reasonable thing, to want to take Ash out of Haven.

Once upon a time, there had been days when Ash wanted to be as far away from Haven as possible. But not right now. Not like this.

"Take me home immediately!" she demanded.

Merewen pushed a stray strand of hair out of Ash's face. Her fingers were ink stained. "You'll be where you belong soon enough," she said soothingly.

"What does that mean?" Ash demanded. "Are you taking me to the empire?"

Merewen shook her head. "If you promise not to try anything foolish, I will untie these bonds and you can come out to share breakfast with us. Uncle Crispin says to remind you that he and Aylin are armed, as well as stronger and faster than you. They won't let you get away, but they will let you eat."

Ash wasn't planning to do anything foolish. In all the books she had read about strategy and tactics, and all her studies with Aunt Jonet, she learned that to make a strong plan she needed as much information as possible. About her surroundings and the people who had kidnapped her. About their intentions. She needed to find their weak spots.

She was planning to do something smart.

"I promise."

"Good!" Merewen clapped her hands. She fiddled with the ropes until the knots came undone and slid away from Ash's wrists. Ash swallowed a cry when blood flooded back into her hands, stinging like nettles.

She rocked her arms back and forth, letting the blood flow. Clenching her jaw, she pushed her arm back into the right position. It snapped into place with a sickening crunch, and Ash felt faint.

"You're in pain." Merewen frowned. She dug in her pocket and considered the star amulet she must have taken from Ash's purse. "Will this help?"

Ash hesitated. She'd only packed one, just in case. If Merewen used it now, even to help her, it would be spent. Ash wouldn't have a chance to try to steal it back later. But her shoulder ached so fiercely. She needed to be able to think. "Please. Do you know how it works?"

"I've never even seen one up close. Do you just tie it near your injury?" Merewen rubbed her thumb over the small gold star braided into a leather band.

Ash held out her arm. "Yes. Smiths at the star temples cast the amulets. According to one of the royal physicians, their secret is in the metal they use, and in the making. They temporarily dull the pain."

Merewen looked skeptical as she tied the amulet's thin band around Ash's arm.

Almost instantly the pain eased. Ash flexed her hand. The amulet would work for a few hours, giving her a reprieve. "Thank you."

"For what?" Merewen asked.

"You had no reason to help me, but you did." Ash forced herself to put on a smile. "Do you suppose I might walk around a bit?" It was a good way to investigate her surroundings, and she wanted to be able to stretch her legs and relieve herself.

Merewen helped her to her feet and, without hesitating, grabbed Ash's cane and handed it to her. "I will stick by you. I'm sure Uncle Crispin won't mind."

She guided Ash out of the wagon and into a makeshift camp. The fake guard—Aylin—was busy building a small campfire, despite the bright sunlight. He carried several knives and daggers on his belt. Seeing him out of his guard uniform, Ash realized how young he was. A few years older than Lucen, at most. She raised her chin. "Guardsman."

He turned away from her.

"I trust Merewen has explained the rules to you, girl." The gruff voice belonged to a wall of a man, with a mess of thick brown hair and a battle-axe taller than Ash by his side. Crispin's eyes were pale blue and full of disdain. "You're worth the gold but not the trouble."

Ash pulled herself up high. She wasn't the type of princess who needed everyone to call her "highness," but here, she wanted to be untouchable. "It's *Princess Adelisa*."

Crispin spat on the ground. "Whatever you say, girl."

Ash didn't cower.

Crispin went back to digging something out of his saddlebags, and Merewen tugged at Ash's arm. "Come. This may not be up to palace standards, but we'll be comfortable here."

She led Ash away from Crispin and Aylin, around the small clearing where they'd stopped the wagon. Sunlight dappled the trees around them, and Ash didn't have a clue where they were. Judging by the lack of noise, they were far from any road or town. It was the four of them and three horses, and if Ash wanted to get out of here, she needed a plan.

Belatedly, she realized Merewen was still talking.

"—must be nice to have a whole palace at your fingertips, but we lived in Haven for a few months and I miss the crickets at dawn and the stars at night. Everything is so *loud*." Merewen glanced sideways at Ash. "Though I did love the spiced chestnut cakes we bought at the market. I can't get those at home."

Ash bit her lip. "Where is home for you?" She wondered how Merewen had gotten caught up in her kidnapping. Was it just family ties? Why would anyone do this, steal another person?

Merewen kicked at a broken twig. "I don't think I'm supposed to share."

"You don't have to tell me the name of the town," Ash said, thinking hard. "Tell me about your favorite food that you can't get in Haven."

Back in the camp, Aylin managed a small fire, and he'd retrieved provisions to prepare a meal. He used one of his knives to chop up herbs. The smell of wild garlic and thyme filled the air, and hunger gnawed at Ash's stomach.

Merewen closed her eyes and savored the scent too. "Aunt Enda makes the best seaberry jams," she admitted.

Ash stored that bit of information away. "My aunt had a few seaberry bushes on her estate, but they never grew well. And no one ever made jam. They dried the berries and used them for pies."

"Aunt Enda says she likes her berries to still have the taste of the sea. They grow best near the coast."

Merewen guided her around the wagon, where the trees and greenery grew thicker. The winter had chased away most of the leaves, but the trees stood like an impenetrable wall of gray and brown tree trunks. Green sprouts and leaf buds heralded the arrival of spring.

Ash could hide here, and she could all too easily get lost.

"I'd love to be able to bake," she said, to keep the conversation going. "Aunt Jonet's cook taught me to make bread, but I'm not great at kneading or shaping the dough."

"I could help," Merewen offered. "Aunt Enda taught me. Once we've settled somewhere, I could teach you all the tricks I know."

Again she spoke like getting Ash out of Haven was meant to be a boon to Ash. It scared Ash more than talk of gold. She'd meant to keep Merewen talking, but fear and anger rushed over her like waves crashing down on the coast. "Why? You're not my friend. What will happen to me?"

Merewen shook her head insistently. "I *am*. I'll take care of you. You don't understand it yet, but you will."

Before Ash could ask what that meant, Crispin called out to them. "Merewen, stop dawdling! Bring the girl back here, and go gather water!"

Merewen nudged Ash along. "He gets grumpy when he's hungry. Come, sit by the fire. Don't worry about Uncle Crispin. He's all bark and no bite."

Ash nodded her understanding, and she let herself be guided back. She didn't know what to say, so it was best to not say anything at all. Instead, she could listen. Try to figure out what Crispin's plans were.

Try to befriend Merewen and gain her trust.

She'd managed that with Mist and Hazel.

The idea left her feeling nauseated.

When Merewen paused to unhook a bucket from under the driver's seat, Ash took advantage of her distraction to run her hand over a piece of rope that hung from the wagon. After she'd managed to tug it loose, she hid it in her sleeve. She could use it to tie someone up. She could use it to fashion a bridle for one of the horses.

She could use it.

Now she only needed a plan to go with it.

The meal Aylin prepared was simple. Cured meat—deer, he said, though Ash wasn't convinced—with dried fruits and oatmeal. She was so hungry she ate it all. Merewen fell silent in the company of Crispin, and Aylin still didn't meet her eye, so breakfast was a quiet affair.

After they banked the fire, Merewen led Ash to a nearby stream where she could wash up. Her arm ached dully despite the amulet, and when she returned to the wagon, she caught Crispin staring at her rubbing it.

He scowled at Aylin. "Tie her up carefully. I don't think Vance *or* the palace will pay for damaged goods."

Merewen rolled her eyes. "Don't be rude, uncle."

Aylin grabbed Ash's shoulder tightly, and she winced. "Vance said he'd sort out our gold, Dad. We don't have to deal with the palace again. That was the agreement."

"We're the ones who're risking our hides. Doesn't hurt to have a backup plan. We can barter the girl for the treasury if Vance doesn't come through." Crispin jerked his head toward her. The implication was clear: Ash didn't need to hear this discussion. "Get her inside, we need to continue on north if we're to meet him on time."

But while Aylin marched Ash into the wagon, Merewen piped up. "We can just take her to Aunt Enda now. You told me Vance only wanted us to get her out of Haven. That's why he came to us, because he knew we'd care."

"You foolish girl. Don't talk about things you don't understand."

"We're not *villains*. She's my—"

"Silence!"

While Aylin yanked her arms behind her back, Ash considered what she'd heard. She was Merewen's *what*, exactly? And who was this Vance who wanted her away from the palace? It wasn't a Ferisian name, but if they were headed north, they were headed toward the Crescent Mountains. Toward the empire.

He had to be another one of the spies Uncle Lam had warned them about.

At least Crispin had given her one piece of crucial information. He was worried about hurting her. So that meant if she was injured, they'd have to stop to find a star temple or a physician to help her—or tempt the wrath of Vance. A single star amulet wouldn't do the trick, and once they were near a village, it'd be a far easier escape than here, in the middle of nowhere.

Aylin wrapped a piece of rope around Ash's wrists. She struggled enough to make it difficult for him, and he grunted. "Careful. You're the most precious cargo we've had in a while."

It was the first thing he'd said to her, and she tried to look at him. "Is that all you care about? The gold? Is it worth committing treason for?"

"Treason, *princess*?" Aylin shook his head. He dumped her on the floor of the wagon and towered over her. "You don't know what you're talking about. You couldn't understand what it's like to be so hungry or cold that people grow sick from it. You're hidden away in that palace of yours. You wear your star amulets, and you have no idea how much people are hurting because of the war. Merewen has a head full of dreams. The gold will feed our family for years to come. It's absolutely worth it."

He climbed out of the wagon, shutting the door behind him.

Ash pulled her knees up to her chest.

As much as she hated to admit it, Aylin had been right. Even in Byrne, away from the luxuries of the palace, she'd never gone hungry or cold. Aunt Jonet's storage cellars were always full, and there was plenty of food at the table. Sterne had once told her his parents saved the scraps of every meal, just in case, but she had never thought about what that meant.

She'd always been taught that comfort and power were part of being a royal, in return for duty and responsibility. Comfort, so they could focus all their attention on doing right by Calinor, without wanting for themselves. Power, so they could protect the realm and its people, to make sure everyone could live well and thrive.

But if that was the case, a tiny voice in the back of her mind whispered, why wasn't everyone thriving? The queen fought to convince the merchants of the floating docks to pay taxes so that the people of Haven could be provided for, but the royal treasury held more than enough coin to cover the cost.

The families of the knights and soldiers who protected

Calinor, the bakers and butchers who provided the realm with food and security, the masons and carpenters who built the streets, the temples, the houses, the palace . . . they all did their duty and they were all responsible for a small part of Calinor. Didn't they deserve comfort too?

Ash bit her lip. She didn't have any answers.

Two of the horses were harnessed to the wagon and pulled it back on the road, where they settled into a comfortable rhythm. Crispin called to Aylin to check out the road ahead, and the hoofbeats of the third horse disappeared into the distance before returning.

As the hours passed, the light that filtered in through the cracks between the panels turned brighter and then, slowly, to a purple-hued dusk.

Ash had pushed herself back into a sitting position in the corner of the wagon. She'd found a rusty nail poking out of one of the planks, and she tried to use it to saw through her binds. The strands of rope caught on the nail and unraveled, one at a time. She didn't know how long it took, but eventually, one hand slipped free. And then, the other.

She pulled at the leather straps of her braces. They were made to keep her hands and wrists in the right position, ensuring that they wouldn't swell up and become painful. It was freedom, to have them strengthen her. Before, when she was smaller, her fingers would snap apart as easily as twigs, and her wrists and ankles would angle in all sorts of odd ways, leaving them completely useless. Once Aunt Jonet's blacksmith had made the braces to keep her joints in place, she could finally play without worry of breaking.

But Ash had learned that if she reversed the bands and rings, the braces could as easily push those joints into opposite directions. Once when she'd sneaked up to Sterne with her fingers bent like bony spiders, he'd run screaming.

It hurt. It would hurt for days afterward, and she didn't have more amulets to ease the pain, but it'd be worth it. Ash clenched her jaw and reminded herself of all the bruises Splinter had gathered during training. If Ash fell into Ferisian hands, her mother would be forced to make impossible choices. She could be as brave as Splinter to escape.

She twisted her braces.

The wagon slowed down, and Crispin called for them to take a break. "We'll have dinner and wait until nightfall, and then we continue on. I want to get as far away from Haven as possible."

Ash inched closer to the door. As soon as the wagon

came to a stop, she let herself fall as loudly as possible, and she screamed in pain.

The wagon rocked as the door slammed open and Crispin darted in, his heavy boots causing the wood to groan and creak. "What is going on here?"

Ash angled her face away from him. Her cheeks flushed and she blinked hard, trying to look as disheveled as possible. "My arm," she moaned. "I fell. It hurts. Please, I need help."

She felt Crispin edge closer, and when he bent down to examine her arm, she cried out again. "No, no, no! Please, don't touch it! I think it's broken!"

He muttered a string of curses, and without care for her protest, he grabbed her by her shoulder and planted her in an upright position. "We can't bring you to Vance like this. He needs you whole enough to travel."

Ash tried to curl herself up in as tight a ball as possible and sniffed for good measure, but tugging at her arm in this position was painful enough that it made her head spin. She didn't have to fake that. She just had to focus on running, the first opportunity she had. And she repeated the same rushed garble of information to herself over and over again.

My name is Princess Adelisa. I was kidnapped. Please bring me to the guards. You'll be well rewarded. Please help me.

Through her eyelashes she could see Crispin running his fingers through his beard while he considered what to do with her. He was green and uncomfortable at the sight of her arm.

"Please help me."

"Where's that star amulet? Merewen!"

"She already used it," Ash croaked.

Crispin cursed. "That girl is too softhearted. We need to find you a physician."

Ash's heart leapt.

Then the wagon door creaked again, and Merewen came in. "No, we don't." She carried the same bucket she'd used to gather water for breakfast. She held strips of cloth and a small bag with dried herbs. She crouched down next to Ash and ran her fingers over Ash's arm.

Ash winced and arced away from her, but to no avail.

"I have a better cure than bracelets and amulets," Merewen said, determination in her eyes. "I used to care for Nanna's aches. I can splint her arm if it's necessary, and wrap it with wet cloths infused with star mint and pink rue. It eases the swelling and cools the ache. She'll be fine."

Crispin coughed. "Are you certain you know what you're doing?"

"Yes," Merewen said confidently.

Ash gaped at the girl. It was the same remedy Brother Nivanil had used, when the star amulets weren't enough, before she got her braces. "How do you know how to do that?" she asked, temporarily forgetting her pain.

Merewen's eyes were dark enough to look like molten silver. Behind her, Crispin retreated, and as soon as he stepped out of the wagon, Ash could hear him retch.

"I know you're trying to escape, but I won't let anyone take you from us," Merewen whispered. "Not again."

"What does that *mean*?"

Merewen poured the dried herbs into the bucket with water and placed the linens in the infusion. Silently she opened the leather straps of the braces. She untied the star amulet, which had grown dull, and tossed it aside, unimpressed. She nibbled on the inside of her cheek, and when she'd taken off all of Ash's rings but the decorative ones, she squared her shoulders. "You need to know who you are." She took a deep breath, and then all the words tumbled out.

"Twelve years ago, when the royal carriage slipped off an icy road, it wasn't just the prince consort who died. The driver died too. And the queen's companion . . ."

"I know." Ash frowned.

"You don't. She was called Talwin. Nanna always said

she was powerful and strong like the sea. Talwin moved to Haven to become a seamstress, and she was allowed to work for the royal family. Talwin and the queen became friends. She became her personal seamstress first, and then her companion. She was with child when she traveled with the royal family that night. The queen's daughter had been born just weeks earlier, and Talwin was convinced her daughter would grow to be the princess's friend too."

Ash felt faint. "What are you saying?"

"Someone else died that night when the carriage crashed." Merewen's voice grew soft. With steady hands, she wrapped the fabric around Ash's arm.

"Talwin's daughter?" Ash asked.

Merewen shook her head. "No. The queen's daughter. The *princess*. Talwin lived long enough to give birth to her baby. When she died, the queen decided to raise the child as her own. She wanted to protect the people from the grief of losing the prince consort and the princess on the same day. Better to pretend the princess survived. But she forgot about us, Talwin's family."

Ash tried to push away from Merewen, but Merewen held her tightly.

"Talwin was Crispin's youngest sister. I know how to tend your aches because I recognize them. Our nanna had bones that snapped too easily and hands and feet that twisted in all directions. Dad too, before the sea claimed him. It runs in the family. Your family. *You're* family."

"You're lying," Ash cried. Her plan was forgotten. She felt like she was tied to the floor and she had nowhere to run.

Merewen wrung out one of the linens and wrapped it around Ash's hand. "That's why Vance came to us for help when he discovered who you are. He wants to cause chaos, but Uncle Crispin cares about family. We could help each other. We didn't steal you. We're finally bringing you home."

CHAPTER EIGHTEEN

SPLINTER

When night rolled in, Splinter and Lucen dashed across the square. A gaggle of guild apprentices gathered around the fountain, skidding stones off the ice and sharing stories about their workday. One apprentice pulled out a flute and blew a merry tune, until an elderly passerby with a sour expression scolded him for making light of these dire times. The boy crossed his eyes at the man. On the ledge of a building, a night crow cawed.

A full day had passed since Splinter and Lucen left the Maronne household and sneaked back into Haven. The sun had come up, and Splinter had realized neither of them knew where Lord Idian lived. Guards had flooded the streets, ordering people to keep an eye out for the missing Princess Adelisa—and the wayward Prince Lucen. Fear rolled through the city like a storm. The palace was in disarray, and the queen was sick with worry.

"You should go back," Splinter had told Lucen.

He'd grown paler overnight, the dark circles around his eyes even deeper. He looked at a loss without the other squires around him. "Will you?"

She'd glared at him. "Of course not."

"Then don't tell me again."

She hadn't. They'd laid low, sticking to narrow alleyways, scampering over walls and rooftops, hiding between buildings. Twice they'd turned a corner and walked straight into a contingent of guards.

The first time, near the central market, Lucen had ducked into a pile of waste and vegetable refuge. He'd picked slimy lettuce leaves off his cloak for hours afterward.

The second time, the guards were so close Lucen had frozen up. Splinter had hooked his arm through hers and dragged him to a store window, as if they were apprentices shopping. In the reflection of the window, amid the jars of colorful candies inside, she'd seen the guards take notice of them, so she'd elbowed him and pointed out a jar full of sugar crowns the size of thimbles, loudly convincing him to buy some. A young street urchin placed her hands against the window, salivating. When the guards passed them by, Lucen's shoulders had sagged in obvious relief. He'd glanced at Splinter before he'd slipped the girl two silver coins to buy all the candy she wanted.

Splinter had considered him. "Did you do that because you wanted to help her or because it made you feel better?"

He hadn't answered.

Now, in the evening light, they were halfway across the square when guards with torches appeared at the far end. This time it was Lucen who reacted first, grabbing Splinter's hand and pulling her into the crowd. The apprentices moved without question, hiding them from view.

The flutist picked up a song again, mocking the guards.

One snarled at him and pushed him aside, but they kept walking.

As soon as the light of the torches disappeared, Lucen and Splinter let go of each other's hands and ran.

In a shaded alleyway, Splinter paused to catch her breath. "And here I thought traveling with a prince was supposed to make life easier, not harder."

She'd meant the words in jest, but Lucen looked away. "I'm sorry."

"Oh." Splinter didn't know what to do with that. She felt off-kilter around the crown prince. It was much easier to think of him only as a bully, but Splinter had seen flashes of worry, loyalty, curiosity. She didn't know this side of Lucen. She wondered if anyone did.

She turned the corner, into a familiar street. "Come along, highness. Let's go ask Camille how to get to Lord Idian."

The moment she'd realized she didn't know where Lord Idian lived—and that maybe she didn't know Haven quite so well as she'd boasted to Ash—she'd known the one person who would be able to help them. She also knew that approaching her home by day would be tantamount to walking up to the nearest guard station, so they had to wait until nightfall.

Now that night crept through the streets, DuLac manor was a haunted house, full of ghosts and bad memories.

She led Lucen toward the mansion, and she clenched her jaw. "The gate will be guarded, so we're going to have to walk around. There's a servants' entrance off the main road."

"You don't look excited about coming back here," Lucen remarked, his eyes dark. He sucked in the corner of his lip, and his unruly hair pushed out from under his hood. He resembled Ash, Splinter thought. She had never been able to see it before.

"I'm not," she said.

"Why? It's your home. Your family. You think they'll help."

She winced. She hadn't explained to him who Camille was. She did so now, in as few words as possible. The housekeeper's son, and her oldest friend. "The only family member left in Haven is my uncle, and he won't help. He agrees with you that people like me shouldn't be squires." Splinter licked her lips. She sprinted past the house and into the side street. She made sure the street was empty before she gestured Lucen to follow her. "He doesn't even know I'm not a girl. He just thinks I'm a *stain* on the family legacy."

Red blotches appeared on Lucen's cheeks. "I . . ."

Splinter didn't want to hear it.

She dashed up to the house, knocked on the door of the servants' entrance, and darted back into the shadows.

For the longest time, nothing happened. Then the first lock opened, the sound echoing against the tall buildings across the street. The second lock. The door opened just far enough for one of the servants to look out.

It was a stroke of good luck after a string of misfortunes when Camille peeked his head out. "Who's there?"

"Camille!" Splinter's voice cracked. Her eyes stung and

she didn't quite know why. "Come out, I need to ask you a question."

Camille slipped out the door, hooking the ring of keys on his belt. He blinked, adjusting to the low light, and shivered. When he spotted Splinter, a smile broke through on his face. "Of course you *would* be the one to get me into trouble."

She ran and wrapped her arms around him. "I missed you."

He squeezed her hands before he took a step backward. "The manor is boring without you. Except for today. Guards were in and out."

"Looking for me?"

"For him." Camille pointed to Lucen, who edged closer.

"Is there any word about my sister yet?"

"No, your highness. They're searching. Court is in a panic, and it's rippling through the kingdom." Camille punched Splinter's arm. "Do you know what your uncle will do if he catches you?"

Splinter shuddered. He wouldn't be thrilled to see her, that much was sure. "We need to find Lord Idian." She tugged at the collar of her tunic. "I don't know where he lives."

Camille stared at her in silence for a heartbeat, then he

rolled his eyes so hard, she thought he'd topple over. "You make a fine rescue team, the pair of you."

"Can you give us directions?" Splinter insisted. "And food?" She would have asked for horses too, if she didn't think it would get him in trouble with her uncle.

"Of course. Stay out of sight."

Lucen leaned in. "What will Splinter's uncle do if he finds us?"

Camille blushed slightly, and he held himself like he wasn't sure whether to bow in the presence of the prince. "He'll hand you over to the royal guard before locking the doors and making sure Splinter never leaves home again." He didn't meet Splinter's eye. His face twisted with regret. "He knows you're no longer a squire. He's been gloating all day."

Splinter set her jaw and resolved that she wouldn't let his cruelty get to her. "We won't be seen. I won't give him the satisfaction." She wouldn't go back again, not unless her brother finally came home.

"Good."

Lucen made a sound in the back of his throat like he wanted to say something, but when Camille raised his eyebrows, he only shook his head. So Camille pointed them to the shadows and promised he'd be back soon. "Be careful."

Lucen didn't speak up until Camille had disappeared and closed the door behind him.

"I'm sorry," he said, for the second time that night.

Splinter sagged down against one of the high walls. "For what?"

"They should be proud of you." Lucen's voice was so low, Splinter had to strain to hear him. Even then, she could hardly believe it. "My sister is lucky to have a friend like you. Trying to find her . . . I think it's brave."

"You're trying to find her too," she pointed out.

He shrugged. "That's different."

"Why?"

"Because it's my fault. What I'm doing isn't brave. I'm too scared to tell my mother and Uncle Lam what I did to you. Why Ash was alone all afternoon." It was the closest he'd come to acknowledging the fight, and Splinter felt her anger at the unfairness of it all simmer inside. She rested her head against the stone wall. She wanted to punch it.

Lucen flashed her a humorless half smile. "You weren't wrong when you called me cowardly and cruel."

"Why?" she snapped.

"Why?" he repeated.

"You're the best fighter among the squires. Everyone wants to be your friend. You have a family that loves you, and Ash looks up to you. One day you're going to be king. You could be kind, like you were to the girl outside the sweet shop. You could be brave, like saying this in front of Camille instead of waiting until he's gone."

Lucen nodded slowly. "I could be."

But he didn't say anything else.

With directions—and a satchel full of raisin buns, red cheese turnovers, spiced meat, and a few wrinkled winter apples—Splinter and Lucen easily found their way to Lord Idian's home. Or rather, his grandmother's home. Lady Lavinia Devar lived in a comfortable house near Haven's eastern gate, far away from the noble quarters. Hers was no mansion or manor, but a three-storied repurposed warehouse made into a well-loved home. On either side of the front door, plants climbed up high along the wall, with fine green leaves and pale white flowers despite the cold. The door had intricate stained glass decorations, and so did most of the windows. Light from inside cast colorful shadows onto the street. A well-maintained garden ran along the full perimeter of the building, with winter roses blooming lavishly. It reminded Splinter of the flower maze where she'd first met Ash, and she decided that was a good sign. As was the absence of any guards.

Lucen walked up to the front door and pounded.

Splinter winced. "What if someone hears?"

"They won't be looking for us here, and it's better than staying out on the street."

The door opened. The weary, curious face of a servant appeared, and Lucen straightened. "Message from the palace for Lord Idian. Please escort us to him."

Splinter crossed her fingers for luck, certain the servant would call the guards or demand proof of identity. He merely beckoned them to follow him.

Lucen smirked at Splinter.

She stuck her tongue out.

The servant led them through a cluttered hallway and up a winding set of stairs. Portraits of family members from ages past hung on the walls, some old enough that the paint had faded. Other portraits were more recent—including a sketch of a younger Lord Idian, proudly showing his shield.

On the second floor, the servant knocked on a pair of lavish doors. "My lord? Visitors."

He stepped aside. Lucen and Splinter entered a large office with high ceilings. Maps covered the walls, and in all corners stood bookcases that reached from floor to ceiling, filled to the point of spilling over. On the far side of the office, past a heavy oak desk, burned a comfortable fire.

A knight's shield hung above the fireplace, as did a finely carved bow. In front of the hearth stood two soft blue chairs.

In one of them sat Lord Idian, a pair of glasses pinched on his nose and a book in his hand. He stood when they entered, and Splinter felt as though he saw straight through their cloaks.

He waved the servant away with a word of thanks, pocketed the glasses, and placed his book on the chair. "Come in, both of you."

Once the servant had shut the door behind him, Idian bowed deeply to Lucen. "Your highness." He squinted at Splinter. "And the princess's squire. The whole palace is looking for you. What can I do for you?"

"Have you heard anything? Has anyone heard anything?" The words tumbled out of Lucen's mouth as he folded back his hood.

Idian pointed him to one of the chairs. Lucen perched on the edge of the seat, while Splinter stood next to him.

Idian sat down again. "The people who took your sister have veiled themselves in silence, and unfortunately it's near impossible for the guard to follow all traffic out of Haven. It's a truly despicable act to steal a girl from her home, and I'm so very sorry for the pain it must cause you."

Lucen blinked and turned away. Splinter angled toward Idian. "We want to find her. Hazel and Mist said we should talk to you." In as few words as possible, she explained the situation. "They mentioned other threats to the crown. The Larks?"

Idian frowned. "You're the youngest of the DuLac family, aren't you?"

"Yes." Splinter wasn't sure what that had to do with anything.

Idian stared into the fire. "If *I* knew where Ash was, I would've gone to the queen already." He seemed conflicted. "What I do know is this. The Ferisian Empire isn't the sole threat to the crown. And the Larks are certainly better positioned to steal a princess."

Splinter and Lucen shared a look.

"Are you talking about spies among the nobility?" Lucen asked.

"Not quite," Idian said.

"Who *are* the Larks?" Splinter prompted.

Idian ran a hand over his face. "Highness, what do you know about your great-grandmother, Queen Eliane?"

"She was powerful," Lucen said. "She protected Haven by building city walls, and she protected the nobility by enshrining its privileges and traditions in law."

"Some would call it powerful," Idian said, choosing his words with care. "Others think she was mighty and cruel. Her word was law. She was afraid of the growing influence of the citizens of Haven, which is why she kept the city from expanding."

Lucen flushed. "She did what was best for the crown."

"But was it also best for the kingdom?" Idian countered. "Those two things aren't always the same. Queen Eliane valued the kingdom, I'm sure, but she chose tradition and power over progress and equality, and unfortunately that's a legacy many nobles now cling to. They want to go back to those good old days." He spoke the words with disgust. "They believe any change is weakness, and trying to improve Calinor for all makes it worse for them.

"And your mother, stars guide her, taxes the nobility. She negotiates with merchants. She provides for the poor. She's willing to defend the border but not push past it into Ferisian territory. She believes that making Calinor fairer makes it stronger, but *they* think she's weak."

"She's willing to break tradition to let people like me become squires," Splinter offered.

Idian nodded. "Some nobles just grumble and complain and don't do anything. But the Larks . . . they've formed a secret faction within the kingdom. A network of nobles determined to return Calinor to its former glory. No matter the cost. They've sworn to depose the queen."

Lucen plucked at the hem of his cloak. His hands trembled. "I never heard about the Larks."

Idian shook his head. "You wouldn't have. The Larks stick to the shadows. But if fighting in the mountains has taught me one thing, your highness, it's to be aware of the dangers around me. And court is a hotbed of danger."

Splinter had never heard about the Larks before either. But she knew Ash trusted Lord Idian. That was what mattered. "Ash once called court a tedious gathering of greedy nobles who only care about having the loudest voice, the most coin, the biggest influence on the queen," she muttered.

The words startled a laugh out of Idian. "Plenty of nobles do care about what's best for Calinor. The problem is, many of us have been taught that because we're of noble blood, we know what's best. That we're better than others. Too many nobles let that go to their heads. They would put their own values and prestige over other people's homes and lives."

"But why would the Larks need Ash?" Splinter asked.

"To undermine the queen. To sow chaos, fear, and doubt. It would be enough to disappear her, but if they do somehow manage to bring her to the empire, they may even think they'll gain imperial support. And the empress can sit back and watch Calinor destroy itself."

Splinter paced. "Do the queen and Lord Lambelin know?"

"Of course her majesty knows." Idian frowned. "But to most people, the Larks are a myth. Those of us who've tried to find them have not been able to prove anything. They fiercely protect their identity."

"You're saying anyone could be a Lark?" Lucen asked. "Even in the palace? How do you know about them at all?"

"There have been rumors about secret meetings here in Haven for years. The old lady got an invite once. A card with a time, an address, and a lark feather, slipped into her purse when she went to one of the midwinter plays. She shared the information with the royal guard, but by the time they investigated, the warehouse was empty. She never got invited again. When she told me, I started asking around." The corner of his mouth turned up in a humorless half smile. "Mist must have overheard me talking to Lord Maronne. He came back from the mountains believing in traitors too. Perhaps that's why she sent you to me."

Lord Idian took a long drink from the cup by his side.

"Stars, I wish it was just a thrilling story. If the Larks are stirring, it means they're becoming more confident—and more powerful."

"You believe it's them, don't you?" Lucen whispered.

Lord Idian looked down at his hands, where thin scars ran from his wrists to his fingers. "I don't have evidence to accuse anyone," he admitted. "But . . . yes, your highness. I believe they're a danger to the kingdom. And right now, they're a danger to Ash."

It was a terrifying and overwhelming thought. Splinter shivered. Lucen wrapped his arms tight around his chest.

"What about when you served in the mountains?" Splinter wanted to know. "Were Larks there too? How do we unmask them?"

Idian's mouth twitched. "I don't think you'll like the answer, squire."

"Tell us," Splinter said. "Please. Anything."

"There were tales. Whispers about a young knight from Haven, who made his way up through the ranks with such ease that people assumed he had high-placed friends interested in his survival."

Idian's eyes filled with pity, and Splinter's stomach dropped.

"Your brother. Anders—"

"*No.*" Splinter's voice echoed. Her world tipped. Her ears rang. "That's not true. Anders isn't some kind of traitor. He's loyal to the crown." She shook her head. "He spends a lot of time behind enemy lines, that's why his commanders trust him."

"The soldiers called him stars-blessed, at first, because he was the only one who could cross into the empire and return without a fight."

"You're *wrong,*" Splinter insisted. Her brother was a hero. He wouldn't have anything to do with this.

Lucen bit his lip, clearly mulling over everything he'd heard. "Splinter, it's a lead. The only lead we have. My mother and Uncle Lam are investigating the empire. We should investigate the Larks."

Splinter met his gaze. "Then let's go talk to Anders. He'll *help* us. He's my brother. Please, Lucen."

Lucen's eyes widened. He nodded.

Idian stood, sending the book perched on his armrest flying to the floor. "Oh no, I'm sorry, your highness, I can't let that happen. I wanted you to know, but it's my duty to keep you safe. It's time for both of you to go back to the palace."

"Lord Idian. It's for Ash," Splinter said. And Anders. He would help. He would.

Lucen approached Idian. Splinter saw his hands clench and unclench by his sides. "Lord Idian. I order you to let us go."

"The palace ordered everyone in this city to report any sight of you or your sister immediately. I cannot and I will not disobey my queen."

"But one day I'm going to be king. You shouldn't disobey me either."

"You're not yet," Idian said apologetically.

"I don't want Calinor to destroy itself," Lucen said softly. "And I don't want my sister to come to harm. *Please.*" The words landed heavily in the office, sucking the comfortable, warm air from the room.

"I can give you a head start before I inform the guards," Idian said after a moment, though he sounded none too happy with the compromise. "It's the best I can do."

Lucen turned to Splinter. "To the Crescent Mountains?"

She put on her bravest smile. "Yes. I promise, Anders *will* help."

When Splinter and Lucen walked out of Lord Idian's office, he still appeared in conflict with himself, but he guided them to his stables. "If you're going to travel, you need to be better prepared," he said. "You need horses. The old lady will send me right back to the mountains herself if she wakes up tomorrow and finds I haven't done everything I can to help you."

He collected two proper swords, and two sets of bows and quivers full of arrows. "Promise me you'll run before you get into a fight. But if you do find yourself in danger, I want you to be able to protect yourself."

"I won't forget this," Lucen promised.

Lord Idian smiled crookedly. "I don't know if that will make a difference to the queen, your highness."

But Camille's provisions and Lord Idian's horses *would* make a difference to their journey.

Even if it seemed to baffle Lucen. "I don't understand why Lord Idian helped us," he admitted later, as they passed the gates amid a group of merchants. "He could have ignored me. Camille too. They'll only get into trouble with the palace if they're found out."

"Because people care," Splinter suggested. "True friends are willing to get into trouble to help when it's necessary."

Lucen nodded quietly. For the first time, Splinter wondered if Lucen had any true friends among the squires. It made her inexplicably sad to think he didn't.

CHAPTER NINETEEN

ASH

The days passed in a blur of creaking wagon wheels, infusions of star mint and pink rue on her uselessly painful arms, and denial. Merewen's words followed Ash like ghosts, and every time she closed her eyes they became louder. Crueler.

They whispered to her that she didn't fit in at court because she had never belonged in the first place.

They told her the queen only brought her back to help with the investigation, and she wouldn't miss her at all.

They reminded her that the physician's assistant had been right all along. Her fragile bones *did* run in the family.

Just not the one she thought was hers.

She tried to banish the whispers.

She focused on Aunt Jonet, who had made a place for Ash in Byrne. She'd told Ash time and again that she was the spitting image of Queen Aveline as a young girl. But what if she'd only said that to convince Ash she was family? Was that why it was so important to her that Ash decided on the kind of princess she wanted to be?

Ash thought of Lucen instead. She resembled her brother, didn't she? They had the same bushy, unruly hair, the same snub nose. Except his shoulders were broader, his eyes wider, his chin pointier. He probably hated the idea of being compared to her, anyway.

She thought of her mother, who'd been so adamant that Ash was her daughter and *not* expendable. She could still feel her mother's arms around her on the day she got back to Haven. The queen had held her so tightly, like she planned never to let her go.

She thought of Splinter too, who had promised to stay by her side, whether she was angry or sad or hurting or scared.

Ash didn't know how and if she could ever disprove Merewen's claims, but she did know this. *They* were her home. Her family. They were hers in all the ways that mattered.

So a week after Merewen and Aylin stole her from

the palace, Ash shoved her worries aside and got up when Merewen brought her breakfast. She'd refused to face the others, but today she flexed her arms and raised her chin when Merewen climbed into the wagon.

"I want to eat outside and wash myself," she said, like she would to any servant at the palace.

A bright smile broke through on Merewen's face. "You're feeling better? I'm so glad. Uncle Crispin says we'll be at our destination soon, so you'll be able to spend more time outside. The wagon must get stuffy." She didn't seem bothered by Ash's haughty demeanor.

"Where are we?"

Merewen went on like Ash hadn't asked. "I can guide you to one of the streams. The water is freezing, but Aylin is baking ember cakes for the road. Those will warm you up nicely. Will you let me help?" She held out a hand to Ash. Ink stained her fingers again.

Ash steeled herself. Merewen was the only one in the group of three who'd been kind to her. Crispin treated her like cargo. Aylin ignored her. Merewen was gentle; her whole face lit up when she laughed.

Ash didn't want to be the kind of princess who befriended people to be able to use them.

But she also needed to escape.

She let Merewen help her out of the wagon.

Outside, sunlight pushed through the cover of evergreen trees, taller and older than in the first place they'd made camp. Thick moss crawled across big boulders on either side of an overgrown road, making the wagon and the travelers look small in comparison.

Neither Crispin or Aylin acknowledged Ash's presence, and Ash kept her focus on Merewen. She tilted her head. "Why do you have ink on your hands?"

"Oh." Merewen hid her hands in her skirt and blushed. She guided Ash to a stream, and only answered when they were out of earshot from the others. "I've been trying to map the roads we pass. I want to be a mapmaker, you see. Have adventures like Aunt Talwin did."

"But you hated Haven," Ash said. She sat down next to the stream and stuck her hand in the water. It was as cold as Merewen had promised, but the moss that grew on the banks was soft and comfortable, and along the stream itself the forest opened up a bit. In the distance, the tall peaks of the Crescent Mountains marked the border with the Ferisian Empire. Ash shuddered.

"I'm sorry it's so cold," Merewen said, misinterpreting.

Ash pushed up her sleeves and let the water trickle over her arms. "It's fine." She longed for a warm bath and clean clothes, but the cold eased the ache in her hands. "Tell me about your maps."

"I want to see more of Calinor. I don't like Haven, you're right. But . . . Clayden is lonely too," Merewen said, identifying her coastal home.

"Is that why you stole me?" Ash kept her voice casual.

Merewen blushed deeper. "I wanted you to come home to us."

"You want a friend," Ash suggested. "I understand that."

"You do?"

Ash nodded. "When my mother called me back to Haven, I didn't like the city either. I wanted to see the midwinter plays, but I didn't want to play a role at court. I wanted to be at home with my family, but instead I felt out of place, like I didn't belong. I think my brother hated me being there." She scooped up a handful of water and splashed it on her face. "It helped to make a friend. My *best* friend." She suddenly realized how true that was. Splinter *was* her best friend. If her eyes were wet, it was only water. She pulled her tunic over her head, leaving just an undershirt. The cold tickled her shoulders and neck.

Merewen gasped. "Your birthmark." Her fingers brushed Ash's shoulder.

Ash craned her neck. She had a small birthmark the

shape of a seven-point star on her left shoulder. She never paid attention to it. "What is it?"

"Look!" Merewen pulled the collar of her shirt down. At the tip of her shoulder, she had her own birthmark. It was lighter than Ash's and slightly twisted—but it was a seven-point star. "It's the same!"

"Oh." Ash turned back to the stream and splashed more water on her face. "I guess."

Merewen shone. "I *knew* it."

Ash felt a stab of anger and cruelty. "Why are you lonely in Clayden, anyway?"

"Oh." Merewen flinched. She stared at her feet. "I . . ."

Guilt crushed cruelty. "I'm sorry. You don't have to tell me."

Merewen angled away. "When Nanna died, I couldn't stay in the house where we lived. It was too big for me. Other families in Clayden needed it. I moved in with Uncle Crispin, Aunt Enda, and Aylin. But without Nanna and Talwin, something inside our family was broken. We didn't lose the people we loved to the war, but we lost them all the same. And we were losing each other too." Merewen pulled her knees up to her chest. "Then one day, a visitor came. A lord, on his way home from fighting, and he told us about you. For the first time in a long time, we had something that bound us together."

"Vance? He told you about me?"

"He wasn't the first. Nanna always said she knew you still lived. She felt it in her bones." Merewen spoke with such clear conviction, the world shifted underneath Ash's feet again.

"But Vance told you where to find me?" Ash squinted at the sunlight sparkling off the water. "*How* to find me?"

"Uncle decided to go to Haven. He's good at moving things unseen. Grain for the other villagers. Wool. Messages."

"Smugglers."

Merewen didn't deny it. "He'd been to Haven before, to visit Talwin. He knew his way around."

"And Aylin infiltrated the guard," Ash mused. To get someone into the palace guard implied that Vance was powerful and well connected.

"It was all for a good purpose! I'm glad he told us," Merewen said. The words sounded like a challenge.

Ash pulled her tunic back over her head and gathered herself. "I'm glad I know more about you."

It wasn't a lie. Ash needed as much information as possible, to escape and to tell her mother. But she knew Merewen would interpret her words differently, and when Merewen beamed, Ash felt a stab of guilt.

"One thing I don't understand," Ash said, facing her. "If you want to bring me home, why did Aylin and your uncle talk about gold? Why does Vance want to see me? Isn't it enough that you took me away?"

Merewen got to her feet and brushed her hands on her shirt. She pulled a small bundle out of her pocket and held it out to Ash. Inside were the rings Ash used to strengthen her fingers, the rings she could wear again now that some of the swelling had subsided. "Uncle told me Vance wants you out of Haven and the palace. I think he wants to make sure we did our job properly. I don't think Uncle actually cares about the gold."

Ash kept quiet, but a pit opened up in her stomach. What Merewen said didn't add up. Crispin had said that Vance *needed* her, not just needed to see her. And Crispin was willing to ransom her to the palace if Vance didn't pay up. But she doubted that Merewen would help her uncle if she thought he meant to trade Ash for gold. "What if he lied to you?"

Merewen shook her head so hard, her hair flew in all directions. "He didn't. He *wouldn't*. You're here, aren't you? We finally get to be a family again."

"Yeah," Ash said. Her arms ached, and her treacherous stomach grumbled when the smell from Aylin's ember cakes drifted toward them. "I'm here."

She plastered on a smile. "When we're back on the road, will you show me your maps? I'd love to see them."

Merewen settled into the wagon with Ash when they got back on the road, and she pulled out a well-used notebook. The pages were uneven, bound together between dyed leather covers. The first few papers were torn out, and the whole book was covered in ink stains.

"It used to be Aunt Talwin's. Nanna gave it to me when I started sketching the town and the roads around it." Merewen showed Ash the first hesitantly drawn maps. Some were nothing than scratches, where she had obviously tried to start a map before she changed her mind and blotted it out. "I kept sketching Clayden until I could trace every street and every house by heart."

"May I see the rest of it?" Ash held out her hands. With Merewen next to her, she wasn't bound, and it was a boon.

Merewen nodded.

Ash traced the edges of the book. "This was Talwin's?" It felt odd and uncomfortable—and also a bit curious. If Merewen was right, this was her mother's. If she wasn't right, Vance had seen the family's grief and lied to them. But how could someone Ash had never met be her mother?

Her *real* mother loved her and was a part of Ash's life.

"She used notebooks for her designs," Merewen said. Her voice dropped low. "There were only a few designs in this one, and Nanna tore them out so I could have a book of my own. I wish she'd kept them."

"I would've liked to see them." Ash leafed through the sketches of a small coastal town. After the first tentative drawings, the maps became clearer and more detailed. The buildings looked realistic enough that Ash could imagine tiny people walking out of them. "You're an artist. Which is your house?"

Merewen bit at a hangnail. She pointed at a small fisher's house at the edge of town. "There."

Ash steeled herself. "And Talwin—where did she grow up?"

"Nanna's house." Merewen pointed to a larger building in the center of the town, with small flowers around its edges and a kettle in front of one of the windows.

Ash smiled.

The sketches slowly morphed to maps of roads and forests and Haven.

The floating docks.

The market. She wondered where the best market stalls were to buy candied berries.

The palace.

Ash stared at Merewen's sketch of the palace for what felt like an eternity. She committed every pencil stroke to memory. Merewen had drawn the curtain walls. The gates. The secret passageway from the second floor to the battlements. Three other passages that Ash recognized, passages she'd explored with Splinter, and a fifth one she didn't know. She needed to tell Uncle Lam about it when she was—

Home.

Ash felt a fierce stab of homesickness. She gripped the book so tightly her hands ached.

"I'm sorry," Merewen whispered.

"For what?" Ash wanted to know. "For stealing me? For showing me this?"

"I'm sorry that you're hurting."

Ash winced. She believed Merewen's words were genuine. She even liked the girl. But that wouldn't stop her. She held the book to her chest. "I know this means a lot to you, but . . . would you mind if I hold on to it today? Until we reach our destination? I'd like to spend more time with it."

Merewen toyed with the leather necklace she was wearing, and Ash ran her fingers over the cover. She knew what it would look like. Merewen would assume that Ash cared. That it was personal to her too. And it was, just not in the way Merewen would think.

Ash *hated* to give a lonely girl hope only to snatch it away, but it was for a noble purpose. Didn't that count for something?

"Until we get to the meeting point," Merewen allowed.

Ash clung to the book. "Do you have to tie my wrists again?"

Merewen shook her head. "I think it'll be fine."

"Thank you." Ash curled up with the book in her hands. She paged through the maps slowly. Clayden. Haven. And finally, when Merewen climbed out of the wagon, the roads that they'd followed. She memorized them all.

The long meandering stone street that rolled out of Haven.

The smugglers' routes that wound through the Royal Forest, across the heaths, across the moors.

And this forgotten path through the Heartian Woods, the centuries-old forest that blanketed the northern hillsides.

Ash compared Merewen's maps to the maps of Cali- nor that her tutors had showed her. She knew how close the woods were to the Crescent Mountains that marked the border with the Ferisian Empire. She was in the most dangerous part of the kingdom, especially for a lost princess. But if she reached the encampment that guarded the border, its knights and soldiers would be able to help her.

Better yet, Splinter's brother was stationed there. Anders. *He'd* help her.

He'd get her home.

She studied the map of the woods until she was convinced she knew every twist, turn, and crossroads of the path they took. She knew her way back. All she needed to do was listen closely to what happened outside and bide her time. So she did.

The light that pushed through the wagon's cracks grew a darker orange.

Crispin commented that he couldn't wait to collect the gold and leave the bulky wagon behind.

They slowed down to a halt, and Ash heard Aylin's boots hit the ground when he dismounted.

Now.

Ash threw herself against the wagon door. It slammed open with a loud crack. Ash saw the heads turn. Crispin. Aylin. Merewen. But she had the advantage of surprise. She leapt off the wagon, the impact like a hundred needles pushing through her ankles at once, but she was fast and determined.

She grabbed the reins of Aylin's horse right when Crispin came to his feet with a growl.

She ducked out from underneath Aylin's flailing arms.

Crispin shouted something, but she didn't hear. Didn't listen. With the reins in one hand, she clung to the saddle.

"Ash, no!" Merewen ran toward her.

And Ash pulled herself into the saddle, shouting for the horse to run.

The horse bolted. Ash knew they couldn't keep up this speed for long—she was barely holding on—but she pushed the horse as hard as she dared.

It had to be enough to get away from the camp.

The last thing she saw was the deep betrayal etched on Merewen's face.

Then the trees closed around them and swallowed them whole.

CHAPTER TWENTY

ASH

The horse, a small blue roan, was fidgety and nervous under Ash's touch. Ash had never been the strongest rider, and she jumped at every sound. The trees rustled on either side of the path, and the clouds overhead cast shadows on the road. They left tracks everywhere. The best thing she could do was to get out of the woods and keep going until she got help. Try to outrun her inevitable pursuers.

Ash turned around. She didn't see anyone yet.

The path ahead was empty too, and after an hour of clinging to the horse, Ash's muscles were screaming in pain. She sat back and tried to relax a little, letting the horse slow to a trot. She laughed. She wasn't a princess who needed to be saved. She could save herself.

Splinter would be proud.

She patted the roan's neck. "I don't even know your name," she whispered. "But you can get me to safety, can't you?"

The horse snorted and Ash smiled. "Thank you, you beauty."

She let the tangy, sharp forest air fill her lungs. Some of the tension of the past days slipped off her shoulders, and the horse calmed too.

She couldn't let her guard down entirely. She needed to plan. Anders would help. Once she reached the Calinoran encampment on this side of the Crescent Mountains, she'd be safe. Or at least safer. She would get word to her mother and Splinter, and she would tell Uncle Lam about the passage Merewen had sketched.

She would find out who Vance was.

Overhead, an owl hooted, and Ash tensed. The reins dug into her hands, and she struggled to unclench her fingers. She had to find a place to water her horse and rest before night fell, off this overgrown path.

She kept going until the path crossed with a broader road. Tendrils of frosty air crawled through the trees. Hunger slowed both Ash and the horse.

"Only a little bit farther," Ash promised.

Once, twice, she thought she heard hoofbeats, but the road remained empty. The roan had outrun the draft horses. And Ash slowed down, to be more careful with their tracks.

"You'll come home with me, and the royal stables will feed you all the hay and all the apples you want."

Eventually night caught up with them, like an inkblot running through the woods. The dark air grew colder still.

The Crescent Mountains' two highest peaks crested over the tree cover, stars beginning to appear all around them, and Ash felt another bubble of laughter pop up.

She was on her own. She was terrified. But she was *free*.

In the distance, another horse whinnied.

Her hands trembling, Ash slipped off her roan. Her knees buckled, and she snatched the reins.

Half running, half falling, she pulled the horse into the thicket away from the road. Her heart hammered. She crouched low to keep herself from falling and to keep herself from being seen, and to her relief her horse started munching on the moss and herbs that covered the ground.

She wished she had a weapon, but all she had was the coil of rope that she'd stolen, which she'd wound around her waist. At least it would help her secure the horse overnight.

Ash shivered. She should've brought the thin blanket too. And food. Anything. It was all the more reason for her to get to the encampment as soon as possible.

Hoofbeats echoed across the road. On the horizon, Ash could make out a single solitary rider. A knight.

"All the knights in the kingdom would fight and die for you," Splinter had told her once.

She let him get closer.

In the gathering darkness, it was hard to make out the colors of his overcoat—it seemed colorless, until the gray softened to light brown and the black to a purple. It was familiar to Ash, but the traveler had a hood pulled over his head, and the fear of the flight still coursed through her.

The knight kept his eyes on the road ahead and whistled a merry tune, one Ash was *certain* she'd heard before.

Then it hit her. The song—though off-key—was one the musicians had played the night of her birthday celebrations. And at that moment, she knew who he was.

The grumpy, judgmental knight captain. The son of the Labanne family.

The Labannes were friends of her mother.

Their son had been Anders's best friend, growing up. Splinter had told her so herself.

He might not think much of her, but he was sworn to protect her.

Ash started forward before she fully realized what she was doing. The roan, eating happily, shook his head and snorted when she tried to move him.

The knight brought his horse to a standstill. He reached for his sword. "Is anyone there?"

"Lord Labanne?" Ash's voice croaked. She stepped out of the thicket. Some of the branches grabbed at her as if to keep her away from him, but she brushed them off.

The knight captain's eyes grew wide, and he slid off his horse. "Stars! Princess Adelisa?" He unbuckled his cloak and wrapped it around her. "Your highness, everyone is looking for you!"

"I was abducted, but I escaped." Ash pulled the cloak tight around her shoulders, and she shuddered. Her teeth chattered despite the sudden warmth. It felt strange to fall into the role of princess again and not . . . whoever she had been in Crispin's camp. "I need to go home."

The knight captain unsheathed his sword and checked the road. "Do you have a horse? Or did you walk all the way here? Where are your captors?"

Ash pointed at the bushes, where the roan was busy trying to find the best greens. "I stole one of the horses."

"You did? How enterprising of you. How careless of your captors," the knight captain said, and some warning tugged at the back of Ash's mind. "I need to go home," she repeated. Her voice squeaked.

The knight captain took a step closer. His eyes were sharp and, to Ash, dangerous. She took a step back.

"No, your highness." He turned his sword on her. "You're not going anywhere."

Ash backed into a tree. The rough bark stabbed at her through her cloak. Relief made way for horror, when everything slotted into place. "You're *part* of this," she whispered.

Lord Labanne shook his head. "I shouldn't have involved that fool Crispin. But there have been rumors about you for years. A fake princess. The story was too good to pass up."

Ash growled. "Why? You swore an oath to my mother! You have a duty to the crown."

"You ignorant girl," Lord Labanne seethed. His face was suddenly closer to hers. "Don't talk to me about duty."

He feinted to the left, and caught her going to the right, wrapping his long arms around her and using the cloak to pin her in place. His breath was hot on her face. "I'm *doing* my duty. To Calinor. Your crown is a *threat* to this kingdom. Calinor was strong once, but no more. Your mother is cutting this country to pieces and giving its riches to commoners, to merchants, to monstrosities like your squire. Everything the nobility fought for and bled for, our lands, our privileges—she's destroying them all. We have to fight for a future for ourselves and our heirs."

"So you'll . . . what?" Ash demanded. "Take me to the empire and hope they'll give you a medal?"

"I could bury you here and revel in the chaos," he said. "But my contacts within the empire will pay well for you. In gold. In favors. And when your mother's throne inevitably crumbles, the empire will remember well who stood on the right side of history."

"They'll trample you like bugs."

He smiled thinly. "The empress knows better. As long as we swear fealty to her, she'll restore us to our former glory. We'll regain the power we lost."

"So you'll destroy your country because you feel slighted? You're *nothing* to the empire. You're a traitor."

"I'll take my chances, princess."

Ash kicked and shouted, until the knight captain stuffed a rag in her mouth and wrapped a rope around her, cloak and all. He carried her back to his horse and dumped her on the ground so he could collect the blue roan.

Ash wiggled and screamed into the gag. She tried to

roll away, but the knight captain returned with the horse by his side. He tethered the roan to his own mount, all the while watching her with barely disguised disgust. "I won't be able to bring you to the empire tonight without alerting the patrols, so Crispin is going to have to keep an eye on you. But he'll learn. Believe me when I tell you that to risk you, to risk the mission, is an unforgivable blunder. And he'll pay the price."

When the horses were ready, he walked up to Ash and yanked her to her feet. Pain burst through her, and she nearly choked on it.

Vance unceremoniously tossed her over the roan's saddle. "You may not be much of a princess, your highness, but you'll serve a purpose. For a better, stronger Calinor."

CHAPTER
TWENTY-ONE

SPLINTER

Seven days after they left Haven, when the night made way for dawn, Lucen and Splinter were deep in the Heartian Woods. On the way, they'd slept by the roadside and in abandoned waystations, they'd avoided guards and groups of travelers, they'd made careful conversations and practiced their sword patterns together. Splinter followed Lucen's example with the exercises, knowing full well that what she'd told Ash was true: the crown prince was the best fighter of all the squires.

On the fourth day, just before they crossed into the Heartian Woods, a spring rainstorm had caught them unawares, and by the time they'd made camp in an abandoned inn, Splinter had felt like she was carrying small lakes in her boots. Lucen hadn't said much, but he'd sat down by their fire, skinned the rabbit he'd hunted, and quietly showed her the best way to clean and wax her sword.

Now the only indication of rain was the smell of fresh earth and young leaves. Birds flew overhead, singing and cawing and greeting the day. Deer crossed the road, as did the occasional squirrel. They'd spent three whole days in the woods, and they hadn't seen any other travelers. Overgrown paths led away from the main road deeper into the forest, and Splinter wondered where they led. Perhaps, under different circumstances, she could come back and explore.

Lucen caught her staring. "It's magical, isn't it? I don't think anyone's ever managed to map all of it." He patted his horse's neck. Quest was a spicy red gelding with strong opinions if they pushed on too long. "Uncle Lam brought me here once. I thought these woods could hide entire castles. You could wander off course and find lost villages and hidden treasures."

The words tugged at a memory. "Or abandoned star temples with magical mists? Ash told me about Sir Riven."

"She did?" Lucen sounded surprised. His face softened. "That was before she went to live in Byrne. I didn't think she remembered."

"I think the story means a lot to her," Splinter said. "Because it's yours. Together."

Lucen turned away from Splinter, and he reached for his necklace. "What if we don't find her?"

"We will."

"What if we're too late?"

"Lucen." Although she still called him "highness" most of the time, Splinter was growing more comfortable using his name, especially at moments when it counted. It was easier away from Haven too. He was gentler here. "We'll do everything we can to find her. And knowing Ash, *she'll* do everything she can to escape. We just need a few lucky stars."

Lucen ran his nails over the reins of his chestnut horse, a nervous tic Splinter had caught several times over the past couple of days. "All the squires in the palace, everyone I know, has lost relatives or friends to the war. Ilsar lost his father. The twins lost their brother. Tobias lost both his mothers. Why should our stars be luckier? And I won't be sent into danger, because I'm *indispensable*." He spat the words. "But I can't shield them all. I wish Ash had stayed in Byrne. At least she was protected."

"You're not responsible for all of their lives," Splinter said.

"If I'm to be king, aren't I?" Lucen replied. "And I *am*

responsible for putting Ash in danger."

"The people who stole her are responsible," Splinter said firmly. Something else occurred to her. "Is that why you were so cruel to her? To chase her back to Byrne?"

Lucen nudged Quest to a trot, as though to put distance between himself and the question.

Splinter caught up with him. *"Lucen."*

"A king has to be strong. If I let myself be vulnerable, people will get hurt," he said. The wind that rustled the trees around them mussed his hair. He let wayward strands fall in front of his eyes. "What if I got used to having her back, to sharing Mama and Uncle Lam with her, to being friends, only to lose her again?"

Splinter shook her head. "Caring for someone doesn't make you vulnerable. Is that what your friends told you?"

"You heard what Lord Idian said," Lucen argued. "The queen cares about our people, and it makes her vulnerable. If the nobility rises up against her, we'll tear ourselves apart. We can't let that happen. We *have* to be strong. And . . . the nobility fights for this kingdom. The knights. The lords. Is it so bad to respect that?" He angled away from her, so she wouldn't see his face.

"The knights. The lords. The soldiers. The bowyers. The farriers. The scribes," Splinter said. "We *all* fight, Lucen.

Who are you to decide who matters more?"

"The crown prince!" he snapped. "Everyone always reminds me of that! Uncle Lam tells me that one day, I'm going to be the most powerful person in Calinor. That power means something, and I'm going to have to make the right decisions. But how do I do that? What if I don't know what the right decisions are?"

Splinter stared at the road ahead and considered his outburst quietly. "You're afraid."

Lucen nodded. Tension ran along the lines of his shoulders.

"I think I would be too, in your situation." Especially when it sounded like more than a few of his friends were sympathetic to Lark ideas.

"You wouldn't be," Lucen said. "I was wrong about you. I know that now."

She hesitated. In for a copper, in for a gold. "What did I ever do to you?"

"I thought you were a girl," Lucen said blandly.

Splinter scowled. "Even if I were, that's not an excuse."

"I know that." His voice cracked. He was paler. "I *know*. I never gave you an honest chance."

"Because I reminded you of everything that was changing?"

Lucen squeezed the reins tightly and straightened, discomfort apparent in his stance, but he tried to smile. "Also, you punched me first."

"Because you were bullying that merchant girl!" Splinter's voice echoed between the trees and she raised her hand to her mouth. "Oops."

"If there is a hidden castle somewhere, they know we're coming now," Lucen said. He sobered. "You're right. I was cruel. You didn't deserve it, and neither did Ash. Or that merchant girl. Sometimes when everything overwhelms me, I just . . . snap. It's easier to be angry than to be kind, you know?"

"A knight is supposed to be courageous," Splinter reminded him.

"Do you think I can learn to be?" Lucen's voice was so small, Splinter had to strain to hear him.

"The boy I met in the palace couldn't," Splinter said honestly. "The boy who's on the road with me, who's trying to right his wrongs—I think he can."

Lucen shifted in his saddle. "If you don't mind me asking . . . what does it feel like?"

"What does what feel like?"

"Not being a boy or a girl, I guess. Does that make you neither? Or both?"

Splinter considered it. "I don't know. When someone calls me a girl, I feel it in my chest. Like this big hand reaches in and squeezes my insides. Because that's not me, and I hate that people see me as someone I'm not." She'd never put that into words. "When I think about being a boy . . . that's not me either. I dressed in Anders's squire gear for Ash's party, and I *liked* it, but his armor still itched and it chafed and it felt like masquerading. I don't want to pretend to be someone else. I just want to be Splinter."

Lucen didn't respond immediately, and she wondered what he was thinking. It made the back of her hands itch.

"So when you're a knight, are you going to be Sir Splinter?"

Splinter coughed a laugh, and it instantly made her feel better. The conversation amid the dawn-lit trees had grown unexpectedly heavy. "When Ash asked me to be her squire, I dreamed of having a knight's sword with gold wire around the hilt and stars etched into the blade, like my mother's dagger. I thought that maybe I would figure out another name. But in case you forgot, I'm not a squire anymore." The words didn't sting so much this time around. They *hurt*, but they didn't carry the weight of anger with them.

Lucen nodded. "I'm sorry. I was wrong."

Splinter held the words close for a moment, and then

she *breathed*. "You were," she said simply.

"I'll make it right by you. I promise." He dug into the pocket of his cloak and produced a slightly stale aniseed biscuit.

Splinter made a face. "Do you walk around everywhere with food in your pockets?"

"This *is* a peace offering."

She took it.

The trees thinned. Jagged rocks protruded from the green, and cliffs and crags pointed up toward the peaks of the Crescent Mountains. Splinter gasped. A large, fortified encampment guarded the Calinoran border. It was over a mile wide, with long stone walls and countless barracks. On either side of the main camp stood other guard structures, and Splinter could make out guard towers dappled across the mountainside. In the distance, along the mountain pass, a ruined castle had been repurposed as a guard camp.

The kingdom's flag flew above the encampment, and the late morning sun bathed the lands in a golden light.

"Wow." When Splinter heard talk of fights in the mountains, when Anders wrote about being stationed here, she'd thought of tents and rock slides and skirmishes. Not a whole city guarding a kingdom.

Lucen shrugged deeper into his hood. "I think it's better if you do the talking here."

Splinter nodded. They'd discussed the plan. She'd be a concerned sibling, looking for her brother with a message from the family. But now that they approached the guarded gate, she felt a flutter of nerves. Her hands were sweaty.

Guards let them pass without a second glance, only pointing out the command center where clerks kept a list of duty assignments, so Splinter could locate her brother. They were used to visitors; merchants, messengers, and soldiers went in and out, and the relative quiet of the endless forest made way for a constant drumbeat of horses' hooves.

Once inside the gate, Splinter and Lucen left their mounts in the encampment's stables, paid for their care, and continued on foot. Splinter kept her head down, and Lucen followed closely. It was like walking down a normal city road, with workshops and stores on either side. A large smithy, a tavern, a messenger service, a bakery preparing loaves for the midday meal. Two apprentices carried stacks of swords from one building to the next, and a farrier led a large warhorse down the street.

Everywhere were soldiers and knights assisted by squires. Several of them showed the scars and wounds of skirmishes, although the last of the winter's snow currently prevented the Ferisian troops from venturing deep into the kingdom. There was a tension in the air, far different from midwinter in Haven.

Lucen stepped closer to Splinter when a group of knights walked in their direction, arguing loudly.

". . . think it's brave for him to try to find his sister."

"He's a junior squire. They can barely find the pointy end of a sword."

"You know what I think? To run away is anything *but* brave. He has a duty to the kingdom, and he's forsaking it."

"Stars, Arden. Don't be so hard on the boy."

"He's not wrong. We've had no sign of the princess either. What if neither of them come back? We might as well open the gates and invite the empire in. We're *dying* for them."

Splinter looked over her shoulder at Lucen. He was bone white. She squeezed his hand. She opened her mouth to say something—and she froze.

Lucen bumped into her, but she barely noticed.

She recognized his hair first. He had the same mousy brown hair that she had, bound back in a braid.

Then the colors of his overcoat. The white flower against a dark gray field of the DuLac crest.

His laugh.

Anders.

Her brother.

Standing in the street, talking to a scrawny young man with curly brown hair and soft brown skin, wearing a baker's apron.

Splinter ran. She didn't consciously decide to do it. She pulled Lucen along and she ran, zigzagging past the other people on the street.

"Anders!" Her voice held halfway between a shout and a sob.

Anders reached for his sword, but Splinter had already flung herself at him. It was as if the world slowed down around them. She saw the sword glint. She saw the baker take a step back. She saw all the ways in which her brother was different—the broad shoulders, the fuzz of a beard, the new scar that ran along his jawline—and all the ways in which he was the same. And in the last possible moment, she saw the spark of recognition—of shock.

Anders dropped his sword back in the scabbard and opened his arms, stumbling as he caught Splinter. The impact left them both breathless.

Splinter clung to her brother. He still smelled of home.

"*Splinter?*" Anders took her by the shoulders and held her in front of him. There were scars on his hands and face, evidence of battles survived. "Stars, can this be real? How did you get here?"

"I *missed* you," Splinter managed. Her voice was thick with tears and her vision blurred. "You never came home and you left me with Uncle Elias and I missed you so much."

He pulled her close again, and she felt the steady rhythm of his heart. His armor smelled like the leathers she'd worn to Ash's party. His hands were firm and strong. "I missed you too."

"You look like Dad," she murmured.

His chest rumbled when he laughed. "What are you doing at the border? I got your letter, but . . ."

Anders fell silent.

Splinter slowly pulled back. Her brother was looking at a point just past Splinter's shoulder. At a *person* just past Splinter's shoulder. He paled when he recognized Lucen. *"No."*

Splinter set her hands by her sides. "We've come to find Ash. We need you."

Anders recoiled.

The ground swayed beneath Splinter's feet. "You will help, won't you?"

"Splinter . . ." Anders said, shaking his head almost

imperceptibly. "You need to go. Now."

Splinter's heart skipped a beat. This was her *brother*. The type of knight she aspired to be. "But we're looking for Ash."

He took a step away from her. "I'm afraid I can't help you."

"Anders."

Lucen cleared his throat. "Lord Idian was right about you, wasn't he?"

A flash of something like anger—or hurt—crossed Anders's face. Then he blinked, and all that was left was a cold, empty mask.

Splinter couldn't breathe. When she'd seen Anders from a distance, he'd been her brother, her family. Face-to-face with him, he was a stranger. "I defended you. I told him you couldn't be—"

Anders pulled her toward him and wrapped his hand over her mouth. "Hush," he hissed. "For the love of all the stars, keep your mouth shut."

Splinter pulled and twisted, but he held her tightly.

"The flour barn," the young baker, who'd watched the proceedings with a frown, suggested.

Anders locked eyes with Lucen and jerked his head in the direction of a tall wooden building. "Come along." He scooped Splinter up and followed the baker, who opened the door for them.

After a moment's hesitation, Lucen followed, his hand on his sword.

The baker stepped back toward the bakery. "Call me if you need anything."

"Thanks, Rian." Anders looked down at his sibling. "Will you stop shouting if I let you go?"

Splinter grumbled and kicked at her brother. She tried to bite him.

"Splinter." Lucen leaned against the door, his arms crossed.

She narrowed her eyes and stilled, begrudgingly.

"Good." Anders set her down on top of stacked bags of flour. He ran his hands through his hair. "My sibling, the squire. It's quite the break with tradition."

Splinter heard the ghost of Lord Idian's words, about the Larks who longed to go back to the old days. "Tradition needs someone to ruffle its feathers," she snapped.

Anders grimaced. "Has anyone told you how much you're like Mom when you get angry?" He turned to Lucen. "You're like your mother too, if I'm to believe the stories told by our commanders."

Lucen scowled.

Anders's voice held an edge of anger. "I don't know what Idian told you, but if you have evidence the princess is close by—"

"You'll have to ask your Lark friends," Splinter interrupted, her voice sharp with pain.

They'd come here for his help. They'd traveled for days. She'd *trusted* her brother.

Anders continued as if Splinter hadn't said anything. "The Larks are a myth. If you have evidence the princess is close by, I'll do what I can to find her. But you *will* leave. You in particular, your highness. You're not safe here."

Lucen walked up to him, hand on the hilt of his sword. Breadcrumbs crunched under his feet. They made an odd pair, the knight and the squire. Anders towered over Lucen, and he carried himself with the confidence of a man who'd stared down blades and arrows, but he couldn't meet the prince's gaze.

"We need your help, Sir Anders," Lucen said formally.

Anders shook his head. "There's danger in these hills. I can provide you with an escort—"

"Sir knight," Lucen started, but before he could say anything else, someone pounded on the wall of the flour barn.

"Anders?" A sharp voice echoed down the street. "Don't

tell me you're with your baker boyfriend again. Come on, we have to talk."

Anders's eyes widened. His cold frustration made way for terror. He pushed Lucen toward Splinter, both of them stumbling into the bags of flour, in a cloud of white.

"Go." He walked to the door, and right before he opened it, he turned back to his sibling. His mouth twisted. "And don't look back."

He slipped through the door, and outside, his voice echoed. "Vance? What is it?"

"Trouble is a-brewing," the second person—Vance— replied. "We need to move up our timeline. I have to cross the border tonight." His voice dropped.

Splinter ran to the door and opened it just far enough to peek through.

"Those are Labanne colors," Lucen whispered, appearing next to her and pointing at the figure next to Anders, a knight captain in purples and browns.

"That's Vance Labanne. Anders's best friend when he was a squire." Splinter could barely keep her voice down. Shock, horror, and determination were all wrestling to come out on top.

"He was in Haven for Ash's party," Lucen remembered. "Why would he need to cross into the empire?"

"He was at the theater, when Ash was introduced at court," Splinter said. "Remember what Lord Idian said? In Haven, anyone could be a Lark. They hide in plain sight. But the Labannes have access to the palace. What if . . ."

Lucen nodded. "It can't be a coincidence."

"It can't be." It felt like the pieces of the puzzle were falling into place, and when she glanced at Lucen, she knew he felt the same. He smiled dangerously.

"He's dealing with some kind of trouble," he said. "It wouldn't be knightly to let him suffer, would it? We have to find out what it is so we can help."

Splinter and Lucen looked at each other.

Splinter had traveled to the end of the kingdom to see Anders again. Once upon a time, she would have trusted him without a second thought. He was her family, after all.

But Ash was her home.

Lucen held out his hand. She clasped it.

They weren't going anywhere.

CHAPTER TWENTY-TWO

ASH

Rope looped around Ash's ankle, binding her to the wheel of the wagon with knots so tight she couldn't untie them. She could walk around in the camp Crispin had set up, but never too far, and never out of sight from her captors.

Merewen sat across from Ash, her face puffy like she'd been crying. She hadn't said a word since Vance had dragged Ash into the camp and dumped her at Crispin's feet. She'd lost her smile. She turned her head whenever Ash tried to speak.

She'd only walked up to Ash once, to snatch the notebook from her pocket and hold it closely, hurt radiating from every movement. "I thought I could trust you. I thought you cared." And then she'd pulled away.

Crispin and Aylin alternated between keeping an eye on Ash and turning to argue. An angry cut ran along Crispin's cheekbone, and a bruise was starting to darken his eye. Vance had backhanded him violently after tossing Ash on the ground. "If anything happens to her, you'll pay for it in blood," he'd promised. "I will come back for her tomorrow night."

"You better bring us our gold—" Crispin had started, but he'd cowered when Vance raised his hand.

"You'll get your due. Do *not* test me."

That had been half a day ago. Now it was nearing midday and Ash had mere hours left before Vance would come to take her to the Ferisian Empire. She'd be a prisoner. Or ransom, to be traded for pieces of Calinor.

The thought made her angry and sick.

She had to escape.

On the far side of the camp, Crispin paced, his hands behind his back, muttering angrily. Aylin dug around in the saddlebags.

Ash looked at Merewen. "You heard what Vance said, didn't you?" she whispered. "He'll take me away. He'll pay off Crispin. And you'll never see me again. There won't be any bringing me home or whatever they promised you."

Merewen pulled her knees up to her chest, but she didn't turn away.

"Vance took advantage of your grief, and your uncle *lied* to you. And I'm sorry I stole your notebook. I am. But we have to stop him."

"So maybe Uncle Crispin used me," Merewen croaked. "But you did too. Let him take you."

The words felt like a punch. "It wasn't about you."

"It wasn't?" Merewen got off the tree trunk she'd been sitting on. She stared Ash down. "What then? Did I just happen to be the fool you could trick into helping you? Someone so desperate that she would believe a *princess* could be interested in her?"

Ash narrowed her eyes. The words didn't sound like Merewen's. "Did your uncle tell you that?"

Merewen jutted her chin out. She pulled the notebook from her pocket. "Aylin did. He reminded me that my head is too full of dreams to see reality. That people like you only use people like us as a means to an end."

She stalked over to the campfire. She looked Ash straight in the eye. "It's time to stop dreaming."

Ash gasped. "Merewen, *no!*"

Aylin and Crispin whirled around in time to see the notebook hit the flames. It immediately caught fire.

Crispin dashed toward the flames, but the pages were already smoldering, and the leather binding began to char.

Merewen stood by and watched the book—and all of her maps—burn. Tears streamed down her cheeks, but she didn't flinch. When her uncle tried to wrap an arm around her shoulders, she shrugged him off.

She waited until the book was fully engulfed in flames before she walked back to Ash and sat opposite her, her arms wrapped tightly around her waist and her face pale.

Ash felt like crying. "Merewen . . ."

"No."

Crispin stared into the campfire, looking lost. Aylin returned to his work, but he kept his head down and his shoulders were hunched up near his ears. And while Ash knew that Merewen hadn't been entirely right, she hadn't been entirely wrong either.

"You're right. I tricked you," she admitted. "You have every right to be angry with me. But don't be angry with yourself. I needed to escape. Don't you see? It's not just about family, it's about the fate of the kingdom. If Vance takes me to the empire, my mother will do anything to get me back, and a lot of people will get hurt."

"Why?" Merewen scoffed. "You're a servant's daughter."

"I'm *not*." Ash fought to keep her voice steady. "I don't

know if the story you believe about Talwin is true, but even if it is, the queen *chose* me. She's been my mother my whole life."

Merewen swallowed.

"But we can choose to be family too, if you'll help me," Ash added recklessly. She was scrambling for a way to make this right for Merewen. "Come home with me. I'll find a place for you at court. I'll introduce you to the royal mapmakers. You could be their apprentice."

A light sparked in Merewen's eyes before she shook her head. She dug her fingers into the frozen grass. "So the royal guard can arrest me for kidnapping the princess? No thank you."

"I wouldn't let that happen." Ash tried to move closer to Merewen, but the rope around her ankle prevented her. "I don't know if we can be friends. But you deserve to be someplace where you aren't lonely, and maybe we can get to know each other." A place where they could find out what, if anything, was true of Merewen's story.

This was the kind of princess she wanted to become. The kind who was gentle with other people's hurts and dreams.

"What about the rest of our family?" Merewen asked. She tilted her head slightly. She looked older. She had had her heart broken, and because of it, it held edges and sharp points where there hadn't been any before.

Ash winced. She didn't have a good answer to that question. Even if Vance had manipulated them, court would want to see justice done.

"I'll do my best to help them," she promised.

Merewen grimaced. "Don't bother if it's so difficult for you."

"You did abduct me," Ash pointed out.

Anger flashed in Merewen's eyes. "So you'll let them rot, and I can be your charity case?" She sounded like she was itching for a fight. "Never mind. Besides, if you're so important to the queen, why hasn't the guard found you yet? Do you think your fake brother cares? He's better off without you."

"Vance said the whole kingdom is looking for me," Ash said.

"Maybe he's lying. Maybe they're happy to be rid of you."

Maybe Ash had never belonged at court at all. Maybe all those nobles who'd laughed at her were right.

Silence roared in Ash's ears, all her worries and doubts slamming into her at once.

She didn't want this.

She refused to let them win. The cruel nobles. The bullies. Merewen.

"I'm not the enemy," Ash said at last, tugging at the rope that tied her to the wagon, though she didn't have the strength to break it. "The Ferisian Empire is. Vance is. And if you don't help, I'll assume you've made your choice between the empire and Calinor too."

Merewen's bottom lip trembled. "I don't care about the empire or about the kingdom," she said. "I don't even know who the empire is. I cared about *you*. About bringing you home. If we can't do that, at least Vance will pay us well. Our family will have enough to survive the next winter and keep a roof over our heads."

Merewen got to her feet and stalked away.

Ash's stomach dropped. "The palace will pay you too," she tried, as loudly as she dared. "Merewen, please. If he takes me with him, I'll never see my family again."

Merewen shuddered, but she kept on walking. She said something to Crispin, who'd remained next to the fire, before she disappeared to the other side of the camp.

Ash felt like she couldn't breathe.

The time ticked away around her.

After Aylin finished preparing the midday meal, he took over guarding Ash. He placed a plate with stone-baked bread and salted fish in front of her and sat down on Merewen's tree trunk. His daggers glinted by his side, and he ate loudly. When he went to grab a wrinkled apple, he nudged the burning notebook deeper into the fire with the toe of his boot.

And Ash *snapped*. She picked up the bread and threw it in Aylin's direction, crumbs bouncing off his shoulders and arms. "I hate you! You pretend that what you're doing is noble and right, but you're a criminal and a bully!"

Aylin froze. Red flooded his cheeks.

Ash threw the fish next.

"Merewen cared about mapmaking, and she's *good* at it. And instead of helping her, you tell her that she's worthless. You call yourself her family, but you want her to be small when she could be great."

Ash picked up the plate. "You lied to her and you used her and you stole me from my home and my friends and my family, and I *hate* you." She flung the plate with all her might, and with a satisfying crack, it slammed against Aylin's head.

He charged. The next thing Ash knew, Aylin was on top of her, pinning her down. His expression was twisted with fury and loathing. "You know *nothing* about me."

Ash spat in his face.

Aylin pulled back to punch her. A large hand wrapped around his. Crispin dragged his son off Ash and tossed him onto the grass. "Calm down!" he roared. "Get away from her until you can behave!"

"But *Dad* . . ."

"Now!"

Aylin stumbled to his feet and stormed off.

Shaking, Ash curled herself into a tight ball.

Crispin forced her to face him. "Are you hurt?" he demanded, with all the empathy of a stonemason making sure his wares were unmarked.

To Ash's horror, tears began to trickle down her face, the weight of everything that had happened catching up with her. "I want to go home."

Crispin's mouth pulled into a tight line. "We all want things we can't have, girl. Vance will be here for you soon, and a good thing too. You're more trouble than you're worth."

Tears clogged Ash's throat, and she gasped. Crispin let go of her with a sound of disgust. She cried until the sobs stopped racking her body. She cried until she was too tired to cry. She cried until her head ached.

And then she balled her fists, took the knife she'd stolen from Aylin's belt when he attacked her, hid the weapon in her shirt, and prepared to fight.

CHAPTER TWENTY-THREE

SPLINTER

Lucen snatched a cloak from a wash line and smeared sand and dirt on his face and in his hair. If people didn't look at him too closely, he could pass for a soldier back from assignment. Probably. "It'll be better once it's dark," Splinter mused.

Lucen scowled.

They'd followed Anders and Vance from a distance, until the two knights entered the barracks. Now they lurked behind the building and peeked through the windows.

Inside, Anders and Vance had talked—and argued— for an hour, until Anders threw his hands into the sky and shouted something unintelligible. Vance had patted Anders's shoulder and laughed at his outburst. They'd shared a midday meal together. Outside the barracks, Lucen's stomach had grumbled loudly, and he'd dug in his pockets until he found a dry bit of jerky.

After the meal, Vance stomped up the stairs to the second floor, while Anders stayed at the narrow table, mindlessly tracing the marks in the woodwork, his knight's sword leaning against the wall.

"You know what you have to do, right?" Splinter whispered.

"We've gone through this twice," Lucen said with an amused smirk. "We split up. You follow Vance. I follow your brother. We meet up outside the stables at the second evening bell. If either of us is in danger, if they try to cross the border, or if we find out where Ash is, we go to the commanders immediately."

Splinter bit the inside of her cheek, suddenly nervous. "What if we're wrong? What if they don't know anything?"

"Your brother is hiding something. And we're Ash's best chance."

According to the stories around the encampment, the Ferisian Empire had sent messenger birds to Haven and denied all responsibility.

"Anything we can learn will help," Lucen said, his voice brooking no argument.

Splinter straightened her shoulders. "You're right. You stay here. I'll find a quiet space to observe Vance. That way, there's less chance we'll both get caught."

Lucen squeezed her arm. "Stars guide you, Splinter."

"And you, your highness."

Lucen smiled.

Splinter pulled her cloak tight and walked away. None of the soldiers paid attention to her, and eventually she sagged down on a crooked wooden bench that pushed against a quiet tavern. She picked up a crudely cut wooden doll and whittling knife that a soldier had abandoned, and with her hood high over her head, she kept a close eye on the barracks.

She pretended to whittle. She pretended not to think about her brother.

But while she sat and breathed out shakily, the tears fell, like dark blotches on the willow wood.

The shadows lengthened. Vance wore a nondescript brown cloak when he exited the barracks. He had a satchel slung over his shoulder, and he held one hand on his sword. Like Splinter and Lucen, he carried a bow and arrows. He was dressed for travel.

Splinter shaved away the sharper edges of the doll's

torso—it was missing its legs—but she followed Vance's movements carefully. He stopped by the other barracks first, and spoke to the soldier at the door. At a bowyer's workshop, he demanded to see a young apprentice. He exchanged a tightly bound scroll for a bundle of broadhead arrows with sharpened blades.

When the apprentice asked him a question, Vance slammed a coin down onto the counter and stalked out.

Splinter pocketed the doll and whittling knife and got to her feet.

From the corner of her eye, she saw Anders walk away from the barracks too, and decisively turn toward the north side of the encampment. After a moment, Lucen appeared and followed him, dashing from building to building.

He spotted Splinter and nodded.

Vance strode past Splinter without noticing her. He walked toward the gates with purpose. Another knight, in blues and greens, raised his hand and awkwardly lowered it again when Vance didn't look up.

Splinter followed him at a distance and tried to keep out of sight, letting a tall soldier with a washing basket on his hip pass her by, falling behind a squabbling group of senior squires.

Halfway through the camp, two heavy carts crossed

the road. Vance spun around, and she leapt to the side at the last possible moment, ducking behind—and partway into—a leafless, frozen berry bush.

Thorns and branches scratched at her face and arms. She didn't move until the carts had passed and people continued on their way.

When Vance entered the stables, Splinter slipped in too, keeping her head down. Travelers' horses were kept in separate stalls, away from the knights' and officers' warhorses, so she made her way to the dun mare Lord Idian had given her. Biscuit eyed her warily, swishing her tale, not thrilled about the idea of leaving the comfort of her fresh straw and oats.

Splinter patted Biscuit's neck and apologized as a young woman with warm brown skin and hay stalks in her dark braids walked toward her. "Come to collect her already?"

"Only for a little while," Splinter said. "We need to run an errand."

The stable hand tilted her head. "You've been pushing her hard, squire."

"I know," Splinter admitted. For once the weight of the title filled her with dread instead of elation. "I wouldn't do it if it wasn't necessary."

"A good horse means a knight's life," the stable hand

grumbled. "See that you remember that."

Heat rose to Splinter's cheeks. "I will."

The stable hand led Biscuit out and crooned softly while Splinter saddled the horse. The mare had been brushed to a shine and watered, and some of her agitation calmed as Splinter prepared her for the ride.

Hoofbeats clattered through the stables when Vance rode out, and Splinter ducked behind Biscuit's belly, tightening the girth. When she mounted, the stable hand held on to Biscuit's bridle. She looked in the direction where Vance had left, before turning back to Splinter. "See that you bring her back in one piece. And yourself too."

Splinter led Biscuit out of the stables and through the gates, and once she had left the encampment behind, the kingdom stretched out in front of her. The sun crept closer to the horizon, and the sky was aflame with deep red light, while the clouds colored purple. Mist rolled down from the mountains.

Vance rode hard, a lone figure on a long road.

Splinter nudged Biscuit into a trot, keeping a careful distance but determined not to lose him. She hoped she'd pass as a fellow traveler to him.

They rode deep into the Heartian Woods. Dusk brought a chill to the air, and Splinter shivered when they passed between the trees, whose shadows grew darker, like thin fingers skittering across the road.

Twice, Vance changed pace. When he pushed his horse into a canter, Splinter had no choice but to do the same or risk losing him. When he slowed down, she had to get closer or look even more suspicious.

A sense of danger crawled up her spine and her ears itched, but Vance didn't turn. He kept going.

Suddenly he spurred on his mount and swerved right, onto a narrow, overgrown path. Splinter followed until she got to the crossing, where she hesitated. The trees on either side leaned across the trail like they were determined to see what happened below them.

Biscuit danced sideways, and Splinter unsheathed her sword. Her hands trembled.

This path looked secret and dangerous. A wild trail, or a smugglers' route.

She pressed forward. As soon as she left the main road, the woods' birdsong and rustling of leaves faded, and silence took over. Biscuit slipped several times on the rough trail before she stopped. No matter what Splinter did, she refused to keep going.

When she shook her head wildly and snorted, the sound echoed through the trees.

Splinter slid down from the saddle and tied Biscuit's reins to a tree. The branches underneath her feet crunched. She knew it was foolish—but what if Ash was close?

Her heart pounded. She squeezed the hilt of her sword.

Then the path opened up into a clearing, bathed in twilight's pale purples.

The first thing Splinter saw was another horse, tied to a tree.

Then, the glint of an arrow.

Vance stepped out from behind a tree, his bow trained on her. "I would demand to know why you're here, but I recognize you. Anders's degenerate sibling. It was too much to hope that you'd just disappeared."

"Vance Labanne," Splinter shot back. "I knew you were ill-mannered. I didn't think you'd be dishonorable too." She clung to the tree line, bringing up her sword as a meager defense.

"Traitor!" she taunted.

To her surprise, the words hit their target. Vance's face twisted. "I swore to serve Calinor. Calinor is better off without a broken princess. You'll never see her again, and you will not stop me." Cruelty lit up his eyes. "But you *will* tell me who you're with and what you know."

Splinter straightened. Vance knew where Ash was. "I won't tell you—"

The arrow zoomed past her, a hair's breadth from her face, before it drilled itself into the tree behind her. The broadhead dug deep.

Vance pointed the second arrow straight at her. His voice grew impossibly soft. "Now."

She squeezed her sword tightly. She ducked to the side, away from the arrow's intended path. She let out a bloodcurdling scream—

And she charged at Vance.

CHAPTER
TWENTY-FOUR

ASH

"Did you mean it?"

Merewen crouched behind Ash. Dusk crept up on the camp, slivers of twilight crawling out of the forest.

Ash immediately stopped sawing at the rope tied around her ankle and hid the knife in her sleeve. She didn't have much time left, but she couldn't risk Merewen seeing what she was doing. "Did I mean what?"

"What you said to Aylin. Did you mean it?" Merewen's voice held a sense of urgency. She leaned in, like Ash's answer was important to her.

Ash frowned. "Yes. Obviously."

Merewen appeared in her line of sight. She was pale.

"Did you mean it when you said you'd introduce me to the palace mapmakers?"

"I guess that depends on whether you believe I'm the princess," Ash said uncharitably.

Merewen crouched near Ash's feet. "I don't know," she said. "I don't know who you are. I don't understand why the kingdom is so important to you. It's just an idea, and we're real people. But you stood up for me. No one ever has." She took out a small knife and started cutting through the rope.

Relief crashed over Ash. "You'll help me?"

"I don't want you to never see your family again," Merewen said. "I want you to be my cousin, but I don't want you to feel lost and small. I know how much that hurts." She bit her lip and kept her head down. Tension rolled down her shoulders.

"Wait." Ash held out the knife she had stolen. "It'll be easier if we work together."

Merewen stared wide-eyed at the blade, and then she laughed softly—if a little sadly. "Aylin?"

"He has a temper."

"He does sometimes."

"I meant what I said," Ash insisted, with a little more force this time. "I'm sorry I used you. Your maps were really good."

Merewen sniffed. She glanced toward her cousin and uncle before she resumed sawing at the rope. Ash joined in silently.

With their combined efforts, the rope around her ankle started to fray. The loops loosened. Ash wiggled her foot. The rope caught on her braces and the remaining knots tightened under the movement, but it was progress. Another handful of heartbeats later, the rope snapped, and Ash pulled her leg free. She rubbed at the raw, painful lines around her ankle.

At the campfire, Aylin complained loudly and Crispin stirred. "Merewen, Aylin needs your help with the meal."

"Coming! I'm just gathering . . ." Merewen's eyes grew wide, and she took in her surroundings. "Heartwort leaves for Aunt Enda. She likes them for her teas."

Crispin didn't notice her hesitation. He grunted. "Hurry, girl."

"Yes, uncle." Merewen helped Ash to her feet. Her voice dropped. "We won't have much of a head start."

"Do you know your way around these woods?" Ash wanted to know.

"A little," Merewen said. "Enough to get you back to the main road and to the soldiers at the border encampment."

"That's all I need." Ash took one last look at the

campfire, where Crispin and Aylin were arguing. After Vance, she didn't know how to trust anyone at the border encampment, but at least Splinter's brother would be there.

She held out her hands to Merewen. "Are you sure?" she asked.

Merewen nodded. She snatched Ash's cane from where it was leaning against the wagon, took her hand, and pulled Ash between the trees, away from the path, where the greens and browns turned a colder shade of blue. The last streaks of sunlight flamed across the darkening sky, and the glow from the fire slipped away.

Ash accepted her cane gratefully, and she squeezed Merewen's hand. "Run."

They ran.

The dim light of the campfire illuminated only the first brush through the undergrowth, before the shadows of trees began to tumble all over each other. Ash used her cane to find a steady path. Merewen pushed ahead without a care for branches and roots, angling away from the camp and the trails.

They tried to be careful, but it was too dark to be quiet.

"Merewen?" Crispin's voice echoed, following them.

Merewen hissed. "Come on." She kept running.

When Crispin called out again, it sounded fainter.

"Merewen? Stars, girl, where are you? Where—" In the distance, Ash could hear Crispin's string of curses. It reminded her of Byrne's blacksmith on the last day of the harvest festival, when he'd struck his thumb with his hammer. Nerves and fear bubbled up inside her, and she hiccuped a laugh.

Merewen frowned. "We have to keep going."

"I know." Ash pushed forward. The giggles dried up. "I'm . . . really scared."

The branches of a tree pulled at her hair and grabbed at her shoulders. The ground was uneven. Cold, hard roots made way for large patches of moss that were so soft it felt like running across mattresses. It hurt.

The last thing they heard was Crispin's roar. Then silence swallowed them, like the whole forest held its breath to see if Ash would make it out this time.

Ash was determined she would.

They followed a stretch of forest where the ground was rolling and uneven and thick bramble bushes had grown all around the trees, their thorny vines covering the forest floor.

Next came a patch of forest where the trees were spread wider apart, and the last light from the evening sky illuminated the way—and the girls.

When the trees grew closer once more, Ash stumbled, hands on her knees and gasping. "What . . . did he . . . do . . . ," she managed, "the first time . . . I escaped?"

She grasped at one of the tree trunks to steady herself. Twigs snapped under her grasp.

Merewen was equally out of breath. "He sent Aylin out to look for you. He didn't want to leave me alone. They'll take both horses now, to cover as much ground as they can."

Ash stretched her legs and winced at the pain that ran up her ankles and knees. Everything burned. "We'll have to be careful."

Merewen pointed at the tall, ancient trees ahead. "The main road isn't far. We can stay adjacent to it, but I don't want to get lost."

Ash nodded. She bit through the pain.

They continued. Ash winced at every snapping twig and every crunching step. They were so loud, and the woods around them had eyes everywhere.

A fox barked and Ash nearly jumped out of her skin. Merewen placed a hand on her arm. "The road should be right there," she whispered. She walked forward with a purpose, pushing bushes to the side—and then she stopped.

She took a step forward and brushed branches to the side, before she looked back at Ash.

Worry settled in Ash's stomach. She walked past Merewen and stared out between the branches. There were only more trees as far as she could see. The light that pushed through the treetops was pale, and it did nothing to show them the right direction. The stars weren't out yet.

"We could keep going," Merewen said without conviction. "Uncle Crispin told me about all the smugglers' paths . . ." Her voice trailed off as she tried to make sense of where they were. It was easy to get lost in the endless miles of forest.

It was dangerous. It was deadly.

But Ash would much rather be here than back in the camp, waiting for Vance to take her away. She wouldn't give up.

She strode forward, using her cane to steady herself. "We'll continue," she decided. "If we can't find the road, we wait until the stars are out and we use them for guidance." Like Sir Riven, she added silently.

She picked a tree in the distance and started walking toward it in a straight line, like an arrow slowly flying toward its target.

Then a scream echoed through the woods, and Ash's

heart missed a beat. She *knew* that voice.

It couldn't be—

It had to be—

Without explaining what she was doing, she started running in the direction the scream had come from. Merewen called out, but Ash barely heard her. She stumbled forward, caught her footing, and shouted, "Come on! We have to go!"

Other sounds flooded toward them. The sharp clanging of metal on metal. The creaking of leather armor. The soft, restless whinnying of a horse.

And a tall knight grunting, "You are brave, I'll grant you that. What a waste of courage."

Ash recognized Vance's voice and derision.

She caught flashes of him through the branches and leaves. He'd discarded his colorful overcoat for a more sensible cloak. One that would mask him better on his intended trip across the mountains.

She couldn't make out his opponent, but Vance lifted his sword above his head and brought it down hard, knocking his opponent's sword to the side.

And everything happened at once.

Merewen grabbed at Ash's arm, but Ash pulled herself free, crashing through the thicket.

Her cane flew out of her hands and she landed on her hands and knees, as Splinter, lying on the ground, kicked at Vance.

Ash drew breath to call out—

Vance brought his sword down a second time. This time, the blade didn't tangle with Splinter's sword. Instead, the sword cut into her, like the leather armor offered no resistance at all, and he cut down deep.

Ash screamed.

Vance withdrew the blade. Blood poured from the cut to Splinter's shoulder. She curled up in pain. Vance whirled around and sneered when he saw Ash. *"You."* He spat on the ground. "You troublesome little girl." He adjusted his grip on his blade and advanced on her.

Ash crawled backward.

Merewen wrapped her arms around Ash's torso and heaved her upright. "Ash, come on. We have to run!"

But Vance burst through the bushes and grabbed Merewen by the arm. He lifted her up as if she weighed nothing.

He tossed her to the side.

Merewen crashed into a tree and slumped down to the moss.

Ash backed away. She took the knife she'd stolen from

Aylin and held it out in front of her, but she wished she had a bow and arrow. Or better yet, Splinter by her side and a squadron of knights at her back.

Vance laughed derisively. He opened his arms wide, as if to invite her to attack. "You think you can win against me? Come on, try your best."

Ash gripped the knife tighter but kept backing away, careful where she placed her feet.

"You're as much a coward as your mother is," Vance taunted.

"No." A voice rang from the clearing. "She doesn't have to fight you. I will."

Ash's heart soared.

Splinter stood between the trees, sword in hand. She was pale and bloody, but her eyes were blazing.

She stared past Vance to Ash, grinning wildly. "I know you dropped your cane again, but you're going to have to find it yourself. I'm a little busy."

Splinter attacked.

She fought like no one could stop her. She drew Vance back into the clearing, taunting him and attacking him, and as soon as they were out of sight, Ash ran to Merewen.

She crouched down next to the girl. When Ash pushed

her hair out of her face, Merewen moaned, but her eyes fluttered open.

Ash bit her lip. "Are you okay?"

"Hurts," Merewen groaned. With Ash's aid, she struggled to a sitting position, and she managed the faintest of smiles. "Go. Help your friend."

Ash squeezed her hand. "Wait here for me. I'll be back."

She got to her feet and then bent down again, gathering up a bunch of gnarled sticks from the foot of the tree. She rushed to the clearing as fast as she dared.

In the clearing, Splinter faced off against Vance. She swayed and stumbled. Her shoulder wound bled heavily, but she didn't let the knight get close enough to score another hit against her. And she kept slashing at him like she was some kind of whirlwind.

Ash retrieved her cane. Standing taller and prouder, she flung the branches at Vance.

One bounced off his breastplate, surprising enough that he flinched and fumbled his attack. Splinter stepped in, and her sword tore open a cut along his left forearm.

Another branch caught him against the side of the head.

A third glanced off his knee.

Vance spun toward Ash and snarled at her, but for the

first time she saw doubt flicker across his face.

He caught Splinter's wild swing right before her sword would have cut into his calf.

With a growl of rage, he pushed her back. "Little fake squire. There'll never be a place for you in our Calinor."

Splinter gasped. "Calinor isn't yours. It belongs to all of us."

Vance's expression twisted into one of utter disgust. He began to attack furiously from overhead, and Splinter was clearly tiring. She was swaying, blood dripping down one hand, and Ash realized Splinter couldn't beat him on her own. But they could beat him together.

With no branches left, Ash took her knife, fixed her eyes on Vance, and *threw*.

The blade sliced into his shirt. Splinter grinned dangerously and redoubled her attack. She went all in, ducking under Vance's defense, feinting to one side, then attacking on the other, jumping back and forth. She was constantly moving, constantly trying to keep him on his toes.

Ash grabbed her cane and crept closer. As soon as she was within range, she locked eyes with Splinter and nodded. Splinter dropped her guard slightly, baiting Vance to lunge at her. And with all her strength and all her desperation,

Ash slammed the end of her cane into the back of Vance's knee.

She felt the resounding snap.

Vance cried out.

He slammed forward, his knees hitting the ground and his sword digging deep into the dirt.

Splinter leapt out of the way. Before Vance could recover, she reversed the grip on her sword and brought the pommel down on the knight's head. The crack of the impact made Ash shudder.

Vance toppled forward like a felled tree and stilled.

Splinter ran.

Ash clung to her cane. But the fear and worry of the past few days crashed over her like waves, and she sagged down on the ground. Her breath came in small gasps. Her vision blurred.

"Splinter?"

Splinter appeared at the edge of her vision, the reins of a horse in her hands. She grabbed Vance by his arms and dragged him to the nearest tree. With quiet determination and bloody hands, she tied him to the tree and used the remainder of the reins to bind his wrists together. "I want him to face justice," she said tightly.

Ash wiped at her eyes, and she smiled. "You saved me."

"You saved me," Splinter countered.

"I think," Ash said, "we saved each other. We make a fearsome team, don't you think?"

Splinter secured the last knot in Vance's ties. She smiled. And then she flung herself at Ash. "Always."

CHAPTER TWENTY-FIVE

SPLINTER

Splinter's stories tumbled all over each other, with everything she wanted to say and everything she wanted to tell Ash. She didn't know where to start, except "I never got your message. I would have been there, but I never got it."

And "Lucen helped. He was with me every step of the way."

And "Are you okay? Did they hurt you?"

And *"Ow."* In the rush of the fight and the joy of finding Ash, she'd forgotten about her own wound. But the memory of the sword stabbing through armor and muscle came back to her now, along with the pain.

"You fool," Ash said gently. She guided Splinter to a tree trunk where she could sit without the world twisting and spinning around her. "When I asked you to be my squire, I hoped you'd be my friend. You have plenty of time to be a hero of the kingdom later."

She used the small knife to cut into her own shirt, and she tore ribbons from the fabric. Confidently, she tied them around Splinter's shoulder, pressing down on the wound to stop the bleeding. "It's a good thing Aunt Jonet taught me how to wrap bandages, but you're going to need a physician."

The pain made Splinter's head feel fuzzy, and Ash's words took a moment to register. "I *am* your friend," she said softly, and then a little louder. "I am your friend." Even if she couldn't be Ash's squire, that would never change.

"You're my home," Ash replied. "Can you move your hand?"

Splinter flexed the fingers of her shield hand, but now that she wasn't in the middle of a fight, it hurt deeply. "I'd rather not," she admitted.

Ash scanned the clearing. She tilted her head as though she was listening for something. "We have to get out of here. All of us," she muttered.

"Biscuit is tied up back there," Splinter pointed with her good arm. "My horse. Take her to the encampment and get help. I'll stand guard over Va—"

She looked past Ash at the bound knight, and her words turned to dust. *"No."*

Vance had come to. He'd pulled his knees to his chest, and in spite of his bound hands, he'd reached for a slender dagger in one of his boots. His mouth twisted into a slow smirk. "All hail the Larks."

He aimed to throw—

In the blink of an eye, Splinter surged upward and *shoved* Ash out of the way—

And at the same time, from behind her, something *zoomed* past them both.

With a dull sound, Vance's dagger fell to the forest floor. The bound knight slumped, an arrow through his throat.

Splinter spun and found two figures running toward them through the trees. Anders, with his sword in one hand and a lantern in the other. And Lucen, holding on to his bow. They were both ghostly in the starlight. Lucen stared past Splinter toward the man he'd shot, and Anders just stared at her.

Next to Splinter, Ash coughed. Splinter's shove had sent her sprawling, and she struggled to stand up. "Splinter? How did he—what happened?"

"Ash." Splinter helped her to her feet. Her shoulder protested the movement. "Look."

Ash turned too. Her eyes flicked over to her brother, who stood still, bow in hand. He seemed rooted to the spot, as if the two sides of Lucen were at war with each other.

Then he ran to Ash, and his voice cracked. "You're *safe*."

In that moment, Splinter couldn't help but notice how much Ash resembled her older brother. The same messy brown hair, made messier by the past week's events. The same bushy eyebrows that arced down when they raised their defenses. The same lanky tension. "You shot him," Ash said, like she couldn't quite believe it.

Lucen kept an arm's-length distance. "He would have killed you. And Splinter too."

Ash reached out a hand to him, slowly. "All that for an interloper in the palace? A fake princess?"

Lucen's expression twisted in pain. "Stars, Ash, I'm so sorry. You're my sister. I will always—"

The rest of the words were muffled when Ash closed the distance between them and hugged her brother hard. There was still much to overcome, but this reunion, at least, was a whole lot better than the first.

Splinter glanced at her own brother.

Anders kept his distance like a guard, his sword in hand. When he caught Splinter looking, he tentatively took a step toward her, but she held her hand on her sword. Despite the fact that he was a full knight and she wasn't even a squire, he stopped. His shoulders slumped, and it was clear he didn't know what to say to her, except "You're hurt. You need a physician for that shoulder."

Behind her, Ash spoke up. "You do. We need to get to the encampment. Before these woods grow darker and none of us knows where we're going."

Splinter wasn't planning on just riding along with Anders yet.

"How did you know to come here?" she demanded.

"We followed you," Anders said.

Lucen pulled at his ear and grinned self-consciously. "Your brother caught me almost immediately, and when he heard that you were trailing Vance, he insisted on following you."

"Why?"

A shadow crossed over Anders's face. "Because I know from years of being his friend *and* working with him just how dangerous he is."

"So you *were* working with him." A pit opened up in Splinter's stomach. The confirmation hurt worse than the sword wound to her shoulder, and all that pain seeped into her voice. "I looked up to you."

"Splinter . . . ," Lucen started. Splinter didn't listen.

Ash came to stand beside her and took in the situation. She rounded on Anders, like a warrior princess with a fearsome grudge. She jabbed her cane in his direction. "You were involved in my kidnapping, Sir Anders?"

Anders dropped to a knee. "Your highness, *no*. If I'd known Vance was responsible for your kidnapping, I would've done everything in my power to stop him. I never thought he'd go to such extreme lengths."

Splinter started forward, but Lucen put a hand on her shoulder. "Let him talk."

Anders continued, "Vance is part of a network of powerful nobles, intending to dethrone the queen." He briefly glanced in the direction of Splinter and Lucen. "He *was* one of the Larks, you were right about that. I saw how he fell for their craven lies. This was his attempt to prove himself to them. He wanted to strengthen his own position and destabilize the crown at the same time. It was brazen and cowardly."

"He meant to trade me to the empire for favors," Ash said flatly. "He was convinced that once Calinor fell, the empire would restore the nobility to its former glory."

"I swear I didn't know." Anders took a deep breath. "The empire invests in the Larks. They have everything to gain by us fighting our own. But Vance was a fool if he thought he could trust them." Anguish colored his voice. "The Larks turned my best friend into someone I barely recognized. Someone angry at everyone and everything. Someone willing to choose his enemies over his friends. But he still trusted me, which made it easy for me to get close to him. It's why I was ordered to let him pull me in too."

"You were ordered?" Splinter's voice cracked. Something like hope surged through her.

Lucen squeezed her shoulder.

Anders smiled wryly. "You nearly gave me a heart attack, showing up like you did. It hurt to let you believe I'd betrayed you, but I couldn't risk Vance doubting me."

"How do I know you're not just saying that?"

Anders met Splinter's gaze. "A year and a half ago, I was in Haven to speak with the queen. She ordered me—and others—to investigate the Larks. She told me she needed proof before she could accuse noble families of treason. Ask her. Take me to any star temple and I'll swear to it."

The words sounded true, but she could only focus on one thing Anders said. "You were in Haven and you didn't come see me?"

"I'm sorry." Anders grimaced. "I didn't know if I could trust Uncle Elias. I still don't."

Splinter considered that. "You think he might be a Lark as well?"

"He's never been one for change—or compassion."

Splinter nodded slowly. It made sense. She *wanted* to be able to trust Anders.

"I believe him," Lucen said clearly, and Ash added her voice to his. "I do too."

Splinter continued to study her brother.

He didn't try to convince her, he just sat on his heels and waited for her to make up her mind. He wore the same expression their mother had perfected. Patient, inquisitive, gentle. Achingly familiar. And for all the ways in which Anders might be a stranger to her, Splinter knew in her bones he'd listen to her and accept whatever she decided.

She made up her mind. "Me too."

Anders sagged in relief. "Thank you."

Splinter scowled. "But I am angry with you for not coming to visit while you were in Haven."

Anders held out his arms to her. "You have every right to be angry. But I couldn't bear to disappoint you."

Splinter ran to him and hugged her brother tightly. "Never," she whispered. "I missed you."

He ran a hand through her hair and held her close. "Stars, I missed you too."

From the corner of her eye, Splinter saw Ash walk over to Lucen. She held out a hand to him. "I want to go home," she said. "But first I want you to meet someone."

Splinter frowned at her friend. "Do you want me to come with you?"

"No." Ash shook her head. "Not this time. You and Sir Anders figure out how we can get out of here."

Splinter didn't like it. As far as she was concerned, she wasn't going to let Ash out of her sight ever again. But Ash would tell her story in her own time. "Shout if you need something. We'll be right there."

"Don't worry," Lucen said. "I'll protect her."

"See that you do," Splinter told him.

Lucen tensed. Then his expression softened, and he laughed.

Ash observed the two of them with a curious smile before she tugged at her brother's hand and pulled him into the tree line. "Come on, I don't need protection."

Splinter watched her disappear from sight and wondered who it was Ash wanted to introduce to Lucen . . . and why not to her. A tiny voice wondered if she'd still have a place if Ash and Lucen learned to get along again and she couldn't be a squire anymore, but she quickly told that voice to be quiet.

"He told me that you're a loyal friend to both of them," Anders said softly. He crouched down next to Vance's body and ran his hands over his clothes, checking for pockets and hidden compartments. He pulled a chain from Vance's neck and a ring from his finger. "Mom would be proud of you too, little spark."

The words squeezed Splinter's heart. She hadn't heard that nickname since their mother died. "I hope so. Did Lucen tell you what happened at the palace?"

"He told me enough," Anders said. He placed a purse and a bundle of letters next to Vance's body before he focused intently on his sibling. "Why do you want to be a knight, Splinter?"

It was the same question Ash had asked her the night they met. It was the same question Lucen had asked the night they ran away from the palace.

She didn't have to think about the answer. She sat down in front of her brother and raised her chin. "I wore your squire armor to Ash's party. I'm sorry, I hope you don't mind. I thought I wanted to be like you, but I felt like *me*. And I felt *happy*."

Anders nodded and listened.

"Mama taught us that Calinor is a place worth fighting for. That as long as we believe in it, the kingdom is what we make of it, together." She glanced at Vance's body. "I want to believe it's a place where everyone is welcomed, where everyone can belong, and where everyone is allowed to feel that happy too."

"I don't presume to know what will happen when you return to the palace, but I do know this." Anders's mouth pulled up into a crooked, proud smile. "Calinor is a better place for having you in it. You are kind, you are loyal to your friends, and you stand up against bullies. That is knightly. There are a thousand ways of being a hero, and carrying a sword is by far the easiest one. You have the heart of a knight. You need no oaths for that, you need no sword to prove it, and no court can ever take it away. I know you will serve Calinor well. And I will have your back, always."

Splinter blinked away the moisture that gathered in the corners of her eyes. "Will you come home with us?"

She knew his answer, even before Anders shook his head. "I'm sorry, spark. I have my duty. Vance isn't the only Lark hiding out at the border. And Haven—Haven isn't my home, the way it is yours. I belong *here*."

Splinter wanted to argue but found she couldn't. She didn't have to like it, but she understood it. Maybe some of that showed, because Anders reached out and squeezed her good arm tightly.

"But I promise I'll write," he said. "I promise I'll come visit you. If you ever need me, I'll be there."

Splinter squeezed back, took a deep breath, and then she smiled. "And if you ever need me, I'll be there too."

CHAPTER TWENTY-SIX

ASH

"Merewen?"

Ash returned to the spot where she had left the girl to find it empty, and she frowned. She crouched down next to where Merewen had rested against the tree.

"Who are you looking for?" Lucen asked quietly.

It was odd to be around her brother. Ash braced for Lucen to lash out at her. It would take time and trust before that disappeared.

But he was here. And he was her brother. He deserved a chance.

It was one of the reasons she wanted him with her now. To share something with him. "The girl who helped me escape."

Lucen knelt next to the tree, running his fingers over broken twigs and moss. "One of the people who kidnapped you?"

"Yes." Ash retraced her steps and tried not to sound defensive. "She changed her mind to help me. It was a brave thing to do."

"It was." Lucen drew breath, as if he wanted to say more. He settled for, "I think she went this way." He pushed through the bushes.

"Merewen?" Ash called out softly, following him. "You can come out now."

Merewen.

Merewen.

Merewen.

Ash kept her voice low, but the name bounced off the trees and echoed through the woods.

In the distance were others. Crispin. Aylin.

Lucen tensed and drew his sword. Ash felt the ghost of the ties around her wrists and ankle. Vance hadn't shown up at the camp. They must have thought they had time. What if they found her now?

"We have to go," she whispered to Lucen. If they went back to the clearing, if she took Vance's sword, they'd be four against two.

"Wait." The bushes to their right rustled, and a slender figure stepped out, hands raised.

Lucen immediately jumped in front of Ash, but she pushed him aside. "Lucen, it's fine."

Merewen walked closer. She moved cautiously, like she was in pain.

"I'll go back to them," she said.

Ash shook her head, confused. "You don't have to. I promised to help you."

Merewen sized Lucen up before she turned to Ash. "I saw you with your friends. You were happy. I didn't get it before. I don't belong in your world."

"You could," Ash said. "You could have your own friends. I will find you a spot with the mapmakers in Haven. They will help you fulfill your dreams. You deserve someone who believes in you."

"I won't be home in Haven." Merewen smiled sadly. "Uncle Crispin and Aylin are the only family I have left. You have to be with . . . with yours." The words took effort, and the way Merewen glanced through her lashes at Ash, she clearly still believed the story Vance had told. But she didn't press on.

She took a step back toward the trees.

"Wait." Ash noticed the pouch on Lucen's belt, and she

elbowed him. She held out her hand. "Give me your purse."

The Lucen who'd not so kindly welcomed her home at midwinter would have laughed at her and scorned her request. This Lucen looked thoughtful. He unhooked it.

"Take this," Ash said, holding it out to Merewen. "Make sure you have food for the next winter and a roof over your head."

Merewen didn't reach for it. "Will you send the guard after Uncle Crispin and Aylin? After . . . us?"

Ash felt Lucen's eyes on her.

She considered it. They deserved to face justice for abducting her and making her believe she'd never see her home again.

But they'd been lied to by Vance too.

"They're criminals and smugglers and traitors," Ash said honestly, and Merewen shrank. "But I don't want you to never see your family again either. I want us both to go home."

They heard Crispin call out again, his voice closer now. "Merewen!"

"Will they be angry with you?" Ash worried.

"Probably," Merewen said. "But Uncle won't hurt me, if that's what you mean. He would never."

Ash looked down at her hands. They bore the bruises

and aches from her first escape attempt, but Merewen had tended them well. She slipped off one of the supports, followed by a slender silver ring with vines circling around each other and around a small blue stone. Aunt Jonet had given it to her on her eleventh birthday. She held that out to Merewen too. "If you ever change your mind about the royal mapmakers, come find me. This should be enough to give you access, or at least pay for the journey."

"Merewen!"

Merewen took a deep, shuddering breath. Then she took the coin purse and the ring both, with the speed of a hungry bird seizing the last crust of bread. She threaded the ring through her leather necklace and pocketed the purse before she threw her arms around Ash and held her. "Thank you."

Ash didn't know what else to do but to pat her back.

"I wish we could have been cousins," Merewen whispered. Then, as quickly as she hugged Ash, she let go again, and disappeared between the trees.

Ash stood, arms flopping back to her sides, until she couldn't see Merewen's outline anymore, until the crunching of footsteps was so distant it mingled with the regular nighttime sounds of the woods.

"Merewen!"

"Uncle! I'm here!"

"Blasted girl!"

The voices came from separate directions, and they were enough to shake Ash. She spun back toward Lucen, who held a thousand questions in his eyes. "We have to go back to Sir Anders and Splinter," she said.

"Cousins?" Lucen demanded incredulously.

Ash grinned weakly. "Long story."

"*Cousins,*" he repeated.

"*Lucen.* Please."

"Ash." He kept his sword at the ready and his eyes on the trees around them. The evening's exertions made the dusting of freckles across his snub nose starkly stand out. "Are you sure you're okay?"

"No." She wasn't. She was exhausted and overwhelmed and she wanted to cry. She began to pull her brother back toward the clearing. "I want to go home. And I'm glad you came for me. I thought you might . . . prefer being rid of me."

"Never," Lucen snapped, but he blushed. He took the heavy words and held them. "Splinter told me you told her about Sir Riven."

Ash nodded.

"I didn't think you'd remembered."

"Of course I did." She bristled.

"I didn't," he admitted. "I told myself it was just a story and the only thing that mattered was to be strong. Like Mama. And Uncle Lam. I know you don't trust me. I know I'm not the prince or the brother I should be. But when we're home, I'll try, I promise. I'll learn to be better."

Ash liked this side of her brother, the considerate side. One who didn't just use his words to hurt but to mend.

She spotted the necklace he wore, and she smiled. She tugged at Lucen's tunic and slipped her arm through his, leaning on him. "Let's go home."

The two sets of siblings watched the sun rise from the edge of the woods. Anders decided it was too risky to travel far at night. So Splinter and Ash slept bundled up in cloaks on the hard forest floor, while Anders and Lucen stood guard, talking with each other.

In the early hours of the morning, Ash woke to find Splinter staring at her, her wounded arm cradled to her chest.

"Creepy," Ash muttered.

Splinter grinned. "I want to make sure you're still here."

"I am," Ash said, curling up on her side so she could face her friend fully. Splinter's face was illuminated by the soft blues and pinks of predawn.

"Good."

Ash remembered the first time she'd shown Splinter the secret passages of the palace. The night when she'd thought the scariest thing about treason was that she couldn't trust the girls who were friendly to her. Now here they were, in the middle of an endless forest, and she wasn't sure if she could trust *anyone* outside of the three people with her. And strangely, she felt safer. "I'm glad you're here with me."

Splinter propped her head up on her good arm. "Me too."

"I can't believe you and my brother worked together without punching each other."

A blush rushed to Splinter's cheeks. "It wasn't entirely without punching each other." She sobered. "I'll tell you on the way home. Will you tell me about what happened to you too?"

She was obviously curious, but she let Ash decide. Like she wouldn't have to tell the story a thousand times over when she was home. Like court wouldn't demand those answers. And Ash was grateful for it.

"On the way back." Most of it, anyway. About Vance and the smugglers. About the girl who dreamed of becoming a mapmaker. Not about Talwin, who may or may not have been a lie. She wanted—needed—to talk with her mother about that first. If she could find the right words.

Splinter sat up, cross-legged, and leaned in close. In doing so, she snatched up one of the cloaks, and Ash unsuccessfully tried to get it back. "When Lord Lambelin talked about spies at court, I thought it'd be one or two people sneaking around and stealing information. Not a whole entire web of traitors. Can you imagine?"

Before they'd gone to sleep, Splinter and Lucen had told Ash all they knew about the Larks, while Anders filled in the blanks. The society of discontented nobles that had its roots in Haven had spread toward the border and the encampment in the mountains. There were two shadowy leaders in charge, but no one knew who they were.

"They didn't sanction Vance's plan," Anders told them. "He told me after you found me. He said he wanted to impress them, so that no one would underestimate him ever again."

The idea that there were other rogue knights running around feeling like they could do ridiculous things to prove their worth scared Ash.

"At least we have his body as tangible evidence," she'd said. "Maybe we can start to unravel their web."

"There won't be a body," Anders had said apologetically.

"I'll make sure of that. Forgive me, but it's the only way to convince them I'm still on their side." Until the Larks could be unmasked, Anders needed to stay where he was, to get as deep into the organization as possible.

"Without a body, without a way to prove it's them, they'll claim a victory." Lucen had sounded pensive.

"They'll tell anyone who's doubting their capabilities that they managed to infiltrate the palace and abduct a princess," Anders had conceded. "They'll say the queen couldn't even protect her own family."

"So it doesn't matter whether they succeed or fail, they win?" Splinter had pulled her knees to her chest and stared up at the stars between the treetops. "That's not fair."

"It isn't." Anders had pulled his sibling close and held her tight. "They prey on people's fear and anger, and they tell them what they want to hear. But they won't always win. We have the truth on our side, and we have each other."

"I'd rather fight with swords," she'd said mulishly.

Anders had ruffled Splinter's hair, which had earned him a glare.

Ash had nibbled on her bottom lip. "What do we do, Sir Anders?" she'd asked. "The queen can send knights to the mountains to defend the border, but how do we fight fear?"

"I don't know if we can fight it," he'd admitted. "But I swore an oath to protect Calinor. And someone very clever reminded me that the kingdom should be a place where everyone is welcome and everyone can belong. So we stand together and hold the line."

Ash wasn't sure yet how to do that. It was just the four of them against powerful and ruthless nobles. If the past week had taught her anything, it was that she knew far less about Calinor and her own family than she'd believed. If she wanted to protect Calinor and her friends, she needed to learn.

She wanted be a princess who understood all the secrets of the kingdom, so that they'd all be safe. Everyone, like Sir Anders had said, who wanted to call Calinor home.

Including the people they misjudged.

"Poor Mist and Hazel," Ash said now. "I hate thinking that we accused their father unfairly when he tried to investigate the Larks."

"Do you think someone thought Lord Maronne was getting too close, and they planted evidence against him?" Splinter wondered. "Or maybe that's what the Larks want. For us to be afraid of each other."

"Uncle Lam will be furious when he finds out."

"It's hard to think Uncle Elias might be a part of it,"

Splinter said. She tugged at the bandage that Anders had wrapped around her shoulder. The wound was clean but still a little bloody. "I thought he was just plain horrible."

"He can be both." Ash wrapped the remainder of the cloaks around her. To her left, Lucen stared out at the mountains, yawning. Anders stood quietly next to him. "The important thing is, your brother isn't. And you're not."

Splinter grabbed Ash's hand, and squeezed it. Her hands were comfortably warm. "Never. Never, never."

"Ever?" Ash teased.

"Ever."

Ash smiled.

Around them, the woods grew brighter, the pinks and oranges of the morning edging across the mountains and streaming toward the trees. From his saddlebags, Anders produced a leather pouch with hard cheese, another with travel biscuits, and a small silver spice container with salt and dried herbs. "We all ride out with standard rations," he explained when he spotted Splinter and Ash awake. "It's not much by way of breakfast, but it's better than nothing."

Ash stretched. "Thank you."

Splinter refilled the waterskins at a nearby stream. When she got back, she took the cloak she'd worn and placed it on the ground like a picnic blanket. She picked up her sword to go through one of her patterns, but after one set she dropped it, rubbing ruefully at her shoulder.

Lucen cast one last glance at the mountains before joining the three of them. From one of his pockets, inexplicably, he produced a small paper bag with pieces of crumbly honey biscuits to add to the collection. "Here."

"How . . . ," Splinter started. She shook her head. "Never mind."

"It's tastier than travel rations," Lucen said. "Right, Sir Anders?"

The knight accepted the bag with a nod and a wink.

Ash wondered what Anders and Lucen had talked about throughout the night after she and Splinter had gone to sleep. They'd kept their voices down, but her brother was calmer around Sir Anders. She hoped that once they were back in the palace, Lucen would remember this. That he'd still be happy to have her home.

"Once we're out of these woods, I can't be seen with you," Anders said regretfully, preparing food for all three of them with quiet intensity, like it was as important a mission as fighting in the mountains or spying on traitors. "Not if I want to protect my cover story. So you'll have to ride on ahead to the encampment and ask for General

Gideon. He's trustworthy. He'll provide you with aid and an escort back to Haven. But you can't tell him about me."

"No one will know what happened here," Lucen promised.

"Your mother can know," Anders allowed with a smile. "But only her." He produced the letters he had taken from Vance and tapped them against the palm of his hand. "I'll send word to the queen if I find anything of interest here. I'll do what I must to protect you. I always will."

He locked eyes with Splinter. "All three of you."

Ash nodded royally before she grinned. "Thank you, Sir Anders."

"Thank you," Lucen said quietly.

As he shared breakfast with all of them, Anders shook off the nerves that settled around him. "You'll have to protect each other too, like you've done so far. Stand by one another, and it will be easier to face whatever the empire or the Larks throw at you. Promise me that you will."

"We will," Splinter said immediately.

"We will," Lucen echoed, a heartbeat later.

While the sun rose and cast the Heartian Woods in vibrant greens and reds, Ash looked at her best friend and her brother with conviction. She trusted no one more than the two of them, and even though the world felt more dangerous now, and even if this was only the start, she knew Sir Anders was right.

Together, they would face whatever came next. "We will."

EPILOGUE

A week later, most everything was back to normal, and nothing was.

Ash and Lucen's return to the palace had been met with shock and relief. The official story was not so different from the truth; it just omitted a few details. According to the tale that spread around Haven, the princess had been taken by rogue guards, working for the Ferisian Empire. While she tried to escape her captors, the crown prince had traveled across the kingdom to find his sister, and the brave soldiers who were stationed in the mountains had helped to bring them all back home.

No one mentioned the not-quite squire. No one mentioned the Larks.

Once upon a time, there was a crafty princess and a brave crown prince, and they lived happily ever after.

Queen Aveline knew differently, of course, because she'd gathered her children in her arms upon their return, and the story had spilled out of Ash and Lucen as soon as they got to the throne room, like melting snow rushing down the mountain caps. Outside of the two sets of siblings, she was the only one who knew the whole story. Lord Lambelin had been away from the palace, investigating the Maronne household.

With her heart in her throat, Splinter had watched how the queen reacted to Ash's mention of her brother, and she breathed a sigh of relief when Queen Aveline confirmed Anders's story. The queen had smiled at Splinter. "Evana's children always serve the crown well."

When it came to Vance and the Larks, Queen Aveline had agreed with Anders's assessment. "Without evidence of Vance's involvement, the only people we can successfully tie to this treason are the smugglers who stole Ash from the palace."

Ash had refused to name them, despite the queen's insistence. There was a shadow in her eyes and a story she hadn't told yet.

"We failed the Maronnes," Lucen said. "We were wrong about them."

"Yes," the queen acknowledged. "We were. And we'll get to the bottom of that."

Right at that moment, Lord Lambelin had come bursting in, out of breath and wide-eyed. In an uncharacteristic display of relief and gratitude, he'd embraced both Lucen and Ash and held them close. When the queen informed him it had been Vance Labanne and not Lord Maronne who had been the spy inside the palace, a whole range of emotions flitted across his face. "We shall release Lord and Lady Maronne immediately. And I'll send my guards to find the disgraced knight captain, though I imagine he fled to the empire as soon as his plan failed."

"I killed him," Lucen said flatly. "And when General Gideon at the border encampment sent soldiers to retrieve his body, it was gone."

Lord Lambelin frowned thoughtfully. "We'll talk to his parents and uncover what drove him to side with the Ferisians. Vance Labanne was an honorable man once. Something happened. Someone must have influenced him." He shared a knowing look with Queen Aveline, and Splinter rolled her eyes.

Lucen, on the other side of the dais, smirked. The guard commander couldn't begin to fathom what they knew about the Larks.

"He helped one of the smugglers get a position within the guard," Ash said. "That's how they got to me. With a fake guard and a hidden passage none of us knew about. I know where it is."

The queen shuddered.

"It won't happen again." Lambelin raised his fist to his heart in salute. "I will see to it that passage is blocked, your majesty. And I'll investigate and vouch for every single one of the guards personally."

"That won't be necessary—" the queen started.

Lambelin shook his head. "It is. I want you to feel safe. All of you."

So it was decided. The Maronnes would be freed with apologies from the crown, the guard would be investigated, and the palace would be made secure once more.

Despite that, Splinter was sure the Larks would find new ways of creating chaos in Haven and in Calinor.

Of course, neither the queen nor Lord Lambelin were thrilled with Lucen sneaking out to go find his sister— or with Splinter for aiding him—but they couldn't fault either of them, since they'd both promised to protect the princess. Lambelin insisted they leave the investigating to the adults, next time.

Splinter and Ash had shared a look and a smile.

Unfortunately, despite recognizing her brave acts, the queen couldn't do anything about Splinter's dismissal as squire. It was a decision the master of squires had made, she explained to Ash and Splinter, and she trusted his judgment. She couldn't overrule him, because to do so would be an abuse of her power.

"I'm sorry," she told Splinter. "I know this is your dream, but I'll find another way for you to stay close to Ash. I won't break up your friendship, and I won't send you back to your uncle."

Five days later, Splinter was still waiting to hear the queen's solution. She'd been cooped up in Ash's rooms. The royal physicians had examined her shoulder and had deemed the work done at the border at best acceptable. They'd changed the poultice and rebandaged it, giving Splinter strict instructions not to work her arm too hard until the wound healed. No sword exercises and no joining Ash on the archery lanes for practice.

"Not that I need sword exercises if I'm not allowed to be a squire anymore," Splinter grumbled. She flopped onto the bed. Ash, sitting at the desk writing a letter to Mist and Hazel, shook her head. "Just be patient."

A slender black-and-brown cat Ash said had come

from the palace gardens lay curled up on her lap.

"I'm not good at being patient." Splinter rested her chin in her hand. "How's the letter coming along?"

Ash winced. "I would rather talk to them, but they don't want to see me." All her invitations had been returned unopened. Ash didn't blame them, but Splinter knew that she felt terrible.

"I'm sorry," she said, not for the first time. She had never intended to break their friendship.

"I thought the hardest part would be making friends," Ash admitted. "Losing friends is much harder."

Word around Haven was that the Maronnes were planning to leave the city for the coast, to leave all the cruel and hurtful whispers behind. Splinter couldn't blame them.

Ash focused on the letter again, nibbling on the pen that left ink blotches all across her hands and face. She'd been quieter since their return. She'd asked the palace scribes for books about the royal family's history and pored over them at night. She'd told Splinter she wanted to spend more time in Haven, to get to know the city better. "I don't know enough about Calinor at all."

Splinter had promised to go with her, as soon as the palace physicians gave her the all clear. "Lord Lambelin will want to send the guard with us too."

Ash had hummed noncommittally. "We could go to the floating docks and ask one of the captains to show me their ship."

"We'll eat candied berries and sugar crowns until we're sick."

"Do you think we can find all the secret corners of Haven?"

Splinter had grinned. "I think Camille can help with that."

"Perfect."

Splinter grabbed the small whittling knife on the desk. She'd found the wooden doll she'd stolen in the encampment in her bags, and over the past few days, she'd focused on finishing it to keep herself distracted. She'd garnered cuts and nicks in the process, and she wasn't *good* at it, but the doll was looking more like something she could display and not like something that would haunt her dreams.

She was carving out a leg when someone knocked on the door. At the threshold, she found the same page who'd failed to deliver Ash's note to her the day she got kidnapped.

He blushed. "Splinter?"

"What do you want?"

He produced a thin note. "You're to report to the master of squires."

Splinter's heart skipped a beat. "When? Why?"

The page shrugged. "Right now."

Behind her, Ash had placed her letter to the side, and she held out a freshly washed silver tunic to Splinter. Ash's face was carefully neutral, but nerves bounced around in Splinter's stomach. "Do you know what this is about?"

"I know you shouldn't keep him waiting."

"Ash . . ."

The corner of Ash's mouth twitched into a half-hidden smile. "Go."

Splinter snatched the tunic out of Ash's hands and ran back to her own room, changing from a wrinkled shirt into formal clothes. She ran her hands through her hair, trying to create a semblance of order. Then she dashed past Ash, past the befuddled page, and through the mazelike halls of the palace.

After they got back, Ash had shown her the tunnel her kidnappers had used, now heavily guarded. They'd wandered the rest of the palace together, because Splinter hated being confined to her quarters and they both needed to get used to being here again.

As she ran through the halls now, the familiar smells and sights were a comfort. Splinter swerved to avoid a scribe with her arms full of books, and when she turned to the master of squires's office, she nearly collided headfirst with Ilsar, who was pacing back and forth in the hallway. Behind him—to Splinter's surprise—was Lucen, his arms crossed and leaning against the wall.

"Oh, look. If it isn't the princess's failed squire." Ilsar checked her with his shoulder. "Go away. You don't deserve to be here."

"Ilsar." Lucen's voice snapped like a whip. "Be quiet."

Ilsar's eyes bulged and his mouth dropped open. Splinter bit her lip to keep from grinning.

Lucen offered her a hesitant smile. They hadn't seen much of each other since their return. Lucen had returned to the other squires, and Splinter had become increasingly convinced that the boy she had traveled with was nothing more than a star shade.

Maybe she'd been wrong.

The door opened, and Lord Brenet, master of squires, appeared in the opening. He nodded at Splinter and Lucen and turned his chair back to his desk, obviously expecting them to follow. Splinter slipped in first, with Lucen closing the door behind them.

At the desk, Lord Brenet leaned forward, his expression unreadable.

Spring showers pattered against the window. A lantern sat on the windowsill, and a pair of glasses lay on top of a stack of papers.

Splinter fidgeted. She wasn't sure if she should say something, anything. Next to her, Lucen had folded his hands behind his back as he stared into the distance, but a blush crept up on his cheeks.

"The last time we spoke," Lord Brenet said in his deep, measured voice, "I asked you if any of the squires had treated you unjustly or acted dishonorably. You lied to me."

Splinter swallowed. Whatever she expected, this wasn't it. "My lord?"

"You led me to believe that you were the one who initiated the fight in the courtyard."

"I . . ." Splinter hesitated. The fight in the courtyard felt like a lifetime ago.

"Well?"

She could hardly tell him that she had expected all of the squires he'd trained to blame her. "Yes, my lord."

"Whether you did it out of noble intentions to protect your prince, or because you thought your word would hold no weight, you were mistaken." Brenet nodded at Lucen.

"I expect my squires to follow the rules of chivalry, to treat one another respectfully and honorably. Tell her what you told me."

Lucen straightened. The only indication of his nerves was that, behind his back, he ran his nails along the sleeves of his tunic. "My lord, I was responsible for the fight in the courtyard. The other squires followed my orders to bully Splinter, and I made sure she couldn't fulfill her duties. I started the fight."

Splinter gaped at Lucen. He met her gaze levelly. "You know I'm sorry. I never intended for any of this to happen."

"I know," she stammered.

"Intentions or not," Lord Brenet spoke, "an injustice happened as a result of it, and it will not stand."

Splinter's mouth grew dry. A spark of hope flared through her. "Sir?"

Brenet made his way to the other side of the desk and faced Splinter. "I misjudged you, and for that I apologize. In the time you've been here—and in your service to the princess—you've proven yourself worthy to be a squire. You deserved the aid and trust of your teachers, and I apologize for not fully recognizing the position you were in."

The master of squires held out his hand to her, and Splinter took it. "You couldn't know, my lord," she whispered, feeling hot and cold all over.

"Then that was a mistake on both our parts. Fighting your own fights is a noble pursuit, but a foolish one. To be brave enough to ask for help is knightly," he said. "Do you understand?"

Splinter glanced sideways at Lucen, who wore the same small smile as his sister had. She did. They probably both did. "Yes, my lord."

"Good." Lord Brenet let go of her hand. His expression was as serious as it always was, with deep lines across his forehead. But Splinter could swear she saw a twinkle in his eyes when he said, "Then return to your duties, Squire Splinter."

Splinter yelped. She jumped and *almost* hugged him. She threw her good arm around Lucen instead. "Thank you."

Lucen stiffened. Then he relaxed. "It's good to have you back. I look forward to sparring with you."

She raised an eyebrow. "I look forward to *beating* you."

"*Squires.*" Lord Brenet coughed, and Splinter and Lucen straightened.

"You're dismissed," he said, nodding to Splinter. He approached Lucen, who pushed his shoulders back but visibly blanched. "You and I, your highness, are going to have a long conversation about all of this."

"Yes, my lord," they both chorused.

Splinter turned. She squeezed Lucen's arm when she passed him. And then she ran. Out of the office. Into the familiar hallways of the palace.

Back to Ash.

Acknowledgments

When I was ten, I read Tonke Dragt's *De brief voor de koning*, a Dutch book about a young squire who dreams of knighthood. I fell in love. With the story, with the world, with swords and knights and grand adventures. It was my comfort book. Some days, I'd get to the last page, flip it over, and read it again. The book made me want to become a knight. It also made me want to become a storyteller.

Years later, I discovered Tamora Pierce's Tortall series, and I fell in love all over again. With these lady knights and spies, their found families, and their courageous choices. I read those books to pieces. Quite literally, actually. It was magic to see words turn into worlds that felt a little like home.

Without a sliver of doubt: Splinter, Ash, and Lucen and the world of Calinor wouldn't exist—and I wouldn't be a writer—if it wasn't these stories. The first time I tried my hand at my own book, when I was eleven, I wrote about knights and castles and intrigue, and so many years later, that spark of joy and adventure has never left me. I'm forever grateful to these authors and to all the books I met along the way that helped me become the author and the person I am today.

Thank you to my wonderful editor, Martha Mihalick, who immediately saw to the heart of *Splinter & Ash* and understood it. Thank you for being my partner-in-fantasy-worlds, for pushing me to make this story shine (in fewer words), for your insight and care. Your editorial pen was clearly forged from starlight.

To my agents, Suzie Townsend and Sophia M. Ramos, who are the staunchest knight-protectors that any book could have. Thank you for being unwavering champions of my work. It's far better to be in these trenches together. And that holds true for all of Team New Leaf, and in particular Olivia Coleman, who makes magic happen in all administrative ways.

Thank you to Vivienne To for the cover of my dreams and to Sylvie Le Floc'h for the cover design of my dreams. Thank you for making Splinter, Ash, and Haven come to life.

Thank you to Sabrina Abballe and the middle grade marketing team. To Samantha Brown and the publicity team. To Patty Rosati and the school and library marketing team. You are the fiercest allies any princess or squire could ask for. To everyone at Greenwillow and HarperCollins who had a hand in bringing this story to its readers, thank you for loving this book and these characters so wholeheartedly. I'm infinitely grateful to each and every one of you for giving *Splinter and Ash* such a supportive home.

Thank you to Katherine Locke and Nicole Melleby, whose anthology *This Is Our Rainbow: 16 Stories of Her, Him, Them, and Us* first allowed me to spend time with Splinter and Ash. It remains an honor to be a part of such a special project, and I knew from the moment I finished my anthology story that I wouldn't be able to let go of these characters. I'm overjoyed to now have the opportunity to build them a whole palace.

My endless gratitude goes to booksellers, teachers, librarians, reviewers, and everyone in the book community. Thank you for embracing my work in all its different shapes and forms. I'm so excited to share this new world with you, and I hope you love spending time in Calinor as much as I do.

To my friends who are always there, every step along the way, with every book. You are my knights in shining armor.

And finally, to you, reader. This book is my love letter to the adventure stories that made me. It's a not-so-little piece of my heart. And it's yours to brave and explore. So to every reader who dreams of heroism and adventure, every reader who's on a quest to find themselves, every reader who longs and fights for a better, more welcoming world, every queer reader, every disabled reader: this is yours. Here's to the adventures ahead.